GIRL, ALONE

(An Ella Dark FBI Suspense Thriller —Book One)

BLAKE PIERCE

Blake Pierce

Blake Pierce is the USA Today bestselling author of the RILEY PAIGE mystery series, which includes seventeen books. Blake Pierce is also the author of the MACKENZIE WHITE mystery series, comprising fourteen books; of the AVERY BLACK mystery series, comprising six books; of the KERI LOCKE mystery series, comprising five books; of the MAKING OF RILEY PAIGE mystery series, comprising six books; of the KATE WISE mystery series, comprising seven books; of the CHLOE FINE psychological suspense mystery, comprising six books; of the JESSE HUNT psychological suspense thriller series, comprising fourteen books (and counting); of the AU PAIR psychological suspense thriller series, comprising three books; of the ZOE PRIME mystery series, comprising four books (and counting); of the ADELE SHARP mystery series, comprising six books (and counting); of the EUROPEAN VOYAGE cozy mystery series, comprising six books (and counting); of the new LAURA FROST FBI suspense thriller, comprising three books (and counting); of the new ELLA DARK FBI suspense thriller, comprising three books (and counting); and of the new A YEAR IN EUROPE cozy mystery series, comprising three books (and counting).

An avid reader and lifelong fan of the mystery and thriller genres, Blake loves to hear from you, so please feel free to visit www.blakepierceauthor.com to learn more and stay in touch.

ALMOST DEAD (Book #3)

ZOE PRIME MYSTERY SERIES
FACE OF DEATH (Book#1)
FACE OF MURDER (Book #2)
FACE OF FEAR (Book #3)
FACE OF MADNESS (Book #4)
FACE OF FURY (Book #5)
FACE OF DARKNESS (Book #6)

A JESSIE HUNT PSYCHOLOGICAL SUSPENSE SERIES
THE PERFECT WIFE (Book #1)
THE PERFECT BLOCK (Book #2)
THE PERFECT HOUSE (Book #3)
THE PERFECT SMILE (Book #4)
THE PERFECT LIE (Book #5)
THE PERFECT LOOK (Book #6)
THE PERFECT AFFAIR (Book #7)
THE PERFECT ALIBI (Book #8)
THE PERFECT NEIGHBOR (Book #9)
THE PERFECT DISGUISE (Book #10)
THE PERFECT SECRET (Book #11)
THE PERFECT FAÇADE (Book #12)
THE PERFECT IMPRESSION (Book #13)
THE PERFECT DECEIT (Book #14)
THE PERFECT MISTRESS (Book #15)

CHLOE FINE PSYCHOLOGICAL SUSPENSE SERIES
NEXT DOOR (Book #1)
A NEIGHBOR'S LIE (Book #2)
CUL DE SAC (Book #3)
SILENT NEIGHBOR (Book #4)
HOMECOMING (Book #5)
TINTED WINDOWS (Book #6)

KATE WISE MYSTERY SERIES
IF SHE KNEW (Book #1)
IF SHE SAW (Book #2)
IF SHE RAN (Book #3)
IF SHE HID (Book #4)
IF SHE FLED (Book #5)

IF SHE FEARED (Book #6)
IF SHE HEARD (Book #7)

THE MAKING OF RILEY PAIGE SERIES
WATCHING (Book #1)
WAITING (Book #2)
LURING (Book #3)
TAKING (Book #4)
STALKING (Book #5)
KILLING (Book #6)

RILEY PAIGE MYSTERY SERIES
ONCE GONE (Book #1)
ONCE TAKEN (Book #2)
ONCE CRAVED (Book #3)
ONCE LURED (Book #4)
ONCE HUNTED (Book #5)
ONCE PINED (Book #6)
ONCE FORSAKEN (Book #7)
ONCE COLD (Book #8)
ONCE STALKED (Book #9)
ONCE LOST (Book #10)
ONCE BURIED (Book #11)
ONCE BOUND (Book #12)
ONCE TRAPPED (Book #13)
ONCE DORMANT (Book #14)
ONCE SHUNNED (Book #15)
ONCE MISSED (Book #16)
ONCE CHOSEN (Book #17)

MACKENZIE WHITE MYSTERY SERIES
BEFORE HE KILLS (Book #1)
BEFORE HE SEES (Book #2)
BEFORE HE COVETS (Book #3)
BEFORE HE TAKES (Book #4)
BEFORE HE NEEDS (Book #5)
BEFORE HE FEELS (Book #6)
BEFORE HE SINS (Book #7)
BEFORE HE HUNTS (Book #8)
BEFORE HE PREYS (Book #9)
BEFORE HE LONGS (Book #10)

BEFORE HE LAPSES (Book #11)
BEFORE HE ENVIES (Book #12)
BEFORE HE STALKS (Book #13)
BEFORE HE HARMS (Book #14)

AVERY BLACK MYSTERY SERIES
CAUSE TO KILL (Book #1)
CAUSE TO RUN (Book #2)
CAUSE TO HIDE (Book #3)
CAUSE TO FEAR (Book #4)
CAUSE TO SAVE (Book #5)
CAUSE TO DREAD (Book #6)

KERI LOCKE MYSTERY SERIES
A TRACE OF DEATH (Book #1)
A TRACE OF MUDER (Book #2)
A TRACE OF VICE (Book #3)
A TRACE OF CRIME (Book #4)
A TRACE OF HOPE (Book #5)

PROLOGUE

With her feet perched on the counter, Christine bent her head backward and eyeballed the wall clock above her.

5:32 p.m.

She spun her chair around, then pulled out her phone to double-check the time.

Ugh, she thought, *I'm sure that clock hasn't moved in an hour.*

It had been a forgettable day, in a forgettable town. Christine Hartwell had long known that most Friday nights were unremarkable once middle age crept in, but she never dreamt it would come to this—willingly keeping her shop open until the evening hours on the off-chance someone needed DIY supplies.

She pulled herself up and strolled out into the first aisle. Beyond the store's stained windows, Christine watched a crimson sun descend below a cluster of trees on the other side of the bayou. The last of the day's natural light gradually dissolved, casting a deep gray hue across the small village.

Christine's small Louisiana town didn't have much to offer, but it allowed her to live a simple life against a backdrop of gorgeous scenery. Sometimes, when her store was empty, she could hear the gentle trickle of the bayou outside her window; rhythmic and comforting in its serenity.

It was a life, and that was all she wanted.

She began to rearrange a small display of hacksaws in the shop window, then glanced over at the time again. There wasn't a soul in sight, nor had there been in the past two hours. *Time to close up,* she thought. *I've got a life to live.*

She made her way to the rear of the store to the switch which closed the exterior shutters, after which she'd leave out the fire exit behind her. She pushed down, then counted to ten. She heard the mechanical whir beyond the storeroom wall and began to contemplate what the rest of her evening might hold.

Television? Dinner? Wine? Browse for holidays I can't afford?

But as Christine reached the count of six, something pulled her from her boredom-induced daydream.

1

Bang.

A startling thud on the other side of the wall.

"Oh shit."

Had something crashed onto the shop floor? Had the shutters accidentally crushed something?

She rushed back out toward the counter and surveyed the room. Nothing was out of the ordinary. Hesitantly, she turned back around, and her peripheral vision picked up on something in the far corner.

Outside, she noticed the silhouette of someone standing next to the shop door. The half-closed shutters concealed the stranger's face, but it was undoubtedly a male. Black jeans, well-worn shoes, the bottom half of a woolen coat.

"Hello?" she shouted. "Who's that?"

No answer. The silhouette didn't move an inch. *Typical,* she thought. *Someone wants something just as I'm closing.*

Christine sighed, then sauntered back to the storeroom with heavy strides. She opened the shutters back up, and as they clinked into place, she heard the silhouette-man open the door. She peered her head back around the storeroom door.

There was nothing remarkable about the man, except for his sheer normalcy. Most men in bayou country flaunted that unmistakable aura of rural living; rough hands from a lifetime of manual labor, or the ingrained scent of manure in their clothes. But this man could have introduced himself as a bartender at the local dive or a banker earning six figures and Christine would have believed him either way.

She couldn't place his age, maybe a young forty or an early-thirties who'd endured a hectic upbringing. Under other circumstances, Christine might have even found him attractive, but the fact he'd put an abrupt stop to her plans overrode all of his appeal.

He walked carelessly and without caution down aisle three, before fixating on the display of hacksaws Christine had spent so long preparing earlier that day.

"Anything I can help you with?" she asked from behind the counter. "I was just about to close. You arrived at the right time."

No reply came. He didn't even register that he'd heard her.

Rude, she thought.

Finally, after what seemed like an eternal stillness, he spoke.

"Antifreeze," he said. His voice was gentle but with a rough edge, like an ex-smoker whose vocal cords were in recovery.

"No problem. It's up here."

Christine pulled out a black container and dropped it on the counter. The gentleman approached and fixated his gaze on the item between them. He pulled out a twenty-dollar bill and pushed it across to Christine.

"Heavy-duty, fifty-fifty," Christine said. "Will that do you?"

Two hands suddenly grabbed the container. Christine flinched, stepping back. Her heart began to pound, and suddenly, an unexplainable sense of dread filled her stomach. Outside, sunset turned to full dusk. There were no lights on in any of the other stores on her row. A ghostly fog danced at the window, bringing with it a distressing awareness of just how alone she was.

"Is that all?" she asked.

But once again, the man offered nothing in the way of a response. He retreated the way he came without collecting his five cents change, leaving Christine's hand outstretched like a mannequin.

The man exited the store, looked in either direction, then faded into the darkness.

Christine kept her eyes glued to him as he disappeared. Before his outline completely vanished, he turned, keeping his head down, and took one last glance at Christine's Hardware 101.

She shook her shoulders, brushing off a sensation of numbness. Composing herself, she ran back to the storeroom and closed the shutters. She reached the count of ten but kept her finger on the switch until she was positive she was barred inside.

Without natural light, the store emanated a sunburnt orange glow from the overhead lights. Christine took out the cash register and placed it inside the safe. Just as she punched the last digit of the six-number combination to lock it, she heard a strange shuffling.

A bolt of ice shot down her spine. She surveyed the floor, praying that she'd see an inquisitive mouse, a rat, a cricket.

Nothing.

Then, the same sound again. Like something was scratching along her wooden floor. Rough shoes, maybe, or a fallen screw rolling between her feet.

Bang.

A bead of sweat collected on her head. Her face began to burn. She stood in place, motionless. The sound had come from the storeroom.

I knocked something over when I was in there, she reassured herself.

But then she heard a clunk, the recognizable tone of metal on metal.

She leaped across the counter and grabbed the nearest display model which could double as a weapon. She landed on a chisel and gripped it with a force she didn't know she had.

Slowly, she sidestepped into the back room. Light was minimal, but everything seemed in place. Further along in her kitchen area, the boiler system chugged away, pushing water through the store's heating system.

Was it just the boiler? she thought.

A small wave of relief washed over her, but then Christine shifted her eyes to something lying beside the fire exit.

A container of antifreeze. Heavy-duty, fifty-fifty.

She struggled to comprehend the scene in front of her. She couldn't find the will to scream or cry or run; she simply stood in place, wordless.

The same clothes, the same nondescript look. But this time, there was something else. He held a rifle, with the gun barrel pointing directly at her.

Terror engulfed her from head to toe. She threw the chisel at the intruder, but the object had barely left her hand before a deafening gunshot sent her sprawling to the floor. She felt her ribs shatter. Her vision failed, but she suddenly felt the familiar sensation of wood against her face.

Struggling for breath, she finally opened her eyes and found herself collapsed against her store counter.

Christine crawled and slithered away, each movement agony, blood dyeing her hands.

A foot pressed on her wrist, almost crushing it.

She looked up and finally made eye contact with the strange man she'd first seen only five minutes before. Her gaze deviated to the weapon clenched in his hands. No longer was he holding a rifle. In its place was a felling ax, raised high above the man's head, its tapered blade glistening silver.

Christine raised her head and screamed, her cries ricocheting off the metal hardware on the shelf beside them. Tears streamed down her face as the ax came down.

And then her world went black.

4

CHAPTER ONE

Ella Dark raised the Glock Gen 5 pistol, aligned her sight, and squeezed until she felt maximum resistance. Her hand vibrated in the recoil, and then she emptied the chamber in less than two seconds, almost severing the neck of the target dummy.

The FBI offices in Washington, D.C., were a spectacle to behold at any time of the day, but there was something impossibly surreal about them when nightfall came. Even the FBI shooting range, access to which was a major perk of her job, was unusually deserted on this Friday evening. She removed her safety goggles and inspected the rest of the alcoves, seeing only a lone shooter at the other end of the range.

It was mid-November. Seven p.m. came and went, marking Ella's fourteenth straight hour at HQ. For two weeks, she had been assembling data regarding missing people in the tri-state area of Chicago. Sometimes, she'd spot a link, a pattern, something that could possibly connect a missing child in Wisconsin with an unsolved murder in Michigan. However, her job was merely to report the facts, not to dig into the finer details.

And this, she thought, was the biggest tragedy of all.

Her job was statistical, analytical, but the subject matter took its toll. Every day brought new tragedies and horrors, the details of which Ella was obliged to consume in full. Nighttime shooting sessions offered a constructive way of shedding the burden.

Ella returned her pistol and safety equipment to the elderly man behind the desk and nodded her thanks as she left. She reapplied her thick-rimmed glasses and loosened her ponytail, letting her raven hair fall to her shoulders. The smell of gun smoke lingered at the tips.

She made her way back across the FBI training grounds under a blackened sky which threatened rainfall at any second. A group of young agents jogged past her in an orderly line, several of whom tried to catch her eye, but Ella kept her head down and continued on her way.

Just as she reached the entrance to the main FBI building, she felt a buzzing in her jacket pocket. She pulled out her crumbling Samsung, four years old, ancient by modern standards. One new message.

Jenna: Party at our place tonight. Hurry up back.

Ella breathed a heavy sigh, exhausted by the mere thought of such activities. She brainstormed a quick excuse to be late home, but before she could apply it to the screen, she heard a voice from behind.

"Excuse me, Ella?" it asked. "It is Ella, isn't it?"

Well-spoken, but with a clear air of authority.

She turned around to find a middle-aged gentleman hurrying to keep up with her. She'd seen his face somewhere before. Not in person, but on email, maybe? Or one of the bulletins dotted around HQ?

"Yes, it is," she said, her hand still wrapped around the silver door handle leading into the building foyer.

"Hope I didn't startle you," he said. "Nice shooting, by the way. I saw you back there."

Not another guy trying to give me shooting advice, she thought.

"Thank you."

"Sorry, I should introduce myself. My name's William. I work in Behavioral."

"Oh," Ella said, "nice to meet you. I'm in Intelligence."

Ella was a little taken aback. The Behavioral Research and Instruction Unit was the almost-mythical branch of the FBI that dealt with all manner of ultra-violent crime; serial killers, mass murderers, cult leaders, school shooters, domestic terrorists. It housed the psychological profilers and special agents that every crime drama did their best to emulate. She'd worked sporadically with a handful of agents from the department over the years, and talked to a few of them socially, but their doors were always closed to anyone not inside their circle.

"I know," said William. "Your department has done a lot for us in the past few months. Without your help in the tri-state missing persons project, we wouldn't have made half the progress we have. I wanted to extend my thanks to the people who do the leg work, especially the dedicated ones. I don't get the chance to show my face much."

A wave of gratitude overcame her. Ella felt like she somehow needed to return the gesture, but couldn't think of anything to say. "Thank you, sir. I appreciate it."

"Your work on the Greenville Strangler case was outstanding, too," William continued. "I know the VCU took the credit, but don't think we're not aware of your input."

Ella wasn't one for grandstanding but welcomed the acknowledgment. "Just doing my part, sir. If I can help in any way, I will."

"Excellent," William said. "Well, I'll let you get home. I'm sure you have a husband waiting for you."

Ella shook her head. "No husband, sir. Not really my area."

A muted ringtone interrupted their conversation. William reached into his pocket and pulled out his phone. He answered, excused himself, then turned his back to Ella. She couldn't make out his words, but she noticed his demeanor change significantly. He held his shoulders back and began to tap the heel of his foot against the granite steps. Within ten seconds, William had ended the call.

"Sorry about that. Something's come up," he said. "Listen, I'd like to talk more with you when you have time. Maybe Monday? Someone with your drive could be of great use to us."

A heavy wind came between them, bringing with it a small dose of rainfall. "Of course, sir," Ella said, not wanting to question him further. "Feel free to shoot me an email or call my extension."

"Perfect. Sorry to keep you," William said. "Have a great evening." He pulled his phone back out and stuck it to his ear. He made his way indoors and up the marble stairway to the second floor of the FBI headquarters.

Ella readjusted her backpack and headed through the foyer, catching a glimpse of a picture of the man who'd just left her presence. On the board which declared all of the FBI's pivotal directors, she saw a plaque with the name *William Edis*. Beneath that, *Director— Behavioral Research and Instruction Unit.*

Outside of her own department, she'd never spoken to a director in person before, least of all one who knew her name. The FBI employed over 35,000 people across the entire United States, a large portion of whom were based out of D.C. Her own team reached into the hundreds, and unless it was a special occasion, she rarely got the chance to talk with people outside of her Intelligence bubble.

Full dark set in overhead. The night would soon be over. Ella headed to her Ford Focus in the multi-story parking lot, contemplating what the remainder of the evening might hold. She threw her bag into the rear then noted a pile of crumbled textbooks behind the passenger seat. *Criminal and Investigative Analysis, The Art of Profiling, Modern Serial Killers & Their M.O.*

Ella started up the car and headed on her way, realizing she was going to have to brave the lion's den at some point this evening. It was a weekly occurrence, being coerced into doing something she didn't want to by her overly eager roommate, but for once, she wasn't too concerned, because there was a new light at the end of the road.

Someone with your drive could be of great use to us, he'd said.

***

Under other circumstances, it would have been an arduous journey, but the day and the hour made the usually infuriating drive between D.C. and Annadale bearable.

But as Ella reached the halfway point to her house, she decided she wasn't yet ready to spend her evening idly chatting with people she barely knew. She took a hard left into the deserted parking lot of the Milestone bar.

If there was one thing Ella had learned from a career in law enforcement, it was that every branch had its secret hotspots. A bar that offered free whiskey shots for officers, or a restaurant that halved the bill for anyone with a badge. The Milestone was the FBI equivalent. A lot of agents and admin staff stopped by on the way home for a quick shot to take the edge off.

A heavy odor of smoke hung in the air, adding to the place's rough-but-vintage charm. During her psychology studies, Ella had learned that modern bars outfitted their interiors entirely with metal and wooden furniture so that the sound inside was amplified, giving the illusion of liveliness. But the Milestone was one of the few bars which still boasted padded chairs and cotton drapes, designed to absorb sound and invoke a homely ambience.

Ella welcomed the lack of bodies inside. She took a seat in a red booth and pulled her laptop out of her bag, using the opportunity to ride out the hours until her roommate inevitably moved her party to a club in town. If Jenna asked where she was, she'd just say her phone died.

The bartender, a graying woman in her fifties, sauntered up to Ella's table and dropped a jug of tap water. "Anything I can get you?" she asked, a Southern twang hanging loosely off her lips.

"Just coffee, please. Refill."

"Can do, sweetheart. Burning the midnight oil?"

"Just needed a quiet place to come," Ella said. "Nowhere better than here."

8

"I hear that. Back in two minutes, darling."

Ella's laptop pinged alive and automatically connected to the bar's Wi-Fi connection. She ran her cursor over her background—a scenic forest shot—before landing on a Word document she'd been working on.

A Psychological Analysis of Norman Bates.

Only 700 words long so far, but maybe she'd get the chance to finish it tonight. She read from the last paragraph.

A primary point to establish is that no analysis of a fictional character could ever reflect similar psychopathology if similar crimes to Bates's were ever to occur in real life. While the seed of which Bates was born was planted by Plainfield murderer Ed Gein in the 1950s, Bates is the fictional manifestation of Gein pushed to his utmost limits, in addition to the fact that Bates must also abide by the laws of linear storytelling. The real-life story of Gein was much more haphazard and followed no such pattern, whereas Bates's deviancy gradually escalated for the purposes of a convenient narrative. With this said, Bates displays clear behavior of a perpetrator suffering from dissociative identity disorder (DID), colloquially known as multiple personality disorder. The first instance appears—

"Coffee. Hot as you like," came the voice, interrupting Ella's flow. The bartender dropped a metal jug and a cup on the table. "Cream and sugar on its way."

The bartender strolled away and Ella turned back to her laptop. Her thoughts went back to Norman Bates, but a familiar pinging sound brought her back to reality.

That was when she saw it.

Out of sheer habit, she'd opened up her email client when she'd turned on her laptop. In the corner of the screen, a small window popped up.

But it wasn't from one of her usual contacts.

From: Edis, William.

His message was brief and to the point, with no unnecessary greetings.

Urgent. Call me when you get this.

She did. She closed up her laptop, moved outside to the green-tinted, smoke-filled patio, and called the number on the email. He answered after three rings.

"Mr. Edis?"

"Ella, thank you for calling me back so quickly. I wasn't sure if you'd get my email."

"I happened to be online, sir. What can I do for you?"

"You know how you said you'd be happy to help in any way you can?"

"Of course."

"I've got an interesting case. It needs someone with a brain. Someone who can think and analyze. You'd be working with the BRAI. Would you be interested?"

A million thoughts sprung into Ella's head, overwhelming her to the point of muteness. Why her? Why now? What about her current job in Intelligence?

"Umm," she began. "I mean, I'd love to. But—"

"Actually," William interrupted, "I want to give you all the details before you make a decision. Are you free now?"

"Yes, sir. I'm just at the Milestone but I can—"

"No, that's perfect. I'll meet you there. I want to talk off the record."

CHAPTER TWO

Illuminated by the fluorescent orange lights, William looked a little stockier, a little more haggard than he had earlier that evening. Ella thought of her early beginnings, and now here she was, about to be sitting in a smoky bar opposite an FBI director.

As a twenty-one-year-old criminology graduate, Ella had taken up an entry-level job with the Virginia state police. In her youthful optimism, she'd thought that maybe she'd get to see some action. Maybe a police officer would call in sick one day, and she'd rise to the challenge and become the day's hero.

This fantasy never came true. Instead, she performed admin duties for two years, then moved into a data analysis role. More responsibility, more money, same amount of fieldwork opportunities—zero.

But at the ripe old age of twenty-five, an ex-colleague of Ella's from the police brought her in for an interview with the Intelligence Branch Director of the FBI. She had the skills, in lieu of a computer science degree, but her work with the Virginia state police spoke for itself. After a rigorous clearance check involving urine samples, polygraph tests, extensive mental assessments, and in-depth scrutiny of her entire life, she was offered a six-month contract within the FBI Intelligence team.

Three years later, now twenty-eight years of age, she was still in the same role.

She'd made no secret of her desire to get away from the desk and out into the real world. Sometimes, she'd speak to special agents and profilers at social events, and the stories they told made her equal parts jealous and electrified. She'd sometimes see a picture of real-life crime scenes if she was amassing data from a Behavioral Research case, sometimes she'd be told something that the general public didn't already know. Maybe a voodoo doll had been found alongside the dead body, or a victim had been strangled with a pair of stockings. These little tidbits filled her head with theories and possibilities, but as she was a mere Intelligence Analyst, no one was willing to hear her out.

Except for one occasion. It was that occasion that she believed prompted William Edis to contact her tonight, but she couldn't be certain. However, she'd soon find out.

A knee-length woolen coat concealed his clothing, and a pair of mahogany reading glasses highlighted the wrinkles underneath his eyes. He joined Ella's table, then threw a thumbs-up signal to someone behind the bar. He removed a black scarf and placed it next to him.

"Hope I haven't spooked you," he said.

Ella gulped down the last of her coffee. "Not yet," she said.

"Good. Anyway, let me give you the long and short of it. We've got a situation out in Louisiana. There's been a murder. Female, forties. Shot and decapitated in her own store."

"Oh, that's dreadful."

"Yeah, he's left quite a mess. We need a couple of agents to get out there tonight and see what they can gather. Who is this woman? Why was she targeted? Was this impulsive or premeditated?"

Ella felt a sudden chill run from her fingertips down to her spine. Was this going where she thought it was going?

"I've got one agent lined up and ready to go, but I want you there too. How would you feel about that?"

There it was. The invitation of all invitations. For years, she'd dreamt of being summoned to an untouched crime scene, still warm from the actions of an unhinged psychopath. Now that it was here, it felt almost surreal. Was there a catch? No, she was chosen for a unique opportunity due to her hard work. It was as simple as that, at least she hoped. She felt the excitement rise up in her.

"I mean, yes, I'd absolutely love to help out on an active case like that," she said. Ella stopped while the same bartender dropped a shot of whiskey in front of William. They both smiled at her as she walked away. "But I have a few questions if that's okay."

"Understandable."

She breathed deeply, collecting her thoughts. "First of all—why me? I'm no field agent. You ask for six years minimum before an agent can even be considered for FBI work."

William sighed and downed his whiskey in one. Ella could almost feel the burn from the other side of the table. It must have been strong stuff.

"The way the FBI does things is antiquated. We use outdated technology to counter cyberterrorism. Our case management system is a total mess. When it comes to field agents, most of them have been

12

molded by us from a young age. They only know what we tell them to know. Some of the directors are working on a new initiative, and it involves taking people with skills in other areas and applying them to active cases out in the field."

"What kind of skills?"

"People who have experience from the other side of the coin, not people born into the job they're doing."

Ella nodded. It made sense, and she wasn't going to ruin this opportunity for herself. "Have I been picked because of my help on the Strangler case?"

"Not exactly. I picked you because of your dedication, your ethic. I've seen you. You're the first one to show up and the last to leave."

"Understood. And what about the twenty-week training?"

"Think of this new initiative as an apprentice scheme. You'll be partnered with a veteran who'll teach you everything. Besides, you clearly know how to handle a firearm from what I saw earlier."

"I do, very much."

"I won't lie," William continued, "this is kind of a risk. Behavioral have a history of trying new approaches to investigative work, and not all of them have been successful. We really want this to work because it would open up a whole new pool of recruits for us, not to mention that open serial cases are up for the first time in thirty years."

"Serial?" Ella asked.

"Yes. This Louisiana murder may be linked to other homicides."

Holy shit, Ella thought. *I'm working on a serial killer case.*

"We need this case closed, so please, apply yourself."

"You have my word, sir. I'm very thankful for the opportunity. I won't let you down."

"I have no doubt. Now, enough talk. You'll need to run home and pack a bag because I don't know how long you'll be out there. Agent Ripley is waiting for you at the airport. We'll arrange a cab."

Ella's eyes widened.

"Agent Ripley?" she asked. "As in, Mia Ripley?"

"The very same."

You gotta be kidding me, Ella thought.

***

Ella heard the music from down the hallway. As she arrived at her front door, she couldn't even hear herself put the key in the lock. No doubt she'd be apologizing to the neighbors on her roommate's behalf pretty soon.

She tried to sneak in unseen, but Jenna was leaning against the inside hallway wall chatting with some jock type guy. She turned upon Ella's entrance, passed her drink to the guy beside her, and ran over to Ella. Jenna threw her arms around her in a way Ella thought was wholly unnecessary.

"Finally," Jenna said, adjusting her skirt. "Where have you been, woman?"

"I can't stay," Ella said. "Work needs me to go on a trip. So sorry. I wish I could stay," she lied.

"Screw work. You're always doing work."

"They need me. It's a big deal." Ella put her hand on the door handle to her bedroom, but stopped herself opening it at the last second. She turned around to her roommate.

"Jen?"

"What?"

"There's no one in here, is there?"

Jenna took her drink back from the stranger. She bit her lip and made a worried face. "No. Well, I don't know. You could try knocking?"

Ella shook her head. She wasn't about to knock on her own bedroom door. She burst inside, and unsurprisingly, found a couple getting acquainted on her bed. They both turned to her, looking like deer caught in the headlights. Ella recognized neither the guy nor the girl. Ella dropped her head in her hands and then pointed to the door. Both of them scrambled off the bed in record time.

Jenna appeared in the doorway.

"Oh, you didn't use Ella's bedroom, did you?" She addressed her question to the culprits, who hadn't yet said a word. "That's so annoying. I'm not happy with either of you."

Ella turned to Jenna and gave a look of disapproval. "Where in our massive duplex did you think they'd be? In the guest suite?"

Jenna laughed. "Good one. Get out of here, you two."

They scrambled away, not making eye contact with Ella. "Go on, shoo." She turned to Ella. "Where are you going, anyway?"

"Louisiana," Ella said. She pulled open her wardrobe and took out the first clothes she found. She found her bag and stuffed them inside.

"Like, the south? Why? That's miles away."

Ella thought of a believable excuse. "Training," she said. She fetched her toothbrush, a few books, and a bunch of hair ties. She threw them in her bag alongside her laptop. The essentials. She assumed her hotel would provide the rest.

"Sounds awful. When are you gonna be back?"

Ella thought about it. She realized that she didn't know. "Could be a few days, could be a week."

"A week?" Jenna asked, dropping her jaw for effect. "But what if I need you? What if I need to reset the security alarm again? What if I need you to fill out those forms for the gas and electricity?"

Ella ran a quick check in her head. She had everything she needed to survive out in the wild. She wasn't really listening to Jenna prattle on. "You'll be fine. Just call me. I'm going to the south, not Mars."

Jenna put her hands on her hips. "Have you ever been to the south, El? It's like going to the past. You won't fit in."

"I'll be fine," Ella said, heading into the living area. She saw about ten people congregating on her sofa and her floor, almost none of them she recognized. In more than one way, she was thankful she was being sent on a case. She headed toward the front door. Jenna caught up with her.

"Good luck and be safe," she said, hugging her again.

Ella looked beyond her to the gentleman Jenna been chatting with, still loitering idly in the hallway. "You too," Ella said, moving her gaze from him to her roommate.

Ella left her apartment and hurried down the hallway. The music gradually faded from her eardrums as she went out into the night toward her new life.

CHAPTER THREE

For her entire career, Ella had bought into the myth that all FBI special agents flew via private jet. But as her taxi dropped her off at the hustling Reagan Washington National Airport, she realized she'd been deceived.

Things outside seemed much clearer than they had earlier. Despite the stiff graze of winter's breath and the endless torrent of rain which soaked her from head to toe, Ella saw a somber beauty in the shadows, like the outside world had taken on a fourth dimension while she had been indoors.

This was what she worked for, and god knows she was going to grab it by the horns.

She collected her one-way ticket and headed straight for Gate 31. It was nearing 9:30 p.m., so security lines were minimal. But when she approached the back of the line, one of the airport staff pulled her aside and escorted her through without question. She'd never had the first-class treatment before, but it was a welcome perk. She was marched directly through the rickety tunnel and onto the aircraft, straight down into the glittering business lounge. Cream leather seats were perched up against long rectangular windows, positioned opposite each other with a gloss white table between them. Up ahead, she saw a marble table with a gleaming white coffee machine perched on the side.

"Rookie?" a voice asked. "Are you the rookie?"

Ella turned around to face the far corner. A redheaded woman, dressed in suede heels and a black suit, sat sipping from a miniature bottle. She had pale eyes and chiseled, distinguished features. She looked around early fifties, although her real age eluded Ella. She looked to be in incredible shape, like a yoga teacher, Ella thought. There was clear muscle definition in her legs and forearms, at least from what Ella could see. There were a few patches of dried skin on her cheeks and forehead, possibly the effects of nicotine or alcohol. Ripley didn't strike her as a smoker, not in her line of work. When Ella saw that the miniature was straight bourbon, she had her answer.

Ella was a little taken aback. She'd never seen Mia Ripley in person before.

"Well?"

"Yes, I'm the rookie, Agent Ripley. It's a pleasure to meet you."

The stern woman returned her gesture, motioning with her other hand to join her on the seat opposite.

Behind them, the rest of the passengers began to board. Ella parked herself on the chair while the rush of footsteps filled the rest of the plane. No one else joined them in business class.

Ripley narrowed her eyes as she read something on her laptop, then she closed the case with a sudden jolt. Tales of Ripley's heroism out in the field were common knowledge throughout the entire organization. She'd caught Iowa's most famous and sadistic serial killer, Lucien Myers, after tracking him on foot through a rural farmhouse. When a kid in Florida had taken his schoolmates hostage, Ripley had been the one to talk him down. Most amazingly of all, at least to Ella, was that Ripley once drew up an offender profile so accurate she predicted they'd catch the killer wearing a double-breasted suit and black tie. A few days later, that's exactly what happened.

There was definitely something formidable about her. Ella wanted to initiate conversation but didn't know where to start. Pleasantries? Ask her about the case? Ask her if all the stories were true?

"So, who are you and why are we working together?" Ripley asked, locking her crystal green eyes with Ella's. "Been out in the field before?"

"Ella Dark. Twenty-eight. Intelligence analyst for the past three years."

"And?"

"I've only worked from behind a desk, but I've dreamt of being a special agent all my life."

"Dreamt about it?"

"Very much so."

"So why have you never done anything about it?"

The question stumped her. The truth was that she didn't have an answer. Sometimes fantasies were best left as just that.

"I never really got the chance," Ella lied. "It must be a fascinating job."

Ripley took a gulp of whiskey and pulled out a brown folder from her bag. She threw it on the table. "Before we get going, let me make some things clear. This job isn't for the weak, and no, it's not fascinating in the slightest. It might be fascinating to crime junkies who get off on gory details and live vicariously through the people who have to see this shit in the flesh, but to any level-headed adult, there's nothing fascinating here. I've got two ex-husbands and two kids I never saw grow up, all because this job demanded my full attention. I've seen more colleagues die than you've seen episodes of *Seinfeld*. Don't think this is a free trip around the country, because it's not. You're going to see horrific shit that'll haunt you until the day you die. Okay?"

A numb silence hung in the air. Ella nodded. "Understood. I'm here to treat things with the utmost respect and professionalism."

"Good," Ripley said. "Now, I'll be honest, I wanted to work this one alone. But Edis told me he wanted you to tag along. Another new scheme by the geniuses in Behavioral, or something?"

"That's what he told me," Ella said. "This is completely new to me, too."

"I was a little insulted, but then he told me something about the Greenville Strangler. Care to fill me in?"

Although she'd said nothing about her career, Ella instantly knew that all of the stories about Mia Ripley were undoubtedly true. There seemed to be a constant fire in her eyes, as though years of investigative work had blunted her enjoyment of life's pleasures. Ella had seen a thousand cops in the same position. Depressed, frustrated, and ill-tempered. There was a reason police officer suicide rates were some of the highest of any profession.

"Last year, an unsub was strangling women in South Carolina," Ella began. "Disorganized sociopath. Reckless."

"I know who he was," Ripley chimed in. "What did you have to do with it?"

Ella quickly considered how much of the story to tell. Should she play herself up, or play it modestly? *I'll stick to the facts,* she thought, *nothing more.*

"When I was reading about the case on the system, I found out the Strangler gained access to his victims' homes by smashing their windows. Yet, all his victims were strangled while they slept. Surely, shattering glass would wake someone up, right?"

"Agreed," said Ripley.

"There was an obscure case in Japan in 1988 with exactly the same type of contradiction, so I pleaded with forensics to inspect the locks on the victims' front doors. I personally believed they had the profile all wrong. He knew exactly what he was doing when he smashed those windows, but investigators read the whole situation wrong."

The plane went into pitch blackness for takeoff. An overhead light came on, drenching Ella and Ripley in a sickly yellow glow.

"The truth was he broke in through the front door, then *left* the house out the window after locking the front door behind him. He then broke the window from the outside to draw attention away from where the real clue was—the front door lock."

Ripley sat back in her chair and crossed her legs. Her arms had been folded, but she now unfolded them to summon over a flight attendant. She motioned to bring them two coffees. Her body language change wasn't lost on Ella.

"Interesting," said Ripley, "but how did that help catch him?"

"Forensics swept the locks and found traces of nylon filament in every single one."

The plane rolled slowly along as it took its position on the runway. Ella took a deep breath and tried not to think about takeoff. In truth, flying terrified her, but she knew better than to mention it.

"And, well, this reminded me of *another* obscure case. Mexico. A killer used guitar strings to break into people's homes. He would bend them, like a paperclip, and thrust it into the lock. The string mimicked the shape of the tumbler, so he could turn it with ease."

"I see," Ripley said. "Well, that's news to me."

Ella picked up her stride. She was in her element. Now that she thought about it, she hadn't talked about her input on the Strangler case to anyone. This was her first time relaying the facts to someone, and it felt incredible.

"Guitar strings are made with nylon filament, but it needs to be a real thick string to work. A bass string, in fact. Forensics narrowed down the type of material to a very specific bass string, then investigators went through all the music shops nearby who sold that same item."

"And?"

"CCTV footage did the rest. The police's greatest ally."

Ripley blinked several times for effect. "Quite impressive. You must have really done your research."

Have I won her over? Ella thought. *Not yet, I need to go further.*

"Not really. The Japan and Mexico cases came from memory. I've studied every serial murder case in existence. I started doing it twenty years ago and haven't stopped. Any killer, any victim, any country in the world. I can tell you victimology, methodology, times, dates, locations. If there's a pattern of history repeating itself, I'll know it."

Ripley motioned to the brown folder on the table. "What do you make of these?"

Ella inspected each photo one by one, silently hoping she'd said enough to impress her new partner. The first picture showed a woman lying on an autopsy table covered in a white sheet. It showed the jagged cut where her head used to be.

"Christine Hartwell. Forty-two years old. Assaulted and murdered in her store around six p.m. this evening. The local PD think the murders might be related to two others in the past week."

Ella took the information in. She nodded. "Were they similar?" she asked.

"No. The first victim was a teenage girl, abducted and dismembered. The second victim was an old woman, killed while she slept. And now this."

Ella didn't have to think hard. "All female, but completely different ages and M.O.s."

"Exactly. If you ask me, they're not connected, so let's focus on this recent victim for now. Any thoughts when you look at these pictures?"

Ella wasn't a stranger to gruesome images, not by a long shot, but something about the photographs was more *real* than anything she'd seen before. This was a real person, who only five hours ago had been contemplating life and dreams, and now she was an exhibition to be scrutinized.

Ella stayed silent. The truth was she saw nothing but a headless carcass. She breathed deeply, praying that she'd find at least *something* to contribute.

"In addition to her being shot, the lacerations along her neck look almost identical to the pattern of the cuts on the Villisca Ax Murderer's victims, so I'd guess he used to ax to decapitate her. The amount of blood at the scene means she was murdered on site, and the fact he came with two weapons means that this was premeditated. He's not impulsive. He knew exactly what he was going to do."

She moved to the next photograph. A pool of dried blood.

And then she noticed something in the corner of the photograph. She felt a brief spark behind her eyes, like two pieces of electrical wire momentarily touching.

Beside the mutilated body, she saw a sign which read *Tungsten Tip Screws $0.99*.

"The victim ran a hardware store?" Ella asked.

"Correct."

She thought back to earlier in the evening.

Norman Bates.

Psycho.

A gun, an ax, a hardware store. It was all there.

No, it couldn't be.

Ripley caught her eye. "What is it?" she asked. "I can see the cogs are turning."

"Nothing."

"You can't hide from a profiler. Come on, out with it."

Even in total darkness, the Washington, D.C., skyline zigged and zagged with elegant poise. And then it was gone, replaced with brief whispers of clouds and stars.

Ella brought the crime scene photo up to eye level. "No, it's nothing," she began, "it's just a lot to take in."

However, what Ella didn't say was she was certain she'd seen this exact scene somewhere before.

CHAPTER FOUR

Around two hours and three whiskeys into the night, their plane landed at Monroe Regional Airport in Louisiana. Ella stuck to coffee, but Ripley hadn't been quite so reserved.

Despite Ella's questions, she realized that she hadn't learned much about the woman in front of her. Ripley's exterior was impenetrable, like that one schoolteacher who never smiled and never let slip any comment that wasn't related to the school curriculum. Whether Ripley liked or hated her was a mystery she'd have to wait a little longer to solve, if ever an answer came.

Midnight dawned. It felt as though days had passed since she was at the shooting range back in Washington. Whether it was jetlag, excitement, tiredness, or a nameless emotion Ella was only now experiencing for the first time, she didn't know. She fought off sleep, not wanting Ripley to think she couldn't handle a little exhaustion.

Once the hum of the plane's engine disappeared, Ella and Ripley were the first to be called off. The runway was alight with a string of orange lamps that formed a path into the airport. The air felt different. Colder than back home, but fresher. It was what her aunt would have called *brass monkey weather* if she was still around. Ella never cared to look up the origin.

Ripley marched on ahead, long black woolen coat with a satchel over her shoulder. Even in her robotic determination to reach the airport lounge, she had a weird elegance about her. Ella put her backpack on both shoulders, and after seeing Ripley's near-empty satchel, worried that she might have packed too heavily.

"Where to first?" Ella called out. "Hotel?"

Ripley led the way, clearly having been here before. "Hold up your passport," she said.

A yellow-vested airport steward motioned for them to follow him. He opened up a side gate in the security area and waved them through. They passed the baggage area, where conveyor belts whirred devoid of any contents or crowds hustling around. Ella found it eerily quiet, with only the automated voice overhead providing any background noise.

All passengers for the twelve-forty flight to Washington, D.C., please board now.

In the lounge area, a row of glass windows overlooked the airport parking lot. In front of them, a solitary figure stood gazing out.

"Sheriff Harris," Ripley called out.

The gentleman turned around. He wore a tweed jacket, both his hands in its pockets. A cigarette was tucked behind his ear. He had short black hair, receding somewhat violently. He reached his hand out to Ripley.

"Please, call me Bill. Thank you, folks, for getting here so quick."

"Special Agent Mia Ripley, and this is—" Ripley nodded at Ella to introduce herself.

Do I say Special Agent too? she thought. *No, of course not. Don't be ridiculous.*

"Ella Dark. Intelligence Analyst." She shook his hand. A wave of stale cigarette smoke washed over her.

"Intelligence, huh?" Bill asked.

"We're trying something new," Ripley said. "She's here to learn."

"Well, you'll definitely learn something here. I'm not sure what, though." Bill led them to his sheriff's car waiting outside, which was being watched over by two weary-eyed airport stewards. It was a black SUV with *MOBILE PARISH SHERIFF, HONOR, INTEGRITY, SERVICE* stenciled in gold lettering on the side. To Ella, the vehicle was unnecessarily large. The kind of car chosen by insecure alphas and football players' wives. Ripley took the front, while Ella resigned to the back.

"I'll be your transport tonight. I'm sure you girls understand why," Bill said as he started up the car. Ripley locked eyes with Ella through the rearview mirror, noticing the blank-but-intrigued look on her face.

"Because local police don't like the Feds interfering," Ripley confirmed.

"Ain't that the truth. They don't like to think there's something out there they can't handle, you see?"

23

Ella nodded. "Do you think this is something they can't handle?" she asked. The car pulled out of the airport parking lot onto a main road. It was Friday night easing into Saturday morning, so a few midnight strollers and partygoers lined the streets, queuing for post-session junk food and overpriced taxis.

"Life moves a little slower in bayou country," Bill said, pulling out the cigarette from behind his ear. He placed it in his mouth but didn't light it. "We get a burglary now and again. Maybe some pervert puttin' his length in a wild pig. That's pretty common. But this kind of thing? Not in my twenty-six years."

An empty stretch of freeway took them from the heart of Louisiana into the much quieter suburbs on the outskirts of the city. Through an old-style village, complete with thatched houses and cobblestone wells, down an endless country lane which seemingly had no speed limit.

"Where to, anyway?" Bill asked. "Hotel to get some rest?"

"Crime scene," Ripley said without hesitation. "We need to see it while it's fresh."

"You the boss," said Bill.

It neared 1 a.m. Ella thought of Jenna back home. She was due to stumble back into their apartment any minute now, after having doubtless moved her party to a nearby club. She felt that comforting feeling of familiarity in her stomach, but at the same time felt a little relieved that she wasn't there.

"I hope you're not tired, Rookie."

"Not a chance," Ella said. It was a lie, and Ripley probably knew it.

"Speak for yourself," Bill said, rolling down the driver's window. He finally lit his cigarette after hanging it between his lips for ten minutes. "Sorry. Need the breeze to keep me alert. Been up since six in the a.m."

Ella had him beat by an hour but didn't say anything when she realized the time difference meant they woke up at the same time. She had watched the world change, from the concrete jungle of Washington, D.C., to the Louisiana backwaters with a sprinkling of stars and clouds in between. The speed of everything almost overwhelmed her. She tried to push everything to the back of her mind; the possibility of failure, the fact she was something of an experiment, the likelihood that everyone in her department would hear about this little excursion and she'd be met with professional jealousy from her whole team. She'd heard stories of people being given opportunities from the higher-ups and very few were met with the expected level of success. What made her think she'd be any different?

They'd been driving for over an hour by the time they reached the small bayou town. In the dark, it appeared even more alien than it did in her head. Houses stood on wooden stilts to keep their ground floors from flooding. Shops were barely any more than tiny cabins, worlds apart from the franchises and chain restaurants of Washington. The entire town circled around a murky lake centerpiece, which even in darkness shone a muted green. It reminded Ella of a Japanese strolling park, with its buildings protruding from water and rocks arranged to create steps, but one which had been left to overgrow for decades. A couple of airboats rested on the water. Some creatures moved in the shadows, gliding into the water when the sheriff's vehicle passed them by.

"Alligators?" Ella asked.

"You don't go to China and not see the Great Wall, do you?"

Ella hesitated. "I guess not."

"Just like you don't come to Louisiana and go home without seeing a gator or two," Bill said. "Gators, water snakes, otters, pelicans. This place is pretty much a zoo without an entry fee."

"Sounds like a lot of fun."

"Yeah. Well, I'll tell you what's not fun. What you're about to see in here." Bill pulled up outside a row of terraced shops, with yellow tape bordering across all of them. Just across a dirt path, Ella spotted her first signs of human life. A crowd had gathered, maybe around ten people, with a police officer standing in front of them. "Speaking of beasts. You girls ever been hunting?"

"Can't say I have," Ripley said.

"Same," said Ella.

"That's unlucky." Bill jumped out of the car. Ripley and Ella followed. "Don't say I didn't warn you."

They jumped out of the car and made their way to the store entrance. Inside, Ella caught sight of two masked forensic officers photographing the store's interior. This was the first time she'd seen such a thing in person, and she found it a nerve-wracking ordeal. There was still excitement in her, but the reality of knowing that she was standing mere feet away from where murder had taken place filled her with a sense of dread and responsibility.

25

A memory came rushing back to her. Two years before, Ella had been talking to a special agent at an FBI celebration event. She knew he was probably trying to get in her pants, and it wasn't going to happen, but that didn't mean she wasn't going to get some gory details out of him for his effort.

He told her that the human brain processes a crime scene in the same pattern every time. First, you smell the blood. Like molten copper left to rust in a sewage plant. Second, you see the body. The familiar profile of a human being distorted in a manner that removes all human elements and leaves an empty shell in its place. Finally, you realize that what you're seeing is life brought to an end in the most senseless way imaginable. Every hope, every ambition, and every creative endeavor this person would have gone on to enjoy ended in the very room you stood in. With every crime scene, the day got a little darker while the night got no brighter.

Maybe it was the smell that jogged her recollection. They say smell is the sense closest linked to memory, so maybe it was that that brought back the memory she'd so badly tried to shed. Even decades on, her subconscious could still recognize that bitter, sour odor of blood.

It hadn't quite happened as the agent had said. The smell of blood came first, crushing her senses to the point of defeat. And that was it. The other parts hadn't come, at least not yet.

"Three murders. One week," said Sheriff Harris. "This here is our number three."

Christine's Hardware 101 was an unremarkable store. Rows of DIY tools, screws, locks, bolts—all the same shade of dull silver or darker. There were four aisles, all with shelves low enough to peer over the top of, allowing a full view of the interior.

A forensic officer supplied Ella and Ripley with latex gloves and slip-on boots. They joined Sheriff Harris in aisle three beside a pool of blood, much of which had dried into the hardwood floor. The area was cordoned off with a plastic barrier.

"Christine Hartwell, store owner," Harris began. "Judging by initial examinations, shot in the stomach with a rifle, probably from around three to four feet away. No CCTV in the store."

"Who found her?" Ripley asked, following the blood-spatter up to the counter at the front of the store.

"If you mean the body, then we did. But a late-night customer came in, sometime around seven p.m. and saw the store was open but empty. He saw the bloodstains and called us in."

"We'll need his name and address," Ripley said. "And the body?"

"That's where things get weird," said Harris. "We couldn't find a body at first, at least not in the store. But when we checked the shed in the back... Well, see for yourself."

Harris picked up a small folder which he'd rested on one of the shelves. Ella was a little shocked by his relaxed manner but didn't say anything. She was too busy putting the pieces together. She had an idea what Harris was about to show them.

"Hanging upside down in the shed. Hooked like a slaughtered pig. Cut right down the middle. Poor woman had almost been separated in two."

Ripley scrolled through the photographs while Ella looked on. They were much more visceral than the few she'd seen on the plane.

"Why weren't these sent along with the first batch of photos?" Ella asked.

"The officers who were first on the scene took these. By the time the rest of us got there, the forensic team had already removed the body and taken their own photos back at the coroner's office. I called you guys as soon as I got here. Your guys then liaised with the local coroners, not us."

Ella didn't buy it.

"Let's see the shed," said Ripley, already making her way toward the exit.

"This way," Harris called. He led them behind the counter and into the storeroom area, cluttered with boxes and panels of wood. Ella thought this would make a great place for a killer to hide. They entered into a small yard area, filled with similar junk like spare shelves and wooden crates. Specks of blood were dotted around on each of them.

But Ella spotted something. She stopped in her tracks for a second, but was interrupted by the high-pitched creak of the shed door opening. She caught up with Ripley and Harris.

"You might want to borrow this, Agent," Harris said. He pulled a small face mask from his pocket, crumpled but still in working order. "Dead bodies don't exactly have that new car smell."

Ella put the mask on while Ripley took no such protection. They entered into a muddled, damp shed, illuminated by two small police lamps sitting on the floor. Their eyes all fixed on the same thing.

Two hooks hung from the shed roof, held in place by four thick nails.

Something about this image filled Ella with a sick awareness of her own mortality. Even through her face mask, the scent of death seeped into her lungs. It reminded her of when her local garbage men didn't remove the communal trash outside of her apartment complex for a week. Rotting meat, moldy food. Even though the victim had only been in here for a few hours, the presence of death still lingered.

Neither Ripley nor Harris said anything. Suddenly, Ella felt out of her depth. She was looking at an instrument of murder and mutilation. No textbook in the world could prepare a person for witnessing these things in the flesh. She felt light-headed at the thought that only a few hours ago, a real woman was sawn in two in this very room, while the rest of this sleepy town went about their business completely oblivious to the horrors taking place a few doors away.

Ella had seen enough crime scene photos to last a lifetime. Both her personal and professional life exposed her to such images on a regular basis. Blood was no different, with certain scenes from her past replaying in her thoughts and dreams nightly. But here, in reality, other feelings crept in alongside the dread and sorrow. These were the actions of a real serial killer, and just being here was enough to potentially put her in his or her crosshairs. Was she a fool to come here, away from the safety of her cushy desk job?

A part of her told her yes, she was.

"Before you ask," Harris said, "no. We haven't found her head yet."

***

"So, maybe he was a hunter? Or a butcher?" asked Harris.

"Possibly," said Ripley. "This kind of setup takes time, planning, coordination. He didn't just do this on a whim."

Ripley marched from the store to the shed and back again more times than Ella could count. She spoke loudly, but to herself, putting herself in the killer's head as she retraced his steps from intrusion to murder to dismemberment. She scribbled notes in her black notepad, then pushed her hair behind her ears. "Sheriff, the three recent murders aren't related," she said without looking up from her pad.

Harris narrowed his eyes. He pulled out his third cigarette of the night and lit it up. "What makes you so sure?" he asked.

"Victimology is different. M.O.s are different. Crime escalation doesn't add up. This isn't the same person."

Ripley wandered back inside the store, leaving Ella and Harris outside. "Mind explaining?" he asked.

"No serial killer, at least not a sexually motivated one, would murder a teenager, an old woman, and a middle-aged woman in the span of a single week, and certainly not in that order. Serial killers have types," Ella said. "Nor would he discard the bodies in such different ways every time—especially if these are his first murders."

"What's sexual about this?" Harris asked. "Just seems like a lunatic to me."

"He's appeasing a very specific fantasy. This is about more than just death. He's been picturing and perfecting this scene in his head for a long time, and usually, that comes with a sexual component."

Ella, still holding the photographs, began to scour through them again. The same thoughts she had on the plane came surging back. These images were oddly familiar, but something was different about them. There was an additional element present. A recreation of something. Like a reboot of a classic film, but one modernized and stripped of the things which made it classic in the first place.

Ripley returned from indoors. It was closing in on 2 a.m. Even in her coat, scarf, and flimsy face mask, Ella felt the windchill against her bones.

"Mr. Harris, we're dealing with three separate murders here," Ripley began. "I'm sorry if that makes things even more difficult, but I'm convinced of it. There's a possibility these three victims may be connected somehow, but given how much they vary in age and character, it's unlikely. It may be a gang operating in the area. I'm hesitant to use the word *cult*, but that's another possibility. In all my years as an agent, I've never seen a serial killer this haphazard. Therefore, my conclusion is that this isn't the work of a single perpetrator. I'd bet my pension on it."

The more Ripley talked, the more Ella was convinced she was wrong. She glanced back at the hooks hanging inside the shed, then at the assortment of junk and back-stock lingering in the yard. A crate of emulsion. Bags of gravel. Cheap stuff.

Then something new caught her eye.

PREDILUTED COOLANT. HEAVY-DUTY. 50/50

Harris took a huge drag of his cigarette and exhaled smoke alongside a heavy sigh. "Well, I guess you—"

"What was the last·item rung up at the store counter?" Ella interrupted. Both Harris and Ripley eyeballed her. Harris pulled out his notes, which flapped in the wind.

"Let me see." He flicked over a few pages.

"I'll save you some time. It was a gallon of antifreeze, wasn't it?"

Harris held his notes up to the light from the shed. He ran his index finger down the page. "Bingo."

"What does that matter?" Ripley asked.

"What's the timestamp on the purchase?" Ella asked, ignoring Ripley's question.

"5:49 p.m."

"Right around the time of the murder," Ella said. "I knew it. One more question."

This was it. This was the detail that would confirm her suspicions. Norman Bates. Psycho. *A boy's best friend is his mother.*

"Was Christine shot with a .22 caliber rifle? Was there rope around her wrists?"

"That's two questions, but yes and yes."

"I know who committed this murder," Ella said with a sure confidence she didn't know she had in her.

"What?" Ripley asked. "Who?"

"It was Ed Gein."

CHAPTER FIVE

Ella was the first to admit it sounded ridiculous. Ripley and Harris seemed to agree.

Ripley didn't give it much thought. "Ella, be serious for a second. Ed Gein's been dead for thirty years, and even if he was alive, he'd be a hundred years old. We didn't bring you in from—"

"No," Ella interrupted. "I don't mean it was literally Ed Gein. I mean someone has recreated one of his crime scenes right down to the last detail. It's all here."

"Gein?" Harris asked. "The weirdo out in Wisconsin?"

"November 1957. Plainfield, Wisconsin. Ed Gein walked into a hardware store a few miles from his house. He bought a gallon of antifreeze, then shot the owner with a .22 caliber rifle. He dragged the body into his truck and took her home, where he hung her up like a deer in his shed. He decapitated her, gutted her, and left her blood to drain. This is exactly what's happened here, right down to the ropes on her wrists."

Ella rushed back inside the store. Before her revelation, she would have been glad to get out of the cold. Now she didn't care as much.

"I'm the victim," Ella said, standing at the counter. "The unsub comes in and buys the antifreeze, right? I'm looking at him out on the shop floor."

"Why bother?" asked Harris. "Why wouldn't he just shoot her right away?"

Harris had a good point, but Ella had a better answer.

"Two reasons. First, he needs to scope the interior. Make sure it's safe. Learn the layout. Therefore, we can most likely say that this guy isn't local. I'm guessing it's a tight-knit community round here, and the killer isn't part of it."

"You're right there. There ain't a face I don't recognize in this town."

"Exactly. Secondly, and most importantly, is that it's part of the fantasy. This guy wanted to *be* Gein; wanted to feel the same rush

31

Gein felt back in 1957. He's probably been dreaming of it for a long time."

Harris looked intrigued, while Ripley looked on with disinterest and suspicion. Ella undid her scarf and threw it on the counter for effect.

"Once the guy leaves the store, he comes back in through the back door. That's a two-way fire exit, so as long as he can get into the yard, he's inside. Once there, he shoots the victim from this angle." Ella maneuvered into position. "Hence the huge blood spatter on the counter. Christine then crawled away to aisle three, where he finished her with the ax."

"That's all well and good," Ripley said, "but Gein didn't do that. All his mutilation took place at his home."

"Gein didn't want anyone to find out about his deviance. This killer obviously does."

Ella saw that Ripley was considering her theory. Harris just seemed lost.

"It doesn't stop there either," Ella continued. She thought back to something she saw in the yard on her first trip to the shed. She hurried back outside. "All of these crates are made of wood. Christine probably got them all from the same supplier."

"And?" Ripley asked.

"So what's this doing here?" Ella said, pointing with her foot to a burlap sack. "And it's the only object here which doesn't have any specks of blood on it. That's because it wasn't here when he dragged Christine outside."

Her exhaustion had subsided. She'd been awake almost twenty-four hours but never felt more alive. "Those hooks in the shed? He put them there. He brought them with him."

"Ella, this is what we call assumption. You're molding facts to fit theories. We have no evidence whatsoever of that being the case."

"There's one more thing," Ella said. "Isn't this scene missing something?"

"It's missing a lot of things," Ripley said.

"This killer *wanted* us to find this, wouldn't you agree?"

"Yes, I would."

"Judging by that carved-up body in the shed, I'd say he has a flair for the theatric, and therefore, he's going to use every means available to shock and terrify us. So, what are we missing?"

32

Harris said nothing, waiting for a revelation of some kind. Of any kind.

Ripley shifted her weight onto one foot. "A severed head," she said.

Harris grimaced at the words. "We don't know where her head is."

"I'm pretty sure I do," said Ella. "When the police invaded Gein's home, they discovered all sorts of items made from human remains. One of those items was in—"

"A burlap sack," Ripley finished.

There was a cold silence between them. Ella and Ripley looked at Harris. Reluctantly, he turned on his flashlight.

He edged toward the sack, which had been discarded between two crates. He pulled it toward him, the bag moving as though it was empty. Whatever was in there, if anything, didn't have much weight to it.

He shone his flashlight inside.

Within a second, he'd dropped the bag back on the floor and jerked his arm up to his mouth.

"Jesus wept. I'm going to be sick."

Ella thought of *Psycho*, and *Texas Chainsaw Massacre*, and *Silence of the Lambs*. All Ed Gein–inspired works which she'd seen countless times over. She and Ripley picked up the bag and peered inside themselves. She heard Hannibal Lecter's voice in her head.

Have you seen blood in the moonlight? It appears quite black.

He wasn't wrong. At the bottom of the burlap sack, the skinned face of Christine Hartwell stared back at her. She resisted the urge to say *I told you so.* Now wasn't the time.

"Get this to forensics immediately," Ripley said.

"This guy killed a woman, gutted her body, cut off her head, and skinned her face in less than an hour. Outside the confines of his own workstation or private area," Ella said. "This isn't an average serial killer."

"I won't lie, Rookie, that was quite impressive. I wouldn't have made that connection myself. Someone would have eventually, but you did it right away. Good work."

The exhaustion finally hit her, but the praise from Ripley provided a little relief.

"But even with that connection, it doesn't tell us who did this," Ripley continued. "Not to mention that it further proves my point that these killings are the work of three separate people."

Ella didn't have an answer for that one. Ripley was right. If this killer went to such extreme levels to craft this scene, right down to the small details like antifreeze and a very specific murder weapon, then wouldn't the other scenes be equally as theatric? She thought to Gein's other crimes. His murder of a second middle-aged woman, grave robbing, even rumors of him killing his own brother. None of them fit, at least as far as she could tell. However, her knowledge of the other killings in the bayou town was limited at best.

"I want to take a look at the files of the first two victims," Ella said. "Maybe there are some other patterns there."

"Fine by me. First thing in the morning, I'll talk to some of Christine Hartwell's family. Harris, can you take us to our hotel? I've got a feeling we're going to need some rest."

***

Their motel was a standard three-star affair, located only a short drive from the crime scene. Harris had dropped them off and told them he'd be back for them in the morning. Ella felt a wave of relief when she learned she and Ripley would have separate rooms. There was such a thing as too much, too soon, Ella thought. She needed the privacy to recharge and ruminate on what she'd seen so far.

After checking in with the receptionist, Ella and Ripley made their way to the first floor. Ella's room was located at the end of a short, carpeted corridor.

"See you in the morning," Ripley said. "Bright and early. That's how I like it."

"Likewise," said Ella. "See you in the morning." She swiped her keycard and entered her room. It was surprisingly modest, decorated in a shade of warm orange. Her first point of call was the bed. She dropped her bags beside it and lay down, savoring the relief of getting off her feet somewhere comfortable. The exhaustion hit her hard. She tilted her head so she could see out the motel room window, but she couldn't bring herself to step up and appreciate the view properly.

Her thoughts were of the crime scene. Since seeing the dead body of Christine Hartwell, she hadn't thought of anything else. Her subconscious wouldn't let her, she thought. Seeing something so visceral and unnatural brought up a lot of strange feelings. She was excited to dig further into the case, especially with the Gein connection, but it was the uncertainty that made her feel anxious.

The uncertainty of what might come next. Would there be more bodies, or was this it? Would she have to endure a similar horror again while she was here, or could she focus her efforts solely on this crime scene?

She didn't want to let down Ripley or Edis. She wasn't concerned with being the hero of the hour, she just wanted to add value to the investigation.

Ella closed her eyes and saw the body again.

CHAPTER SIX

It was a new day, but to Mia Ripley, it simply felt like an extension of the one before. That was pretty common these days, days blurring into years, sometimes waking up unable to remember if she was still married or not. After the blissful sensation of morning obliviousness passed, reality always came crushing back. No marriage these days, just the grim details of federal crimes clogging up her brain capacity.

A decapitated, strung-out corpse. A dead skin mask. A copycat crime of one of the world's most infamous murderers. Just another day.

She'd been in the job so long that she was able to view crime scenes with an unbiased eye. The first few years of the job were spent playing the what-if game. What if this victim was my daughter? What if someone else had been present when the killer walked into the store? What if she'd had a weapon under the counter? Eventually, the what-ifs gave way to acceptance

Mia took a cab to the home of Harry Hartwell, the brother of Christine Hartwell. Few tasks filled her with as much dread as visiting the home of the bereaved family. Her humanism, or rather her learned ability to lack humanism, didn't aid her well when she had to sit beside someone and help them process the death of a loved one. And it was made all the more difficult when the circumstances around that death involved dismemberment and flayed skin.

On the journey, Mia gave Ella's theory some thought. While she was impressed that Ella connected the dots so quickly, all it did was establish a *modus operandi*. It didn't provide a motive, or even any leads whatsoever.

Harry's home wasn't one of the lavish waterfront properties. Far from it. The town's central lake glimmered in the distance, morning sun reflecting off its surface, but the area Harry lived in would be considered the town's slums. Her cab trembled along a dirt path which led to a row of detached houses, modest in size and neglected in quality. A handful of the homes appeared abandoned, judging by the overgrown weeds slowly reclaiming their exteriors. Harry's place was at the end of the row.

Mia exited the cab and walked up the steps of his white porch. Before she could knock on the door, someone opened it from the other side.

"Police?" a man asked. He was on the large side, innocent-eyed, with a long beard from the chin down. Mia would have assumed he was a biker, if not for the 2009 blue Ford in his driveway. His T-shirt proudly declared *THE OLDER I GET, THE BETTER I WAS.*

"Close enough," Mia said. "Are you Harry?"

"I am," he said. Mia saw the grief right away, although he was trying his best to keep it hidden. She saw how weak and pale he looked, and she recognized he was talking with a dry mouth—obvious signs Harry was struggling to come to terms with his loss.

"I'm Agent Mia Ripley with the FBI. Do you mind if I talk to you about a few things?"

Harry shook his head. "No. Come in, please."

Mia entered to a surprisingly well-kept hallway. A small terrier, unsure whether it was excited or scared, yapped away from another room.

"Sorry about Loki. We don't get many new visitors," he said.

"Don't apologize. I'm sorry we had to meet under such circumstances."

Harry's living room was a perfect square. One brown sofa along the wall, a TV propped in the corner, and no single chairs. The single person's setup.

"Take a seat," Harry said, pointing to his sofa. He pulled in a stool from the adjoining kitchen.

"Thank you," said Mia. She pulled out her notebook and flipped to a new page. She needed to get the awkward part over with first. "Have you been told what happened?" she asked.

"Yeah. I mean, the sheriff told me the basics," Harry said. His eyes were swollen red, but he spoke with composure. "He seemed like there was a couple o' things he didn't wanna tell me, though."

"First, can I ask about your relationship with Christine?" Mia didn't want to overload Harry with the sick details just yet, for fear Harry might lose his calm.

"Best sister I ever had." He smiled. "We were pretty close, I guess. No one from our family is left, so it's just me and her."

Mia watched Harry's body language closely. Her first point of call was always the interviewee's feet. If they were pointed away from her, it was often a sign the interviewee wanted to escape. Her second point of call was their hands. If someone had something to hide, they'd use their hands to create a literal barrier between themselves and the interviewer. Covering their mouth when they talked, folding their arms, holding their head in their hands while they answered questions.

So far, Harry exhibited none of these symptoms. There was one more dead giveaway, but Mia hadn't gotten there yet.

"Please don't think of this as a suspicious question, Mr. Hartwell, but can you verify your whereabouts between five and seven p.m. last night?"

"I was playing darts with some friends. They'll be able to vouch for me," he said. He ran his hand through his hair and composed himself. Mia saw his eyes begin to swell with tears.

"Thank you. What else can you tell me about Christine? Was she generally well-liked? Was there anyone who might want to hurt her?"

"No," Harry said confidently. "There's two types of women out there. The ones who party and end up puking in the toilet, and the ones who hold back their friend's hair when they're puking in the toilet. Christine's the latter. She's the kindest soul you'd ever meet."

That was all Mia needed. She was certain Harry wasn't involved. Another major red flag was when an interviewee, particularly one who claimed to be grieving, referred to the deceased in past tense. For the first forty-eight hours, their subconscious would still be coming to terms with the fact they were gone, so they'd be more likely to refer to them as though they were still alive. Mia had caught out countless suspects with this little trick.

"Well, actually, I tell a lie," Harry continued. "There is one person—maybe."

Mia pulled out her pen. "Please, tell me anything you can. Any minor detail is useful."

"It's her ex-husband," Harry said. He stood up and released his terrier from the other room. It rushed toward Mia's feet and began sniffing violently. His yapping ceased once his curiosity was satisfied.

"Name?" Mia asked.

"Rick Cornette. Christine dropped his last name after their divorce. Messy, it was. The guy is a total sleaze. Drinks like an Irish sailor. Used to abuse Christine something rotten until she wised up and left."

"Their split wasn't amicable?"

"Oh no. Christine walked in one night and busted him with a couple o' working girls. Confronted him and she got a smack for her efforts. Me and the darts boys went around the same night and set him right."

"And that was the last you saw of him?"

"Me personally, yeah. But Christine went through the whole divorce crap with him. Got in a battle over their assets and the like, but Christine came out golden. She got full ownership of their shop and Rick got jack shit. What he deserves."

"How long ago was this?" Mia asked.

"Couple o' years. Rumor down the darts club is that it sent Rick loopy. Drinks himself to death now. That business was everything to him."

It was a solid lead. Given the overkill at the crime scene, Mia suspected Christine may have been killed by someone with a personal vendetta against her.

"Thank you, Harry. One last question. Did Christine have an interest in serial killers at all? Or anything true crime related?"

"Serial killers? God no. She's the most squeamish woman you could ever meet. Why do you ask?"

"Unfortunately, I can't divulge any details about on ongoing investigation. But it's nothing important, really."

"Understood. Rick, on the other hand. Well, that's a different story. That man's butchered a few carcasses in his time."

Mia pulled her notepad back out. "How do you mean?"

"When he wasn't running his hardware shop, he was at home cuttin' up pigs and deer and the like. He was a skilled hunter."

***

Ella suddenly realized why so many cops were wound up tight. The hot desk she'd been designated at the local precinct was like something from a high school exam hall, and the hard leather chair was like sitting on a cactus.

39

Some snide glances came her way from the surrounding officers. They huddled together on the other side of the office, occasionally peering over at the new girl. Every few minutes, a chorus of laughter would break out.

Now she knew why they'd been so hesitant to send across their crime scene photos to the FBI. Sheriff Harris was right. They didn't like the idea of someone else coming in to take charge of their investigation, least of all a young woman. Law enforcement was a place for the masculine to thrive. It had always been this way. And even in the progressive modern age, there was no sign of this changing any time soon.

She started to feel like she was on display, like a museum curiosity to be gawped at. With Ripley's downplaying her Ed Gein theory, the loneliness and self-doubt began to creep in. A wave of light-headedness came, but Ella took a few deep breaths and steadied herself. What was it Bukowski said? *Decide you want it more than you're afraid of it.*

What she wanted was to catch a killer. It might be a long journey, but all journeys start with small steps.

"Here you go, sweetheart," said a voice from behind her. It was another officer, young, maybe early thirties. Boyishly good-looking too. A stark contrast to the middle-aged circle jerk a few feet away. "All the files we have on the cases you requested." He dropped them on the table in front of her.

"Thank you for your help," Ella said.

"I gotta say, we get a few out-of-towners, but not many as good-looking as you. Where are you staying while you're in Louisiana?"

Oh Jesus. I can do without this right now, she thought.

"Depends. But I can tell you a few places I'm *not* staying."

"Okay, honey. No need for that. Just trying to help. I'll be over the way if you need anything."

"I'll be fine," Ella said.

She idly wondered if she'd been too harsh, but her aunt always told her never to get involved with a policeman, a soldier, or a carny. Every time they left the house, you'd be left wondering if they'd ever come back.

She opened up the first report and read from top to bottom. The noise of the precinct was a distraction, so she pulled her iPod out of her bag and plugged her ears. She played the soundtrack to *The Prestige* on repeat. It had to be something without lyrics.

She read the report of the first victim. Her name was Julia Reynolds, a seventeen-year-old girl whose body parts had been discovered in the nearby High Gate Woods a week ago. Ella pulled out the autopsy report and saw that the cause of death had been strangulation, meaning any dismemberment had been carried out postmortem.

Ella saw that Julia Reynolds's hometown was Lake Charles, Louisiana. She performed a quick search and found that Lake Charles was some hundred miles away from where her body was discovered. She scanned the police report further, landing on something that caught her attention.

Julia Reynolds had been hitchhiking on the day of her disappearance.

A teenage girl. Hitchhiking. Dismemberment.

"You gotta be kidding me," Ella said out loud, making a brand new connection. She looked up and saw a handful of officers ogling her. She dropped her eyes back to the page, but was lost in her head. She piled up case file one and turned to the second.

The second victim's name was Winnie Barker, an eighty-one-year-old woman who was killed only two days after the first victim. The police report said that she was stabbed in her bed as she slept, with stab wounds to her chest and abdomen and a severe laceration across her throat.

She skimmed the police report for any minute details. Two things jumped out at her. The first was that numerous items had been stolen from Winnie's home, something that the killer hadn't done with either of the other murders.

But more alarmingly was that the victim had been discovered with a small lipstick mark on her leg.

To others, this might be inconsequential. There could have been a number of reasons how such a mark arrived in that place.

But Ella knew better. This mark was no accident.

The wheels began to turn. Yes, these victims couldn't be any more different. Victimology was inconsistent, but that didn't mean there wasn't a pattern to be found. The M.O. changed with each murder, but was it possible that this unsub's *modus operandi* was that he changed it each time?

The more she thought about it, the more everything fell into place. Ripley was wrong. This *was* a serial case, but the perpetrator was a serial killer playing the part of other serial killers.

Julia Reynolds. Hitchhiking across the country but was strangled, dismembered, and discarded in the woods. This was a copycat of Edmund Kemper's murders, the Coed Killer who murdered ten people in California.

Winnie Barker. Stabbed repeatedly, throat slashed, and burgled as she lay in bed. This was a copycat of Richard Ramirez's murders, the Night Stalker who terrorized Los Angeles and San Francisco in the eighties. During one of his murders, he drew a pentagram in lipstick on his victim's leg.

The evidence was all right there. And now it was Ed Gein. He wasn't copycatting one serial killer, he was copycatting all of them.

"Everything okay?" a voice asked. "Heard you talking to herself. This stuff will send you insane if you let it."

The boyish officer again. Ella pulled out her earplugs. "Just thinking out loud."

"Anything we can help with? We are the experts on this stuff, you know?" He perched himself on the edge of Ella's desk.

Heavy footsteps sounded behind them. Another voice interrupted.

"Peddle your shit somewhere else, Rick Astley. Miss Dark is more than capable of collecting her own thoughts, thank you."

Ella turned around to see Ripley waiting for her. The officer hopped off the table and held his hands up in mock surrender. He walked into the break room, slamming the door with more force than was necessary.

"You might have embarrassed him," Ella said. Suddenly, her short outburst from earlier didn't seem so bad.

"I couldn't give a monkey's. You'll meet plenty of guys like that, so get used to it. Same goes for that gaggle of limp-dicked oldies in the corner."

Some of them looked up. Ella tried not to laugh. "Anyway, forget them. We've got a suspect to question. Get your shit together and let's go."

"On it," said Ella as she picked up her bag.

"Did you find anything?" Ripley asked.

"Yes. You're not going to believe this."

CHAPTER SEVEN

Ella sat in the passenger seat while Ripley drove. Despite her tough demeanor, Ripley operated the same way a grandma might drive her grandkids to soccer practice on a Sunday afternoon. Slow, obedient, and dared not rush a red light. Sheriff Harris had commandeered a vehicle for them to use to avoid relying on cabs.

"Trust me, as an agent, you don't want to ever get caught fucking around on the road. We're supposed to set an example. Besides, nothing says *frigid old bitch* like trying to own the road."

Ella wasn't much listening. "Edmund Kemper. Richard Ramirez. Both victims match the M.O.s of them to a tee. We're dealing with a copycat, I'm sure of it."

The midday traffic was picking up, although in this town, even rush hour would be a leisurely experience compared to the horrors of D.C.

"Winnie Barker, the second victim, even had a pentagram drawn on her leg. That was one of Ramirez's hallmarks. How can that be just a coincidence?"

Ella turned to Ripley for some kind of confirmation. Anything. Ripley pursed her lips and squinted her eyes as she navigated the roads. "Don't you think?"

"It's a great connection, Dark, and it's a link I'd never have made myself, but it's a stretch."

"It's a stretch? How?"

"What I see when I look at those pictures is a blotchy red mark on an old woman's leg. I don't see a pentagram. We don't even know for sure that it was the unsub who put the mark there. It could be anything. Not to mention that it might not even be a lipstick mark. It could have been marker pen or some kind of abnormality from the excessive blood loss. We can't just jump to conclusions."

Ella was taken aback. She drummed her fingers on the Honda's dashboard. An awkward silence hung between them. She had a sudden urge to turn the radio on but resisted. She mulled over Ripley's comments.

"But why would she have a blotch on her ankle? Someone must have put it there. An old woman like her would have had difficulty reaching down there. She was in her eighties."

"You want to know what I think it is? I think it was a carny mark."

"A what?" Ella asked, not wanting to sound amateurish but her curiosity getting the better of her.

"Winnie Barker was burgled, yes?"

"Yes."

"Bands of criminals sometimes literally *mark* potential victims with recognizable symbols. It goes back to the days of dishonest carnival workers who'd mark gullible people with chalk so other carnies would know to target them. This is the modern equivalent. I've seen it a lot."

Ella thought on it. She'd heard of similar things in the past, without a doubt. As she considered the possibility, her theory began to slowly float away from her grasp. She decided to claw it back a little.

"But burglaries don't usually end with homicide," she said.

"Very true, but plenty of burglaries *have* ended in homicide. The perp could have gotten carried away, or may have had a personal vendetta against the victim. Winnie may have caught him in the act and he didn't want to leave a witness. Until we know more, we can't say anything for sure.

"Edis sent me out here because I notice patterns," Ella said, finally. "If not for me, the Greenville Strangler would still be out there. To predict the future, look at the past." Ella decided she wasn't going to let this go.

"You know how many hitchhikers get killed? Lots. You know how many people get stabbed? Even more. Even if it wasn't a carny mark left on Winnie's leg, I've seen unsubs leave star marks, circles, and all kinds of crude drawings at crime scenes."

Ripley had a point, Ella admitted to herself.

"Your Ed Gein theory struck a chord with me, that much I'll admit. But you're just grasping at straws here. You're trying to find patterns where there aren't any. That's what conspiracy theorists do, not professional detectives."

"Do you think it's just a coincidence that three murders in the same week have links to infamous serial slayings, then?" Ella asked calmly.

Ripley turned a stiff corner onto a trailer park site and entered onto a rocky dirt path. They came to an abrupt stop where a row of trailers either side of them began. Ripley leaned forward and surveyed the area.

"Looks like we've reached the slums," she said. "And to answer your question, yes. If you look closely at *any* murder, you'll see some kind of pattern to a famous crime or serial killer. Stabbings, gunshots, strangulation, sawing off dicks—everything that can possibly happen has happened at some point in history. It doesn't mean it's a connection, it just means it's happened before. Likening these murders to events which happened decades ago doesn't help us find the culprit."

Ella bit her lip to stop her from retorting without thinking her response through. Ripley had a point, and given her track record, she certainly did her job well. But Ella couldn't shake a niggling suspicion that Ripley had other reasons to dispute her findings.

"And the Ed Gein link?" Ella asked. "You don't think that's a copycat?"

"It may have been inspired by. But outside of movies and podcasts and all that other sensationalized stuff, the truth is that copycats are rarer than rocking horse shit. In my thirty years, I've only ever come across *one* copycat killer."

Ella racked her brain for the killer in question. A few copycat killers came to mind, but none which were investigated by the FBI. "Who was it?" she asked.

"That's not important right now," Ripley said. She jumped out of the car and shut the door with vigor. Ella followed. "Now, is your head in the game? Or are you going to be thinking of these theories while we're interrogating this guy?"

"I'm ready," said Ella.

"Good, now let's go. It's trailer number thirteen."

They walked past two overturned trash cans. On the side of one trailer, someone had spray-painted *PEOPLE LIVE HERE*. The entire row of cabins opposite number 13 were completely blacked out. No lights from any windows. However, two doors down, number 17 was playing annoyingly loud music. It looked to Ella like they were having a party, despite it having only just turned evening.

Ripley banged on number 13's door. It reverberated with a clanging sound. "Mr. Cornette? We're with the FBI. Open up, please."

45

Ella heard a shuffling sound inside, then a sudden thud. The walls were so thin that she could probably kick through them, she thought.

"What?" a voice shouted back. It was rough, muffled. "What you want?"

"Oh for Christ's sake. He's hammered," said Ripley.

"How do you know?" Ella asked.

Ripley turned to her. "He's speaking from his throat and not his diaphragm. Instant sign that alcohol is in the system. Not to mention those empty cans in his trash."

"Oh. Good spot."

"Mr. Cornette, if you don't open up, I'm afraid we're going to have to break this door down and take you under arrest. Something tells me that wouldn't be too difficult."

"I'm comin'," the man shouted. The lock clicked and the door swung open. "Yes?"

Something told Ella that once upon a time, Rick Cornette was a good-looking man. A luscious head of hair, a lean frame, gleaming eyes. Now, however, that was all gone. Rick had small patches of gray hair dotted around his worn-out face. Emaciated frame, like he hadn't eaten for months. Yellow skin, breath so bad it could strip paint. He was a sixty-year-old man who should still be forty-five.

"I'm Special Agent Ripley and this is my partner, Ella Dark. We understand that you're the ex-husband of Ms. Christine Hartwell, correct?"

"Here's me thinking you were the hookers I ordered."

Ella and Ripley said nothing.

"Fine. Come in. Don't be long."

Rick's trailer only had a single chair, pointed directly at a TV blaring Fox News. His kitchen area was overloaded with unwashed plates. One of his cupboards had no door. Ella spotted a number of prescription pills inside.

Rick slumped back into his chair and faced away from Ripley and Ella. They walked around to face him. Ripley turned off the TV at the plug.

"Whoa, what do you think you're doing?" Rick shouted. He picked up a half-empty bottle of whiskey from beside his chair and jumped to his feet. Ella flinched, thinking for a second that Rick was going to hurl the bottle at them.

46

Ripley threw the plug down on the floor with force. "Friend, we might not be the prostitutes you expected, but I'll definitely put something up your ass if you don't cooperate here."

There was a stunned silence by both Ella and Rick. Ella expected some kind of masculine retaliation, but amazingly, none came. Instead, Rick dropped back into his seat.

Then he started crying. Head in his hands.

Ripley and Ella swapped glances. Ella assumed it was the booze talking.

"I loved her, you know. I still loved her. Our marriage was perfect. It shouldn't have ended. When she took my shop, that was the end for me."

"We're sorry to hear that, Mr. Cornette, but if you could answer some questions we'll leave you to your business. Where were you yesterday evening between five and seven p.m.?"

Rick shot up, wiping the few tears which had collected under his eyes. "I was here. Why?"

"Can anyone confirm that?"

"No."

Ella and Ripley exchanged a look. "Fair enough. Mr. Cornette, is it true that your relationship with Christine included some physical abuse?"

Rick moved over to his kitchen area and fetched a half-finished bottle of brandy. He laid it on the kitchen counter then perched himself over the sink. He stared at his reflection in the small window opposite.

"Yeah, our relationship had its ups and downs, but that doesn't mean I killed her."

"We're not saying it did," offered Ripley, "but given the circumstances of her death, we feel it's necessary to rule you out."

"Circumstances? What?"

"Is it correct you're a hunter, Mr. Cornette?" Ripley asked.

"I was. Not anymore."

The agents waited for Rick to elaborate. He didn't. He ran the tap, splashed water on his face, and returned to the living area.

"Can we ask when you last saw Ms. Hartwell?" Ripley said.

"Hartwell." Rick laughed. "Wouldn't even keep my name."

"Isn't that what usually happens when people get divorced?" Ella said, trying to ease the burden of Ripley carrying the conversation. She saw Rick's pity for himself turn to frustration.

"She was seeing someone else, you know? While we were together." Rick took a gulp of the brandy. "Everyone took her side. Scumbags."

"That's not the picture her brother painted," said Ripley. Ella saw something change, felt the atmosphere change. Rick clenched his teeth, gripped his bottle hard around the neck. He turned away from the agents and launched his whiskey bottle across the room, where it collided with the kitchen window. It cracked down the middle, then the bottle crashed into the pile of dishes. The clang was almost deafening. He reached down and grabbed the whiskey bottle already lying empty beside his chair. "You stupid lady cops come in here, thinking you know me, accusing me of all sorts of shit. I told you, I loved the bitch. I wouldn't kill her."

Ella tried to calm him down. "That's all well and good, but we—"

"Shut your mouth," Rick interrupted. He stumbled over to a wall, cracked his head against it. "Is that not enough? That I loved her? Don't you believe me?"

There was a heavy pause from everyone in the room. Ella could still hear the irritating drum-and-bass from two trailers down.

"No," said Ella.

And before she or Ripley could say anything else, Rick lunged across the room in the blink of an eye. The last thing Ella saw was Rick's stained vest, his brown teeth, his enflamed eyeballs, inches away from her face.

And she froze.

***

She'd always been told that no training could prepare someone for the real thing. People always said that experience was the best teacher, although the test always came before the lesson.

But as Rick's hand, still clutching a glass bottle, filled her vision, a surge of adrenaline shook her from head to toe. Better yet, it was a familiar feeling. Visions of her martial arts sparring classes rushed back. She recognized the pressure points by instinct—wrist, groin, temples, eyes.

Ella quickly strafed to her left as Rick hurtled toward her. She reached out, grabbed his wrist, and then thrust her knee straight into his stomach. The bottle flew from Rick's hand and clattered against the TV as he keeled over. With a fleeting moment to capitalize, Ella mentally marked out two to three centimeters above her attacker's eyes. Still with one hand wrapped around his wrist, she drove the palm of her other hand directly into Rick's temple. His head trembled violently, sending his brain ricocheting around his skull and incapacitating him for around five seconds.

Rick dropped to his knees as he lifted up his arm to shield his head. At that moment, Ella hooked both of his arms around to his back and then pressed her knee into his spine. Rick's body fell limp in her arms as she pushed his face into the cheap blue rug on his living room floor.

Ella looked up at Ripley, who was staring wide-eyed at the scene in front of her. "Help a rookie out and throw me those handcuffs?" Ella said.

Ripley did exactly that. Ella caught the handcuffs and snapped them on Rick with flawless technique. Rick began to writhe as the pain from Ella's strikes subsided, but she held his face down so his cries were muffled.

"God damn," said Ripley.

Ella eased off. Rick wasn't going anywhere. He rolled onto his back and spat up a thick stream of phlegm.

"Yeah. Twenty years of martial arts classes finally paid off," Ella said. She jumped to her feet. Up until now, she'd never seen Ripley at a loss for words. "What? You never heard of Bujinkan?" Ella asked.

Ella saw a look on of something that resembled astonishment on Ripley's face."

"No," said Ripley.

"Japanese. Focuses on pressure points. Hit certain areas until they're disoriented. Temple, abdomen, spine."

"Good old paralysis. It's extreme, but seems to have done the trick," Ripley said. She bent down next to Rick. "Didn't expect it would be *you* in the restraints tonight, did you?"

Rick coughed up another ball of fluid. "You've got nothing on me," Rick shouted. "I've done nothing wrong." He tried to pick himself up to his feet but fell under the weight of his drunkenness.

"We'll see about that." Ripley lifted Rick to his feet. Ella helped steady him. Rick desperately tried to free his hands but he quickly admitted defeat when he realized it was a lost cause. Ripley and Ella marched him to the trailer door, and when they opened it, two young women were standing outside. Both of them were platinum blonde and barely out of their teenage years. One of them had a cigarette lodged between her lips.

"Change of plans," said Ella, shooing them out of the way with a wave of her hand. Her battle with Rick had given her a newfound sense of authority. The adrenaline was still coursing through her. She was the law, and they damn well better respect it. "We'll be doing the escorting from here."

CHAPTER EIGHT

Ella held open the precinct doors as Ripley pushed the handcuffed man through them. Rick stumbled occasionally, purposely slowing down his pace to annoy the agents. But Ripley's sharp jabs to his spine soon hurried him up.

Down the corridor and into the main office, their footsteps drew the attention of the night shift officers. Up ahead, Ella spotted Sheriff Harris staring into a pile of paperwork. He jolted out of his chair when he saw them approaching and rushed over to give them a hand. He placed his pen behind his ear and looked the arrestee up and down. A disproving head shake followed.

"Old Rick Corny," Harris said. "It was only a matter of time before you wound up in here again."

Rick, dressed in a stained vest and sweatpants and clearly feeling the effects of the cold, snarled at Harris as he swayed between Ripley and Ella. "Just give me my phone call," Rick said. "I gotta tell your mama I won't be seein' her tonight."

Harris shook his head in disapproval. "Stick him in the ice room, ladies. End of the hallway on the right."

The entire journey back, Rick had become more obnoxious by the minute. At first, he'd just made lewd comments, something which both agents were used to. But the liquor in his system had slowly reduced him to an incoherent mess. The sudden pang of cool air had given him a second wind, but once Rick was thrust into the interrogation room at the precinct, he went back to mumbling nonsense and zoning in and out of consciousness. Ripley sat him in a hard wooden chair, purposely designed to be uncomfortable. Rick didn't utter a word. The two agents took a seat opposite him.

"Ice room?" said Ella. She addressed the question to Ripley.

"It means interrogation room. It's an old police trick to turn the air conditioning up to the max to put the suspect under additional stress."

Ella was a little surprised Ripley revealed such information in front of Rick, but given that his eyes were shut and he was slumped forward against the desk, it didn't seem too much of an issue. She idly put herself in his position as she let the room's prickly temperature settle into her nerve endings. She felt the cold air seep into her lungs and throat and eyes. It was sharp, unpleasant.

"Mr. Cornette, you're not here to sleep. You're here to answer our questions. Understand?" Ripley said.

Rick gave nothing in the way of a response. He stirred in his chair, rocking from side to side. Ella looked at Ripley and shrugged.

Ripley suddenly booted the underside of the table, lifting the whole thing off the ground and jerking Rick back to life. He blinked furiously and caught a stream of drool from his lips.

"What?" he said. "What do you want?"

"I want to put you in jail for the murder of your ex-wife, and you're making it very easy for me," Ripley said. "Are you going to talk, or shall we take your silence as an indication of guilt?"

Rick spurted out something that almost resembled words, but neither Ella nor Ripley understood any of it. "I think we're wasting our time here," Ella said. "He's too sloshed to give us any real information."

Finally, Rick collapsed face down onto the wooden table in front of him. Ripley sighed. "I hope that hurt. Come on." She motioned to Ella. "Let's leave him here. You're right, we're wasting our time."

The two agents stood up and left the room. Ripley summoned Harris over to lock Rick in for the night.

"We can try him again in the morning," Ella said. The agents headed back to the desk Ella had been working at. She picked up her bag which she'd stashed underneath. There were still a few dreary-eyed officers dotted around the room, pushing themselves on with the aid of coffee and confectionary.

"When I say we're wasting our time, I mean by talking to this drunkard at all. He's not our guy, and I'll bet my life on it," Ripley said. "We'll keep him here until morning. Harris, charge him for being drunk and disorderly and attempted GBH. After that, he's free to go."

Glancing back at Rick through the small window, Ella realized that all she could determine from looking at Rick was that he was a man, with all of the features that made him human and nothing else. She could visualize Rick carrying out the murder of Christine Hartwell, but at the same time couldn't imagine him doing anything of the sort. It occurred to her that she had no idea what Rick might be thinking, or what secrets he might be hiding. She saw an impenetrable wall of human anatomy, with all of the truth concealed and impossible to uncover. The fact that Ripley could so easily claim with such certainty that Rick wasn't responsible for this murder filled her with awe, jealousy, and a dread that she didn't possess this ability herself.

"How can you be so sure?" Ella asked.

"Look at the state of him. The man is a mess. Physically, mentally, emotionally. He couldn't have pulled off a crime scene as elaborate as the one we saw. Besides, if he wanted his ex-wife snubbed out, why go to such lengths to kill her? He would have done it discreetly and with as little mess as possible."

Now, Ella saw it. Ripley was right, but she pushed her further, desperate for a deeper explanation. Not just an explanation into her willingness to free Rick, but an explanation into how Ripley was able to simply *see* these things.

"What if he did it as a way to throw us off the scent? Like, he purposely went overboard with the kill to make us think it *wasn't* him?" Ella asked.

"Like I said before, get your head out of those books. Very few killers would be that smart. When we met Rick, he barely knew what day it was. And judging by his trailer, he's been living like an ape for months. He drowns his sorrows with booze and buys hookers. That's his life. He doesn't have the mental or physical capabilities to be our perpetrator. I could smell it right from the get-go. We needed to bring him in," Ripley continued, "because we're stuck for leads here. And abusive assholes like him really test me."

Ella nodded, taking it all in. The exhaustion of the past twenty-four hours hit her, sending a spike of sharp pain through the center of her brain. All of the traveling and rushing around was a whole new world to her, and the adrenaline comedown had completely depleted her energy levels. "Call it a night?" she asked.

"Already? It's only nine p.m."

Ella felt her heart sink.

"Sheriff," Ripley called out, "can you take us down to the coroner's office? Rookie here wants her first taste of bodies on the slab."

"The other victims?" said Ella. "Now?"

"Now?" Harris echoed Ella's statements from the other side of the room. "It won't be open this late. All my guys are drained and

I've gotta get myself home too. My wife is starting to think I'm playing away with all these late nights."

"All right," Ripley said. "Come on then, Rookie."

Thank heavens, Ella thought. *I need to be alone to reenergize.*

"Want me to drive to the hotel?" Ella said.

"Hotel? No, no, no. We're heading somewhere else. And we definitely aren't driving there."

CHAPTER NINE

Freya's Tavern reminded Ella of the Milestone pub back in D.C., which was the go-to place for any law enforcement personnel. But here, there was a much different clientele. Judging by the looks she and Ripley got as they walked in, something about their appearance was worth gawping it.

An independent bar located within spitting distance of Christine Hartwell's hardware store, it was haunted by a strong scent of stale beer and boasted décor ripped straight from a British pub of the nineteen eighties. Circular tables, gambling machines, and not a single neon sign anywhere to be found. Its drab interior was almost impressive.

On a Saturday night, Freya's was the go-to place for locals looking to drink away the stress of the working week. But tonight, only the most hardened booze hounds had ventured out of their homes. Ella had a good idea why.

Ella found a small booth near a window and looked out as she sat. She could see the cordoned-off row of shops. Two officers sat in a police car outside, keeping any curious visitors at bay.

"What are you having?" Ripley shouted from the bar.

"Coke, please."

She felt a little dirty drinking alcohol while a murder victim's blood dried only a stone's throw away, which was why she stuck to soda.

Ripley, on the other hand, wasn't so reserved. She came back to their table clutching a whiskey tumbler half-filled with golden brown liquid. Ripley gulped the whole thing down in one and relaxed back in her seat. Ella sipped hers slowly, feeling like perhaps she was being judged for ordering something soft.

"No, I don't have a drinking problem," Ripley said. "Except when I can't get a drink."

Ella laughed. "I would never suggest such a thing. I'm just trying to keep a clear head myself. The last thing I want is to wake up feeling more tired than I already do."

"It's fine, I know you were thinking it, but what's life without a drink or two? Especially in this game."

Ella got an urge to prod around, to maybe ask some things which weren't related to murder or profiling or FBI protocols. If there was ever a time to do it, it was now.

"Do you think your job drives people to drink?" Ella asked.

"Oh yes, it does, and for two reasons. A lot of law enforcement drink to forget, but I'm not quite there yet."

"No?"

"The way I see it, I'm already in the green. Most agents don't make it to my age. I've probably got less than ten years left in the job before I have to hang up my badge. When that day comes, I give it another few years before my number gets called, so I might as well enjoy *something* while I'm still around."

"You mean you don't enjoy much anymore?" Ella asked, keeping it as casual as possible.

"It's difficult. In my thirties, I always swore I'd never be one of those career types who were married to their jobs and had nothing else to live for. Twenty years later, that's exactly where I am. My sons are off doing their own thing, only coming back to see me at Christmas. I got a four-hundred-thousand-dollar house with three empty bedrooms waiting for me back in Washington, and a couple of ex-husbands who don't want to speak to me."

Since the bar was relatively quiet, Ripley simply called the bartender from her seat for another whiskey. He flashed her an "OK" sign.

"But you've done *everything else*," Ella said. "There are people all across the country who look up to you. You've got accolades people would kill for. You get to travel the world and get paid well for it. Sounds like a dream to me."

"Exactly. It *sounds* like fun, but so does camping out on Mount Fuji. People tend to change their minds when they've got icicles on their nipples in the middle of the night."

Ella laughed again. Who knew that the battle-scarred, FBI Hall of Famer Mia Ripley actually had a sense of humor? Maybe it was the drink talking, but this was the most Ella had learned about Ripley since meeting her. The bartender came along and dropped a whiskey in front of Ripley and a multicolored cocktail in front of Ella.

"Sorry, this isn't for me," Ella said.

"I know, it's—"

"Don't say it," Ripley interrupted. "A present from those gentlemen propping up the bar over there?"

"Correct," the bartender said. "I can take it back if you wish?"

Ella looked across to see two guys, probably late twenties, desperately trying to look like they were in mid-conversation. They looked like farmer types, a far cry from the usual city slickers who pulled the same trick in bars around Washington.

"No, I'll keep it, thank you," Ella said. The bartender left. She didn't want to upset whoever it was who sent it. It was more trouble than it was worth. Besides, there was a part of her that appreciated it.

"Lucky you. I can't remember the last time that happened to me," Ripley said. "It must be nice to know you've still got it."

"It's a really nice gesture, but it always feels so empty, you know?"

"I know exactly. Do you have a boyfriend back home?"

"Nope. No boyfriend."

"Girlfriend?"

"Does a housemate count?"

"Sure."

"Then yes, I have one girlfriend," she laughed. Ella pushed the cocktail over to Ripley's side of the table. "There you go. Consider this my first gift to you."

"Well, it's probably sweeter than a diabetic's pee but a free drink is a free drink. She clinked the cocktail glass against her whiskey tumbler to attract the attention of the two gentlemen, then raised it to them. "Thank you, boys," she shouted, "but it takes more than a cheap cocktail to bag a rookie like this." Ripley took a gulp, then winced. "Ugh. Hideous."

Ella slid along her chair to hide away from the two guys. She felt a little embarrassed. From her past experiences, there was no such thing as a free drink. They always wanted something in return. The moment where they usually come over and introduce themselves passed slowly and painfully. Ella breathed a sigh of relief as the two men left the bar.

"Why the questions, anyway?" Ella asked. "Trust me when I say my life isn't all that interesting outside of my Intelligence bubble. If anything, I should be the one grilling you. Isn't that what an inquisitive student should do?"

"Go on then. Hit me with your best," Ripley said.

"Most intense case you ever worked on?"

"David Parker Ray. 1999."

Ella expected a little more but nothing came. She already knew all about the David Parker Ray case, and the details went beyond disturbing into another realm entirely. Ripley turned her attention toward the outer world while a brief silence lingered in the air. Ripley took a big gulp of her drink. Ella thought it best not to push any further, so she changed the topic. "Biggest regret?" she asked.

Ripley placed a now-empty whiskey tumbler on the table and swallowed heavily. Next to it, the cocktail still sat half-full.

"Not retiring at fifty," Ripley said, settling back into her seat. "But I knew if I was just sitting around at home I'd want to get back out in the field. But when I'm out in the field, I regret not giving it all up. It's a constant battle."

"Like Rocket Man," Ella said.

"Who?"

"Rocket Man. The story. The astronaut who misses his family while he's in space, but misses space when he's with his family. It's about the struggle between contentment and chasing that one last high. A lot of people find themselves in your situation when they hit retirement age."

"And the best advice I can give is don't let it get to that point. Don't make the mistake of romanticizing this job, or the people we chase. Serial killers aren't some kind of exotic species to be admired. They're normal people who shit and stink just like the rest of us. They're pond scum, and they're certainly not worth dedicating your life to," Ripley said. "If I give you a hard time, it's because I see a little of me in you. But I see a version of me that could have a different ending. Once this is over, go back to your desk job. Make a life outside of work and don't neglect it. Don't spend your life hunting killers, or you'll end up another victim."

Ella was taken aback. She wasn't sure what to say. The last thing she expected was to receive a compliment from Mia Ripley, however backhanded it might have been.

"Or even worse, you'll end up a Rocket Man like me."

They both laughed.

"The idea of going back to my desk seems really weird," Ella said. "It's only been a day, but it feels a million years away."

"Why did you join the FBI in the first place?" Ripley continued. "A girl with your skills could be making big bucks in the technology world."

The question she dreaded the most. She'd been asked it a hundred times in her life, and never once gave the honest answer. Maybe it was time to finally open up. She moved her gaze to a low-hanging light above the bar area where the two gentlemen had been sitting. The light blinded her, consuming her vision entirely. For a few moments, she was in a different place and time. Freya's Tavern dissolved into her childhood bedroom, and she found herself staring at a flashing digital clock.

It was 5:02 a.m. Ella couldn't remember ever seeing the numbers start with *05* before. She shut her eyes tight in the hope that when she opened them, it would be closer to her usual wake-up time of 7:30.

But it didn't work. Something had stirred her and now she was wide awake. She sat up in bed and peered behind her curtains. Outside was still pitch-black. Her dad's sedan was parked crookedly outside their house. He said it dissuaded car thieves from trying to take it.

Ella listened closely to the midnight sounds she'd never been privy to before, the songs the night sang. No cars sped past her window and she couldn't hear any sign of life from her own house or her neighbors'. Everything was so still and motionless, to the point that she felt a sudden urge to cry. She'd never been the only person awake in the house before.

Outside her bedroom door, she could see the hallway light was still on. Her dad always kept it turned off when he was asleep, so maybe he'd woken up early too. Ella hopped off her bed and opened up her door as quietly as possible. She just needed to see his face, whether he was awake or not. She needed to make sense of this, then she could go back to sleep. If her dad questioned her on why she'd gotten out of bed, she'd just say her scrunchy had fallen out and her hair was itching her forehead.

Out in the corridor, the orange light burned her eyes. She blinked until they adjusted then listened out for her dad. Nothing. Dead silence.

Suddenly, she noticed something unusual.

Her father's bedroom door was wide open. He hadn't kept his door open since she was a baby.

59

"Hello?" said a voice. This time, the voice came from outside of her inner acoustics. She snapped back to reality, seeing Ripley in front of her again.

Music filled her ears. Hard rock from the eighties. It sounded like AC/DC but she wasn't sure. Suddenly, she was back in Freya's Tavern, a long way away and many years removed from that night as a five-year-old girl. She always tried her best to keep the visions at bay, but they crept up on her like a spider from the floorboards. Once she knew they were lingering, it took a lot of willpower to not let them in. The slightest mention of family or work or trauma could bring back all of the pain and crush her under the weight of her memories. She had always prided herself on being approachable, honest, authentic, but there were certain subjects she avoided like the plague. This was one of them.

"Sorry, went off into dreamland there," Ella joked.

Ripley narrowed her eyes in her direction. Ella felt her stare. The same stare that had seen right into the heart of a hundred of America's most violent offenders was now turned on her. It burned. It made her feel exposed, like Ripley could see everything she'd just been imagining.

"I've only ever worked in law enforcement," Ella said, trying to revert back to the original question. "Started with Virginia state police seven years ago and never looked back. I guess I've been typecast," she laughed.

"Something was bothering you just then. What was it?"

Ella stuttered. "Bothering me? Nothing."

"They don't call me the Human Lie Detector for nothing. A moment ago, you went somewhere else in your head. Tell me about it."

Ella felt herself freeze up. She couldn't tell Ripley the truth. She'd never told anyone, let alone someone she'd only known for twenty-four hours. But if she tried to lie her way out of it, there was a chance it could affect Ripley's perception of her. Ella could sense Ripley was warming to her, or at least she hoped so. The last thing she wanted to do was quench that.

"I was trying to think about why I joined the Bureau. Around the time I did, some bad stuff was happening in my personal life. That's all."

"Like what?"

"Family drama I guess is the term." Ella hoped the lie was convincing enough.

The moment hung and gradually died out, but then Ripley revived it. "Talk about it. I think you should. "

Ella brainstormed some ideas to shut the conversation down, but nothing solid came to mind. She decided to be direct. "Can we talk about it some other time?" she asked. Ella saw Ripley give her the three-point look, moving her gaze toward her feet, her hands, and back to her eye level. It was the look that said she knew the truth regardless of what came out of her mouth.

"Bottling up trauma isn't good for you. If you want to do this job for any longer than a week, you'll need to find a way of letting that trauma out."

"I get that, it's just that it's a long story and today has really tired me out."

Ripley smiled with a sympathetic look. Ella couldn't tell if it was mock or genuine.

"Sure, let's get out of here," Ripley said.

They exited Freya's Tavern and walked out into the night, following the streetlamps toward a wooden hut that doubled as a taxi stand. Ripley poked her head through the glass partition and booked the next cab available to take them to their hotel.

Seeing Ripley engage in something so mundane was a strange feeling, Ella thought. She then realized that she'd stopped seeing her as the mythical figure she was known as and started seeing her as a person made of flesh and blood, with her own troubles and worries and regrets.

Most interestingly of all, Ella was starting to realize that Ripley wasn't always right. There were blind spots in her rationale. Ella's copycat theory seemed so airtight in her head and yet Ripley refused to accept it, or even consider it in any way. Ella visualized the whole thing like a jigsaw—the victims, the M.O.s, the references to infamous serial killers, even the locations. She couldn't see any holes, but then again, she also couldn't tell that Rick Cornette wasn't a killer. She hadn't known that criminals often marked potential burglary victims with strange symbols. It dawned on her that there were plenty of things she didn't know, and perhaps there were aspects of this murder which could potentially blow her whole theory apart.

In the distance, Ella could still see Christine's Hardware 101. One of the guarding officers had fallen asleep in the police car. Ella began to wonder how easy it would be to slip past them. She wondered if the killer had come back to inspect his handiwork over the past twenty-four hours. It wasn't uncommon for serial killers to inject themselves into investigations in any way they could, whether it be offering to help or calling the police to provide bogus information. The more Ella thought about it, the more confident she was that he would have at least surveyed the scene in some way, even if it was just a fleeting pass-by in his car.

Ella thought of the two gentlemen who'd bought her a drink. She thought of the bartender, the sleeping policeman, the midnight strollers casting an inquisitive eye at the crime scene tape as they walked by. Any of those people could have been responsible for Christine Hartwell's murder. Whoever it was could have been in the same bar as her and she wouldn't know it.

"Get some sleep tonight, Dark," Ripley said as they waited. "We're going to be seeing some dead bodies in the morning."

CHAPTER TEN

He hung back in the shadows, watching his prey. He recalled a paragraph from one of the textbooks he'd memorized.

The serial killer continuously evolves towards becoming his own god and executioner. With each subsequent killing, the homicidal drug, blunted by habitual use, creates a diminishing and disappointing impression. The extraordinary becomes increasingly ordinary.

They were the words of one of the many men he admired. His heroes, he called them. The human monsters whom he'd lived through vicariously for as long as he could remember. They were the words of Ian Brady, the serial killing, psychopathic genius from England whose insights into murder had taught him so much and brought him great success already.

But insights only took him so far, he'd realized. He knew now that acquiring knowledge was only half the battle; putting it into practice was what separated the real artists from the amateurs. And he was going to be the Picasso of his new world, he'd decided. No one would be better than him. People would talk about him for decades to come.

With each subsequent killing, the homicidal drug, blunted by habitual use, creates a diminishing and disappointing impression. However, he'd made sure to keep things fresh this time, to avoid any so-called diminishing impressions. Outside of murders of convenience, how many serial killers crossed gender boundaries? Hardly any. They chose their victim type and they stuck to it.

Bundy, Ramirez, Kemper, Gein. They all killed women.

But there was a certain cannibal from Milwaukee who had a penchant for young, gay, black men. Tonight would be that man's resurrection.

And as he watched the man stumble out of the club and into the road, these thoughts of dismemberment came rushing back, and excited him to the point he began to tremble in anticipation.

The man began to walk away from the club, and so he followed. His plan was simple. Follow him home, enter behind him, and begin the process. The man was Shawn Kelly, and he'd met him in the same club he'd just stumbled out of only the week before. Shawn made the perfect victim for what he wanted to achieve. The second they had engaged conversation on their first meeting, his mind had jumped to the Dahmer crime scene photos, and that was when the pieces fell in place.

Shawn sang as he made his way home, leaving the main street and entering into an eerily quiet side road. He knew the exact route Shawn would take home, and by his calculations, it would take him around twelve minutes of walking. So far, things were on track.

Shawn used the wall for assistance as he clambered down the side street, managing to stay on his feet. Shawn turned into a large cul-de-sac bathed in orange light.

He didn't like the cul-de-sac. It was too open, too visible. There were houses in every direction, making it easy for someone to spot the strange man following the drunk man.

But he knew that Shawn's house was located on the next street over. He kept his distance, occasionally staring at his phone to give the impression he was searching for a nearby establishment. He looked up and saw Shawn reach the small walkthrough which led into the street his house was on, and so he edged slightly closer to keep Shawn in sight.

But then the voices came. Somewhere over the wall. They were numerous and jovial in tone. The unmistakable sound of drunken youth.

Irritation clouded his thoughts. He hated that sound, and even worse was that it threw his schedule into disarray. He was standing at the entrance to the alleyway when, in his panic, he turned and rushed further out of sight.

He could hear Shawn now, talking to them. Something about the club he'd been to and how he'd gotten *completely shitfaced. He must know them,* he thought.

"We're going to Freya's," one of the strangers said. "Coming?"

No, no, no. He was almost sick with worry. He leaned against the wall, feeling a sudden emptiness in his stomach. *Don't you dare ruin my schedule,* he thought. *We've come this far. If you ruin this, you pricks will be next in line.*

They continued talking, then footsteps came his way. He panicked. His first thought was to run, but that would just draw attention to him. He knew he couldn't risk anyone seeing him.

Whoever it was came out of the alleyway. They were about to see him, and Shawn might too. If that happened, everything would be ruined.

Out of some instinct he didn't know he had, he leaned his arm against the wall and arched himself over. He coughed to the point that bile rose up through his stomach and into his throat. He felt their presence behind him, watching him.

"You okay, bud?" one asked. It wasn't Shawn.

He held up his thumb, then continued spluttering. He spat some phlegm out onto the ground.

He waited for what felt like an eternity. But then he heard them leave. Still perched against the wall, he glanced at them and saw they were both white, both teenagers. Shawn wasn't with them.

Relief washed over him, and once the kids were out of sight he rushed through the alleyway to continue on with his plan.

He reached the other side and saw Shawn still staggering up ahead. He arrived at his small, detached home which boasted an impressive view of the lake. Of course, the killer already knew Shawn's home address. He knew his job, and he knew that he afforded his place with a helping hand from his daddy.

He edged closer, ensuring that he stayed cloaked in shadows.

Shawn walked around the back of his house, unhooked a waist-high gate, and entered his backyard. Since most of the bayou houses were located in wide grassy areas, privacy was hard to come by. Public walkways usually circled entire blocks, leaving rear yards open to the view of any passersby. He had no problem circumventing his way around to Shawn's backyard and still remaining obscured.

At last, Shawn made it into his house. A downstairs light switched on. It had been around ninety minutes since the killer had dropped the pill in Shawn's drink and made his escape, so their full effect should kick in any second. Then it was time to strike.

He took a short walk to the end of the street and back just in case any prying eyes had spotted him. He made sure to hold his phone in his hand as he walked back. If anyone asked, he'd say he was talking to a local fellow on a dating app and was meeting up for a midnight rendezvous. If any of the neighbors knew Shawn, and he was sure they did, they'd no doubt believe him.

After three minutes had elapsed, he moved closer to Shawn's backyard.

As expected, the killer's tools were still in place from where he left them earlier. Shawn had been too drunk to notice them, despite them being right by his fence.

One power drill. One gallon of antifreeze, courtesy of Christine's Hardware 101.

The back door opened with a click. He entered into a dark kitchen with black-and-white tiled panels. Five steps later, he was in the living room, staring at a man sitting on his sofa staring at his cell phone.

"Hello, Shawn."

The man jumped up in fright. His phone flung from his hands. "Whoa, shit. You scared me." He put his hand on his chest then smiled. "Come in." He motioned for the stranger to join him on the couch. "What's your name? Or shall I just call you JD213?"

"You can call me Jeffrey."

"Jeffrey? Seriously? What are you, eighty?"

He let out a fake laugh. "Very funny. I might not be as young as you but with age comes experience."

"Don't I know it?" Shawn said. "Listen, I'll be honest, I've had a shitload to drink and I feel woozy as hell. You're a top, right? Because there's no chance I'm gonna—" Shawn stopped himself, putting his hand on his new friend's shoulder.

"What's wrong, Shawn?"

"Just a little light-headed. You couldn't get me some water, could you?"

Shawn's eyelids began to flutter. The killer watched in fascination. It was almost too easy. He wanted to inject some fear into the equation. He wanted Shawn to know that he was in the throes of death.

"Shawn, I think I should call you an ambulance. You don't look good. Have you been drugged?"

"How am I supposed to know?"

"Is your vision blurred? Is your heart elevated? Is there a burning feeling in your temples?"

"Yeah, but I'm hammered."

"You don't get those symptoms with drunkenness. You've been drugged. I've seen this before. I don't have my phone so give me yours and I'll call for help. This is serious."

"Phone is behind you," Shawn said, collapsing backward in his seat.

"Got it," he said. "Let me get you some water." He moved into the kitchen and ran the tap for effect. He waited a few seconds, then picked up the bag he'd stashed near the back door. When he returned to the living room, Shawn had reached the eyes rolling back in his head stage.

Shawn focused his vision. "Bag? Toys?" he said, slurring both words. "Kinky."

"You could say that."

"You call them? I think you're right. I'm starting to..." Shawn trailed off.

He held up his phone. "No. I haven't called anyone." He threw the phone on the floor and brought his foot down onto the screen, smashing it to pieces. He continued to stamp until wires and circuit boards were visible.

"Yo, what the f..." Shawn began before falling back again. His motor skills had faded, rendering him close to immobile.

"No one is coming, Shawn. It's just me and you, and yes, you've been drugged. Any second now, you're going to pass out, and then I'm going to kill you."

Shawn's fight or flight response kicked in, and he began kicking his legs out toward the stranger. But he was too weak, too vanquished.

"Be careful who you talk to online, Shawn, because they might be watching you from afar. They might be in the same bar as you, armed with date rape drugs to use on a horny, unsuspecting kid. Then they might arrange a midnight hook-up with you."

Shawn's eyes fell shut, his nervous system forced into shutdown through foreign substances and utter dread. There was a brief sign of life, and so the killer pounced, wrapping his hands tightly around Shawn's neck and squeezing until he passed out.

CHAPTER ELEVEN

Footsteps woke her up.

They weren't her dad's. They were heavier and more careless.

Ella stepped off her bed. Her nightlight cast green and blue shapes against her bedroom ceiling, hypnotically rotating clockwise. She thought that she was too old for it now, but whenever her dad turned it off, she missed the gentle buzzing noise which she'd come to associate with sleep.

Outside was still dark, so it must be the middle of the night. She never woke early, unless something interrupted her. Maybe it was it her dad, checking on her? She'd told him a hundred times to stop. She didn't need to be checked on.

No. Her dad treaded lightly. She knew his rhythm. She'd heard it every night for five years.

Her door was slightly ajar, giving her a small glimpse into the landing area beyond. Shadows moved and danced, but something told her that those shadows didn't belong to her father. She wasn't sure how she knew. Perhaps child's intuition, the same way she could tell when her dad was angry or irritated. They had a different presence, an alien aura.

Ella treaded lightly as she approached the door, being sure to avoid her blue rug on her bedroom floor. That was where the creaks were the worst.

She peered out to see a figure making its way into her dad's bedroom. She only caught a glimpse, but there was enough to tell her that she was right. There was someone else in their home.

She suddenly felt sick and dizzy. There was an icy chill in her fingertips, but she slowly crept out of her bedroom and followed the strange figure.

Then the darkness consumed her. For a few seconds she saw nothing except brief flashes of light, but when her eyes adjusted to the room's conditions, she saw the outline of a man holding a knife in his hand.

He was standing over her dad as he slept. Ella tried to scream, but no sound came out. She tried to run toward him, but she was locked in place. She picked up a small vase off her dad's table and threw it at the strange man, but it just bounced off him and landed on the floor. He didn't even notice she was there.

He moved closer to her dad. All she could do was watch.

In a series of violent thrusts, the figure plunged the knife into the heart of her sleeping father. The sudden attack rendered him completely motionless. He couldn't struggle or fight back or make an escape. He was at the stranger's mercy.

Ella froze in place, as though her feet were nailed to the ground. Then, everything came in small fragments, as though the picture had been smashed to pieces and she was assembling the jigsaw back together.

She saw blood seeping from the bed onto the carpet. She heard her dad screaming for her to get out of the house. The attacker turned around, pulled back his hood, and looked her in the eye. His face was unrecognizable, reminding her of a badly drawn composite sketch. Whoever it was, she didn't know him. She hadn't seen him before.

Leaving her dad in a bloody heap, he launched toward Ella with his blade pointed toward her.

Bang, bang, bang.

A silent scream. Then everything disappeared. The world dissolved in front of her. The man, the bedroom, the bloodstained sheets. Reality came crushing back, and she was suddenly aware that she was looking at the back of her eyelids.

Bang, bang, bang.

Her eyes opened, adjusting to focus on the window blinds a few feet away. A trickle of sunlight seeped through. She sat up in bed and grabbed her phone off the table beside her. 7:05 a.m. Only now did she realize that the banging noise had been in the present, not in her dreamworld.

"Who is it?" she called out. The cold air hit her hard and jolted her awake.

"It's me, Rookie. Time to get going." Ripley's voice from behind her motel door.

"Sorry, I didn't think we'd be leaving so early."

"Being early is on time. Being on time is late."

"Give me a minute and I'll meet you downstairs."

Ella heard Ripley disappear, then she composed herself on her bed. She breathed in and out slowly then used the *COUNTDOWN* technique to slow down her fast-beating heart. She acknowledged five things in the room she could see. A TV, a leather chair, a motel-issue pen, a pile of books, her laptop. Then came four things she could touch, three things she could hear. After thirty seconds, she was calm.

The visions were always the same. Unexpected and cruel, and they always taunted her with their obscurity. She'd been having them since that night twenty-three years ago, and while she'd learned to cope with the emotional aftermath a little better, they did nothing to paint the story any clearer. They'd distorted the events so much that she struggled to remember what was real and what wasn't.

Maybe her mind was making it all up, she thought. Maybe she never laid eyes on the murderer, or even knew he was in the house at all. Perhaps her five-year-old self had been oblivious to the whole thing, and trauma-cum-guilt had filled in the blanks.

Or maybe she did see the murderer. She might have looked the man who killed her father dead in the eye. But if that was the case, why was she still alive to tell the tale?

***

Ella expected the Mobile Parish Coroner's Office to have a much more sinister aura than it did.

It was located four miles away from their motel. It was a quaint, oddly shaped building with a gothic roof, multi-paned windows, and two chimneys. Outside, the sculpted lawn was decorated with a memorial bench to the building's founder, and two evergreen trees stood either side of the glass entranceway. The interior was lined with a welcoming oak finish.

From the small reception area, a member of staff escorted the agents to Room B3, where the bodies of the victims involved in the ongoing investigation were located. A sliding steel door blocked their entrance to the room. Before unlocking it, the staff member handed them latex gloves and plastic ventilation masks. He then unlocked it and motioned for Ella and Ripley to go inside. He shut the door behind them with a heart-skipping slam.

Inside was a heavy odor of medical fluid. Green-tinted walls stood behind several rows of what looked to Ella like filing cabinets, but she knew better. They were slots for bodies. A steel table sat in the center of the room, with a white sheet covering what lay beneath.

A man walked in from a small side room, hurriedly wiping his hands dry with a towel. He threw it to the side and then greeted the agents with a handshake.

"Good morning, Agents. Sorry for the lack of preparation. It's been all go today. I'm Dr. Scott Richards, the on-site coroner here. I hope you found us easily enough."

Dr. Richards was striking figure. Ella couldn't help but admire his looks. He was boyishly attractive, what her roommate might call *bubblegum hot.* He had short, curly black hair that boasted no particular style. Rectangular glasses magnified his caramel-colored eyes. He was wearing standard blue scrubs that were tainted with a couple of small stains around the chest. Ella placed him in his thirties, but she couldn't be sure. He was one of those *eighteen or thirty* guys.

"Good to meet you, Dr. Richards," said Ripley without looking up from her notepad. "Could you walk us through what you've found so far?"

"With pleasure," Richards said. Ella dropped her bag and pulled out her notepad too. She watched as Richards applied fresh protective gear and pulled the sheet off the central table. A headless, mutilated body appeared. Even through her ventilation mask, Ella could smell the decay. She almost heaved.

It took her a few seconds to process the visual. She thought back to all of the corpses she'd seen in books and crime scene photos, but the real thing was an entirely different story. This was all that remained of Christine Hartwell, a woman who only a few days ago was living her life while believing that death was many years away. And now she was here on a slab, all her dreams and hopes crushed to dust so a psychopath could enjoy a brief high.

"Victim number three," Richards began. He picked up a small metal instrument and passed it over her body, and then began to use it as a pointer to highlight areas of Christine's corpse. "One bullet entry wound in the stomach, exiting through her back and clipping her spine in the process. This would have incapacitated the victim significantly. Lacerations to the neck and abdomen, caused by trauma from a tapered instrument like a felling or scythe ax."

71

Next, Richards wheeled in two more steel tables from the adjoining room. Ella maneuvered around to create enough space to fit them in. "Sorry. Not much room in here. We don't usually get this many dead people at once," he laughed. Ella just nodded, unsure how to respond. It seemed Ripley and Richards were a lot more comfortable around corpses than she was.

Richards pulled off the sheets covering the remains of the first two victims. Their state of decomposition was much more severe than Christine's, giving them a yellowish, skeletal appearance. He moved his pointer to the head of Julia Reynolds, victim number one. She'd been dismembered, and so had been pieced back together like a human mosaic. A final indignity.

"Do you see these brown marks on the neck and arms?" Richards asked. "Blunt force trauma, most likely caused by hands rather than a foreign object. Cause of death was strangulation."

Ripley ran her gloved finger along the lacerations on the arms and neck. She looked back toward Christine Hartwell's corpse and breathed out heavily. Ella did the same, comparing the wounds of the two bodies and trying to determine a pattern or similarity of any kind. However, the only thing they had in common was decapitation. Nothing else matched.

"And victim number two?" Ripley said. The three moved around toward the dead body of Winnie Barker.

Richards moved his pointer to her midsection. "Thirteen stab wounds to the abdomen and one to the neck. I found traces of manganese and vanadium around the inflictions, so the murder weapon was most likely a carbon steel carving knife. Nothing special. Can be bought anywhere. Chances are she died from excessive blood loss during the attack, but she may have still been alive when he lacerated her neck. Once again, these cuts are chaotic and haphazard. He cut through two main arteries but I doubt it was intentional."

"Looks to me like he hacked away without any real idea what he was doing," Ella said. On the surface, it looked to Ella like the three victims were the work of three different perpetrators. But of course, she also knew that that's exactly what the killer wanted.

"Not quite," Richards said. "There's more. Something I found very strange indeed. You see, while the death blows are incredibly violent and reckless, the—"

"The posthumous mutilations were careful and steady," Ripley interrupted. "I know, that's exactly what I was thinking."

Ella leaned closer to inspect the neck wounds on each victim one by one. Ripley was right. The cuts were clean and relatively smooth, like they'd been carried out with professional equipment.

"I'd go farther than that," Richards said. "These mutilations were carried out with almost surgical accuracy. I've been doing this fifteen years and I've never seen any kind of cuts like this before. Let me tell you, there's not many folks in this neck of the woods who could pull off something like this. This is some Alfredo Treviño stuff."

He suddenly caught Ella's attention. "Alfredo Treviño?" she asked. "You know who he is?"

"Sure do."

"I've never met anyone who knows who Alfredo Treviño is."

"Serial killers make great reading for an up-and-coming surgeon," Richards laughed. "I spent most of medical school reading about serial killers who cut their victims up. It's been a while, but I guess I still remember a few things."

Ella was a little taken aback. She hadn't expected to run into someone who knew about an obscure Mexican serial killer from the nineteen fifties. Ella looked over at Ripley, who was inspecting the mutilations and taking pictures on her phone. Ella couldn't help herself. It seemed like the perfect opportunity to ask.

"Do you remember anything about Ed Gein, Richard Ramirez, or Edmund Kemper?"

Richards placed down his equipment and removed his mask. He took off his glasses and cleaned the lenses with his scrubs. "Absolutely. Everyone knows those guys. I'm very familiar with their methodology."

"Well, I'm working on a theory that our unsub is copycatting different serial killers. Christine Hartwell's murder is reminiscent of what Ed Gein did to one of his victims. Winnie Barker's murder involved elements from Richard Ramirez's crimes. And Julia Reynolds was strangled and dismembered, just like Edmund Kemper's M.O."

Ripley looked up at Ella disapprovingly. "Rookie, is this something you should really be sharing? Think about it."

She was right. Big mistake. "Sorry. I shouldn't be talking about things like this."

Richards laughed. "Don't worry, I won't repeat it to anyone. But now that you mention it, I can absolutely see what you're talking about," he said.

"Really?" Ella asked. She knew she'd made a mistake, but having her theory validated gave a small sense of accomplishment. She thought that maybe it would show Ripley that she knew what she was talking about too.

"Sure. I mean, I remember those Gein crime scene photos as clear as day. Ms. Hartwell over there is pretty much a perfect replica. If I remember rightly, Ramirez hacked his victims with a knife while they slept, correct? And Kemper abducted teen girls and cut them to pieces? Damn, I can't believe I didn't make that connection myself. That's absolutely amazing."

Ella didn't expect such an enthusiastic reaction from the coroner. His fascination almost seemed to rival hers. "You know your stuff," Ella said. "All that detail from memory?"

"Quite. It's been a while but there are some things you just don't forget."

From the other side of the small room, a ringing phone interrupted their conversation. Ripley breathed a heavy sigh. She pulled herself away from the lower half of Christine Hartwell's corpse and removed her mask and gloves. She reached into her pocket and pulled out her cell. Ella turned her attention back to the coroner.

"Is there anything else you've noticed that we might have missed? Ligature marks, defensive wounds, things like that?"

Am I trying to impress him? she thought.

"Nothing outside of what was listed in the initial police report," Richards said. "But your theory has opened up a new world of questions, so I'll keep digging."

"Great, thank you. Give me a call if you find anything."

She felt a sense of pride, even though she could feel Ripley's eyes burning her from across the room. She felt that revealing these details was worth it, since it gave Dr. Richards some ammunition to work with. She just hoped that she could make Ripley see her rationale.

"Maybe I'll give you a call even if I don't," he laughed. Ella didn't quite know how to respond. But suddenly, Ripley's frustrated tones broke the tension.

"Are you kidding me?" she said down the phone. "Corner it off. We'll be there in twenty." Ripley shoved her notepad back into her coat pocket. She caught Ella's eye. It was only two days into the job, but Ella knew exactly what Ripley was about to say.

"We need to get out of here. He's killed again."

CHAPTER TWELVE

Their destination was a house some three miles east. Ripley was at the helm, and the sat-nav told them they were six minutes away. Ripley hadn't shared the details of her phone call, other than the fact they were heading to see a dead body in the flesh.

"Did they say anything else on the phone?" Ella asked.

"No," Ripley snapped, keeping her eyes glued to the road. Since getting in the car, Ripley hadn't turned the radio on. Something she'd done on every journey they'd taken so far.

Ella felt resistance. She could sense something was wrong, and she had a good idea what it was. Ella took the plunge.

"Is something wrong?" she asked.

"What the hell were you thinking back there?" she said, hardly pausing to let Ella finish her sentence. Ella didn't need to inquire for more details.

"I'm sorry. I just thought that if someone else believed my theory, it might help persuade you."

They pulled up at a traffic light with an abrupt stop. Ella felt the recoil. She'd pissed Ripley off something fierce. She didn't dare look at her. Instead, she gazed out of the passenger window and saw a man opening up the shutters on his small liquor store. The shop was called *LIQUOR OUT*.

"It was unprofessional, not to mention very stupid of you," Ripley shouted, her voice laced with venom. "What happens if that coroner goes and tells someone else your little theory? That's how rumors start. Not to mention that it's unconfirmed and, at worst, could be completely incorrect. Can you imagine how that would reflect on us?"

"But he has an obligation to keep things on the down low, doesn't he?" Ella said.

The car started rolling again. They were four minutes away from their destination.

"No," Ripley said. "He's not a police officer. It's no different than telling a stranger in a coffee shop."

Ella hadn't yet seen Ripley so irate. She felt she was being scolded by a parent.

"But he said it was a good theory. I thought that if he made the same connections I did, then he might look for additional things coroners might usually overlook. That could really help us. He even said he'd look further into it for me."

"And he couldn't possibly have said that because of an ulterior motive? I know interpersonal skills aren't your strong point and I know you're new to all this, but lesson number one: Don't trust anyone with confidential information about murder cases. That's how you find yourself up shit creek without a paddle."

"I'm sorry. I feel like an idiot for it. I got carried away."

She shouldn't have done what she did, and looking back, it seemed obvious to her now. She felt a pang of embarrassment. She felt she'd let herself down. At the time, she thought it was something minor which Ripley might overlook. She didn't truly know how damaging revealing confidential information could be.

"I understand your enthusiasm but you can't just go around spouting your theories to anybody who'll listen. This isn't a high school class. How would you feel if Julia's parents caught wind of these rumors? Or Christine's brother? Or Winnie's grandkids? Have you ever lost someone you love?"

Ella thought back to the dreams. They'd only happened a few hours ago, but it felt like days. "No," she lied. "It won't happen again."

"Good," Ripley said. Up ahead, a row of detached houses came into view. There were three houses either side of the street, all of which featured modest front and backyards. A winding pathway encircled all of the homes, allowing pedestrians to pass by and enjoy clear views of the town's more scenic areas.

"My biggest concern is that the press get a hold of any information about our investigation, particularly your findings," Ripley continued. "Far-fetched theories like yours are a journalist's wet dream. The press would run with it and sensationalize it to death. Then our unsub would know we're onto him and just like that, the FBI looks like a bunch of incompetent fools. Suddenly, we've got a media shitstorm on our hands. I've seen it happen."

"Understood," Ella said, her embarrassment burning up her temples. "From now on I'll keep things to myself."

"Tell me. Tell the Sheriff. Don't tell anyone else."

Ella let silence do the rest of the talking as their car passed a cul-de-sac and finally pulled up outside a house on Lakeside View. Yellow crime scene tape surrounded the entire house with four uniformed officers surrounding it. Across the small path, two neighbors watched without shame.

Ripley flashed her credentials at a waiting officer. He lifted the tape up for her and nodded her through with Ella close behind. Two masked forensic technicians walked out the front door of the victim's home, took off their masks, and breathed in the fresh air. One of them gave Ripley a thumbs-up, then pointed to the back entrance. Ella and Ripley followed the path around where they found Sheriff Harris waiting with a cigarette held tightly between his lips. His skin was flushed of all color. He blew out a plume of smoke toward the ground and flicked his cigarette over the backyard fence.

"Never in my thirty years," he said without looking at the agents. "I'm starting to wonder if it's me or if the world is getting crazier by the day."

"What do we have?" asked Ripley.

"Wish I could describe it. Follow me. Don't forget your masks. You're gonna need 'em."

They stepped into a long kitchen area. It was designed in a modern, rustic style with wooden surfaces and brown stools perched up against a small dining table. On the work surface to their right, forensics had left masks and gloves for newcomers. Ella and Ripley put them on for the second time in as many hours.

Ella surveyed the kitchen area, her eyes landing on an empty cat food bowl, then moving to a gloss white fridge-freezer that was dotted with selfies and photographs of parties and club nights. In every picture, she saw a young, good-looking African American man, usually with his arm wrapped around another similarly attractive young gent. All of the pictures had been placed artistically around the fridge handle. Whoever this owner was, he had good taste, and he was certainly a popular fellow, Ella thought.

It only lasted a few fleeting seconds, but there was the spark again. The connections were made, and Ella already knew exactly what was about to reveal itself as she ventured further into the house. As the three made their way inside, Ella felt like she'd entered a crime scene photo she'd seen a hundred times before. It was all oddly familiar in some way.

But even so, nothing prepared her for what appeared in front of her. A man sat on a brown sofa, leaning slightly to one side as though he was merely sleeping. A mask of blood decorated his face, running down his neck and not stopping until it collected in a pool on his thighs. It had dried a dark, mahogany color.

From now on, I'll keep things to myself, Ella thought. She wasn't going to say anything unless she absolutely had to, out of fear of another scolding or worse. However, she was sure of it. The scene in front of her confirmed her theory with almost absolute clarity. The victim type, the modus operandi, the cause of death. This was another copycat crime.

"Shawn Kelly, twenty-five-year-old male," said Harris. "We only got here thirty minutes ago so we're still figuring things out, but it looks to me like he's been shot and left for dead."

Ripley approached the body and inspected it more closely. Ella stood back, struggling to take everything in. This was the second crime scene she'd attended in her seventy-two-hour career as a special agent, and the first with a dead body present. At least, one which was still fully whole. The psychological pressure seemed to mount day by day. Setting eyes on the corpses in the coroner's office was difficult enough, but seeing a fresh victim still in the very spot they were killed wasn't something she could easily brush aside. She knew this was an image which would stick with her forever.

Keep it together, she told herself. *If you want to do this job, you have to learn how to handle these kinds of things.* Ella thought back to a disassociation technique she'd learned in her early days at the FBI, but applying it was harder than she thought. The fact she was standing on the same carpet that a real-life murderer stood on only hours before brought up a feeling of nausea. Despite the low temperature, she felt a river of sweat collect on her brow. Her breathing intensified. It was a hard visual to consume.

"Who called it in?" Ripley asked, resting her knee on the sofa and peering into the hole left in the victim's temple.

"Anonymous caller, about an hour ago," Harris said.

"Of course he was anonymous. Aren't they always? Have forensics taken a preliminary swab yet?"

"Just finished. Should take a couple of minutes."

"Good. Did they find a bullet? And what the hell is that smell?"

"What do you think that smell is?" Harris asked. "It's a dead body, ma'am."

I know exactly what that smell is, Ella said to herself, but after her scolding, she decided now wasn't the time to interject. She didn't want to push Ripley's buttons any further by offering her apparently unfounded theories. The thought of being reprimanded once again, this time in front of others, scared her into silence. She thought back to her high school days, when she'd solved the problem on the whiteboard immediately but had to wait for the rest of the class to figure it out before she could raise her hand. It was frustrating, but she reassured herself that her chance to speak up would come in time. She could see Ripley had already come to some conclusions about the dead body in front of them, judging by the look of disbelief on her face. Ella thought back to how Ripley had blown apart her previous theories and didn't want the same to happen here.

"It's not that, it's something else."

"I'm sure it'll crop up in the forensic report. What do you think so far, Agents?" Harris asked.

Ripley stood up and pulled out her notepad. "This whole scene is one huge middle finger to us. This guy knows we're onto him, and he's showing us exactly how capable he is."

"How do you figure?" Harris asked.

"Given the lack of blood anywhere else in the room, the victim was killed right here on this sofa. That means one of two things. Either the killer broke in undetected and blitz-attacked the victim, subduing him and killing him without ever letting him leave the sofa. Or he gained the victim's trust enough to execute his plan while he sat right next to him. Both scenarios show organization, interpersonal skills, and manipulation. He also notified the police himself, something he didn't do last time. He wants us to be here. He wants us to admire his handiwork."

One of the forensic officers walked into the room and handed Harris a clipboard. Ella couldn't tell if it was man or woman behind the mask. "Swab is complete, sir. There were high levels of alcohol in his system, along with a significant trace of hydroxybutyrate from his cheek lining."

Harris scanned the notes up and down, lifting up a few pages. "Right. And what's that mean in English?" Harris asked.

"Date rape," Ripley interrupted. "The victim was drugged."

"Drugged?"

"Spiked, more likely. The killer likely slipped a pill in his drink, that's the most effective and efficient way to get hydroxybutyrate into the system."

"Well, I've got the officers searching for people who knew this guy. Wife, girlfriend, friends, family."

"He won't have a girlfriend," Ripley said. "He's gay, and single. He might have met our killer in a bar and they ended up back here together. Start there." Ripley turned to Ella. "Rookie? You're quiet. What do you make of this?"

"Just taking it all in."

"Look, I said you could share your thoughts with me and Harris. We're the only ones here, so out with it."

It was time to fit another piece to the puzzle. But she didn't expect Ripley to take it on board. "First of all, I don't think the victim was shot." Ella moved and ran a gloved hand near the wound in the victim's temple.

"No?"

"Definitely not. I think he used a power drill to make this hole."

Harris muttered an unidentifiable sound. "I hate to say it, but it could be. Nothing this guy does can surprise me anymore. Not to mention that this report says there's no exit wound anywhere on this fellow's head. Unless he blasted from a mile away, there'd be two holes in his head at the least."

Ripley considered it. "Interesting. The hole is certainly thin, but it's hard to see with the blood clotting."

"And that smell you mentioned?" Ella continued. "I think that's acid, or bleach. Our killer drilled a hole in the victim's skull and filled it with a fluid of some kind."

Harris scrunched up his face. He shook his head. "Why in God's name?"

"Because that's exactly what Jeffrey Dahmer did to two of his victims back in the eighties."

"Dahmer? The Wisconsin nut? That's a name I haven't heard in years."

"Dahmer was obsessed with the idea of creating a human zombie. He thought he could do it by pumping hydrochloric acid into their skulls, but obviously it didn't work."

"Another copycat theory?" Ripley said.

"The M.O. is identical. Our killer meets a black, gay man in a bar and goes home with him. Then he plies him with alcohol, drugs him, and drills into his head while he's still alive. Then he fills him with whatever liquid he can get his hands on. It's all right here, down to the last detail."

Ripley rubbed her forehead with her fingertips. Ella anticipated a rebuttal.

"That's it," Ripley said. "I've got it. The smell. It's antifreeze."

It took Ella and Harris a few seconds to connect the dots. A wave of realization washed over them both.

"Jesus," Harris said. "The same antifreeze he grabbed from the hardware store."

"It's highly likely, but I couldn't say for sure."

Then Ella thought of something. It was another pattern which her subconscious pieced together from various snapshots taken over her short life. She thought of Dahmer's crimes, the mutilations, the cannibalism, the photographs he took.

"So, we can safely say the guy who did this is the same guy who murdered Miss Hartwell?" Harris asked. "I hate to put a positive spin on something like this, but that's a good thing."

"Again, I can't say with absolute certainty, but I'd say it was probable." Ripley took photos of Shawn Kelly's body with her phone. She dialed a number in her phone, but Ella interrupted.

"Sheriff, have forensics combed this place top to bottom?"

"Not yet. That comes next. Why?"

"I think I know a way we can confirm this is the work of a sole perp."

Ripley and Harris turned to her. "We're all ears," said Ripley.

"The other murders really hit on each serial killer's most famous elements. Dahmer only injected acid into two of his victims. He's much more known for a few other things."

"Like?"

"Keeping body parts as trophies."

Ripley eyed up the victim again. "We're not missing any body parts, Rookie."

Ella prayed that she'd made the right connection. Ripley seemed to be coming around to her theory and she didn't want her enthusiasm to wane. "Yes, we are. Maybe not from this victim, but we're still missing something from before."

She rushed back into the kitchen, past the lavish rustic furniture, and stood in front of the fridge. Ripley and Harris followed.

"See those photos?" Ella said, pointing to the pictures around the door handle. "I thought they were just stylized like that, but they're not."

Ripley took a step back to see clearer. "Well, they're arranged like a question mark."

"Exactly. He's drawing us here. Dahmer kept some body parts in his fridge."

"You gotta be joking me," Harris said. "Get forensics in here now," he shouted out the back door. He moved back toward the fridge and opened it up. The usual suspects were all present; two bottles of milk, canned cat food, vegetables, butter. Harris gradually pulled out produce before uncovering a large plastic box jammed in the fridge's bottom left corner. Its sides were blurry so its contents were obscured from the outside.

But Ella knew exactly what was in there, and Ripley and Harris quickly realized the same.

Harris pulled open the lid and a sickly odor filled the air. It was the scent of stale death, having been left to rot and stir for days before being lodged into its new resting place.

Ella saw it in Ripley's eyes. Her theory was right, and Ripley looked like she was all but convinced of it too.

Harris's mouth dropped open. "Sweet mother of God. What the hell is this thing?"

***

Ella, Ripley, and Harris stared at their new discovery as two forensic officers rushed to their side. Harris's hands quivered as he passed the object to them. The forensic team took it and gently placed it on the work surface beside them.

It was the skinned head of Christine Hartwell, faceless and hairless, with two crystallized brown eyes locked in an eternal death stare. There were remnants of eyebrows and a full set of teeth still in place. All of the tendons running from the scalp to the cheek were visible. The whole thing made Ella retch. While Ripley and Harris looked it over, Ella ran out of the house to get some air.

Her theory now had substantial weight, but it was still the grimmest of mornings. Overcast skies up above and muddied grass at her feet. She felt the moisture from the lawn soak into her shoes. Uncomfortable at first, but then she felt grounded back in reality. All of the death and decay she'd been subjected to the past few days made her feel like she was in some kind of surreal dreamland.

The past few days had taught her a lot, including the important lesson that textbooks and crime scene photos couldn't prepare a person for the real thing. Ella always thought she'd be able to leave her emotions at the door if she was ever in a situation like this, but the reality was much different than she could have ever imagined. Each crime scene left an imprint, diluting down all of the pleasant memories with images of brutality and human suffering.

Maybe this wasn't the role for her, she thought, but the idea of letting down the people who'd given her this chance made her anxiety levels shoot up.

Suddenly, she felt a hand on her shoulder.

"It never gets any easier, Rookie, if that's what you're thinking."

Ella took off her glasses and rubbed her eyes. She didn't turn to face Ripley. "I wasn't. I was thinking maybe I'm not cut out for this."

Ripley laughed. "Are you kidding? Your theory is suddenly looking pretty good. Don't let a couple of gory details dissuade you."

Ella felt the anxiety levels drop. The relief came slowly and gradually as she realized she was being complimented by the mythical Agent Mia Ripley. "Well, thank you. It's just... seeing all these fresh dead bodies is a tough lesson. When I see them in textbooks, it's like I'm just consuming facts. I'm just reading history, you know? There's nothing I can do to change what happened to them."

"But now it feels like you're responsible for them," Ripley said.

Ella breathed heavily and nodded. "I guess so. It's tough to explain. It feels like if we'd have tried harder, theorized more, talked it through, then maybe there wouldn't be a dead body in that house."

"Yeah, I remember when I used to think like that. But believe me when I tell you that nothing short of being psychic would have stopped this. You can't blame yourself for the actions of a psychopath."

"I know. It's just hard."

"It sure is, but you should be proud. You pretty much called this theory right from the start, based on one crime scene and a few brief details. That's some impressive shit. Even with today's findings I wouldn't have made that connection myself. I'd have assumed it was some disorganized schizophrenic experimenting with different killing techniques. But your theory spins it in completely the other direction. Even I might be out of my depth on this one."

Ella put her glasses back on and turned to Ripley. An icy breeze collided with them. It chilled Ella to the core. The whole morning had felt surreal, but even more surreal was that Ripley was complimenting her. Ella had to replay her words in her mind to make sure she'd heard her correctly. For forty-eight hours, Ripley had debunked Ella's theory with haste. Now, she was coming around to them. It was a success, no matter how bittersweet. A sense of gratification overcame her.

"Really? Even you?" Ella asked.

"Even me. If I'd have drawn up a psychological profile and sent it out to the cops, imagine how bad I'd look when it came out he knew exactly what he was doing with each murder."

"Pretty bad," Ella agreed. "But you know the truth now."

"There are still things I might not see clearly. You notice the little things, like the burlap bag at the Hartwell scene, the lipstick mark at the Barker scene. Those are the things that make the connections and allow for a more thorough psychological profile. That's why I want you to write one up."

Ella looked at her, shocked. "What? Me?"

"Yes, you. Have you written one before?"

This was it. The crowning achievement. The highest honor that could befall her. She'd dreamt of being the one to provide an official psychological profile to the FBI since she was in high school, when she used to give class presentations and imagine that was exactly what she was doing. Everything she'd worked for, all those years spent working until midnight to stand out from the crowd, all those hours of research she did in her spare time, every time she'd felt invisible despite working herself to exhaustion. The validation she secretly yearned for had arrived in this one tsunami of responsibility.

This was the apex; a moment she'd remember for the rest of her days, regardless of how her career panned out.

"No. Nothing official, anyway."

"Unofficial ones are good enough. Let's give this scene one last look-over and then get going. Do you think you can handle it?"

It was an honor to say the least, and an honor she never expected to receive. It came with incredible responsibility, but there was every chance she could predict this unsub's next moves. There was every chance that her abilities could help catch a real-life serial killer.

"Yes, I can handle it."

"Good."

CHAPTER THIRTEEN

Ella was exhausted. She checked the clock on the precinct wall. Four hours she'd been writing up this profile, changing and adding sections as the thoughts invaded her mind.

She read it through from start to finish, although the words were all beginning to blur.

That's enough, she said to herself, confident that she'd covered every avenue she needed to. She printed off a few copies and readied them to show Ripley.

Thinking about Ripley's reaction to her profile made her nervous. What if the profile didn't hold up, or paled in comparison to some of the profiles Ripley had written? What if she'd overlooked some obvious components of the crime?

She reassured herself that that wouldn't be the case, as if somehow that would make it true. Ella exited the office with the printouts in her hand and found Ripley typing away on her laptop in the main precinct area.

"Done?" Ripley asked before Ella could say anything.

"Done."

The nervousness rushed back. A psychological profile was supposed to be a blueprint to catch an offender. It had to be nothing but perfect, and here Ella was delivering her first official profile to the FBI's most mythical living agent. This felt like more pressure than anything she'd ever done in her Intelligence role.

"Go," Ripley said. She sat back in her chair and looked toward the ceiling.

"Go?"

"Read it out."

Ella felt like a kid in class. Ripley was the stern teacher telling you to show your presentation. Even more pressure. Ella checked her surroundings to make sure no other officers could eavesdrop. Ella started at the beginning.

"All of the men emulated by the unsub have been the archetypical all-American serial killer. White males, sexually motivated deviants, loners who killed to satisfy their own perversions. While they all struggled to present themselves as socially capable, they weren't so inept that they were shunned by everyone they came into contact with. They all had acquaintances, no matter how minor. They managed to fit into their own little circles where they were considered part of the clique, but still, outsiders sometimes considered something to be *off* about them. Since the unsub sees something in these killers which he craves himself, something which he consciously or unconsciously believes he lacks, chances are he will exhibit these same characteristics. He'll be in the same age range of these killers too, so anywhere from mid-twenties to mid-forties."

Ella waited for the rebuttal. She scrutinized Ripley's facial expression. She closed her eyes and nodded.

"Perfect. I absolutely agree. Carry on."

Ella was shocked. The positivity propelled her forward, and she felt herself speak with more authority this time.

"If he were to kill again, the killer would no doubt emulate another offender similar to the ones already referenced. All murders thus far have paid tribute to a different well-known serial killer each time, so it's likely that this pattern will repeat. If so, it would be safe to assume it will be similar lust killers as his previous tributes, such as John Wayne Gacy, Gary Ridgway, or Dennis Rader. Similarly aged white American males whose murders all carried a sexual component. However, he would not choose a killer whose murders were nondescript. The crime would need to possess a recognizable component in order to make the tribute clear."

"Exactly," Ripley said. She stood up from her chair. "Every kill has something unique about it. Something noticeable. His first kill of Julia Reynolds was fairly ordinary by his standards, but ever since then, he's progressed. He's stamping these crime scenes with a unique but different signature every time."

Ella turned the page, no longer reading the words she'd written but speaking her opinions.

"In each scenario, victimology has played a significant role. Every victim type matches that of the killers he's referencing. Additionally, each of the serial killers chosen had *stuck* to their preferred victim type during their own killing sprees. Or at least, the murders they committed which they did for sexual gratification. They didn't deviate. Therefore, if the unsub was to emulate John Wayne Gacy, he would choose a young adult male or teenage boy. If he was to emulate Gary Ridgway, he would choose a female sex worker. The victim choice is as crucial as the act of killing itself."

"Nailed it," Ripley said. "Right in the face. Keep going."

"Likewise, location is also a vital factor. All of the unsub's victims were killed in the same places that the original killers killed theirs; car, bedroom, store, lounge. However, the unsub's disposal sites differ from the original killers'. This can be attributed to the idea that this unsub craves media and police attention in addition to killing for his own gratification."

Ripley picked up a pen and spun it between her fingers. Any other time, Ella would have remarked on her skill, but her focus was solely on this. The dreariness she'd felt a few minutes before had completely subsided. "Bingo," Ripley said. "So if we combine the last two parts, we can determine the victim type and the murder site. Disposal site may differ, but that's something we just can't predict. So, what historical killers might he copy next?"

Ella picked up where she left off, reading aloud again. "This would rule out widely known yet non-unique killings such as those of David Berkowitz and the Zodiac, since the elements present in these crimes were common amongst everyday murder victims the world over, including the fact that these offenders occasionally changed up their victim types and the locations which they killed. Similarly, it would also rule out any possibility of a tribute to Charles Manson, since he lacked the characteristics of the other offenders already referenced by the unsub. It would also rule out any offenders who weren't white, male, American, and acted alone. He would not reference Aileen Wuornos, Jack the Ripper, the Hillside Strangler, or any similar offenders."

Ripley dropped her pen but didn't bother to pick it back up. "You know what? That's a great insight," she said. "That actually narrows down the pool quite significantly, right?"

"Absolutely," Ella said. "If we know we're just dealing with white American males, that makes things a little easier for us."

"See, Dark? You got this. I knew you would."

Ella felt relief. *Thank god,* she thought.

"Talk to me about M.O.," Ripley said.

"The unsub fits into the organized category of psychopath. He is highly capable, methodical, and emotionally controlled in the presence of his victims. These killings have been planned out in advance, during which time he acquires the necessary tools in order to carry them out. In order to subdue his victims, he blitz attacks them when they're unaware in order to gain immediate control over them. Pre-murder intimidation is likely not present—a possible sign of physical inadequacy; however, this aspect may be present in order to sit in line with the M.O.s of the killers he's copying, since they also gained control through the same means."

Ella took a deep breath. She looked around her, seeing her quasi-speech had drawn the attention of a few straggling officers. Ripley's stare made them turn around.

"Since his victims are purposely chosen for their physical traits, it's unlikely that he knows them personally," Ella continued. "He picks them out in advance, stalks them, learns their routines, and then strikes at the most opportune time. He objectifies his victims, and while he sees them as toys for manipulation, he may personalize the victim by talking to them in order to add emotional and intellectual depth to the crime."

Ripley slammed her hands on the desk. "Rookie, I couldn't have done this better myself. You hit every mark. Do you have anything on his childhood, his job, his family life?"

Ella was ecstatic on the inside, but she didn't show it. Now wasn't the time. "Yeah." She tapped the last page. "It's all here."

"Come on. We gotta get this to Harris right now. Someone in town matches your profile, and we're going to pay them a visit tonight."

***

"Harris, we need you to do a search for us," Ripley said. "We've drawn up a psychological profile of the offender and we need to see if anyone in town matches his description."

The sheriff shoved a mound of paperwork into his drawer and summoned the agents to his side of the desk. "At your service," he said. "What am I looking for?"

"A white male, age twenty-five to forty-five," Ripley began. "Unmarried, single. He would have lived in this area his entire life, or at the least within two miles of the town. He works a skilled job which requires manual labor and is possibly self-employed. He would seek a position where he could work alone, and might involve some element of butchery. Hospital attendant, woodworker. His employment history would show him having multiple jobs when he was younger but would have stabilized in the past five years or so."

Harris filled in the boxes on the database screen. The search results began to lessen. "Over a hundred names in there, ladies. Everyone from the baker to the candlestick maker. What more can you tell me?"

Ripley scoured the names and the crimes they were arrested for. "He would have a history of minor offenses, most likely sexual in nature. Voyeurism, public indecency, sex worker usage. There's also a possibility of arson, animal cruelty, and domestic violence in his early years. He may have been orphaned or ran away from home as a child. His parents would either be dead or live in another state entirely."

"Working on it," Harris said. "Three results. Let's see here." Harris leaned closer to the screen. "First guy, nineteen, lives in—"

Ripley cut him off. "No. Too young. Next."

Harris clicked on to the next mugshot. "Second guy. Twenty-six, moved here a year ago after being done for touching up minors in Louisville."

"No. He's Latino. Our suspect will be white."

Harris nodded and moved on to the next name. He leaned closer to the screen.

"Hold up, I recognize this fella." Harris skimmed his details. "Oh boy, this guy is a real piece of work, let me tell you."

"Tell us everything." Ripley said.

"Clyde Harmen," Harris said, tapping his screen with his pen. "A total creep, and not exactly the sharpest tool in the shed."

Ripley scrutinized his basic details. White male, thirty-six years old, single, and lived alone. His work history was staggered, with huge gaps of unemployment between manual labor positions. "What was he arrested for?" she asked.

Harris clicked into the suspect's profile. A colorized mugshot appeared of a scrawny, haggard man with mid-length black hair dangling down to his chin. His forehead was swallowed up by a huge scar which stretched in a diagonal line from his scalp to his right eye.

"He flashed some poor old woman in the town one night. He was dressed like an oddball, trench coat, huge boots, so we found him on the quick. This woulda been about eighteen months ago," said Harris. "He confessed and we charged him. Case closed. But that's not why I remember him so vividly. Something else happened a little while after."

"What was it?"

"We ran into him about two months after the flashing incident. A woman came in here and said she busted someone on her property. Apparently he made off with her dog. She said whoever it was had a huge scar on his forehead."

"Dog theft?"

"It happens sometimes. Usually for dog fights, but we checked out Clyde again and guess what? The deviant had started up a taxidermy business right around the time of the theft."

Ripley and Ella exchanged glances. Their faces said the same thing.

"If he has a history of animal cruelty, then it's possible he's progressed to hurting real people, especially if he's had a year to evolve."

"We didn't have nothing to charge him on, though," Harris continued. "No proof, no sign of the dog. So he got off scot-free."

"Where's he located?" Ripley asked.

Harris checked the records. "Black Lake. Same place we busted him last time. It's out in the sticks, about five miles from here. Horrible place."

"Isolated?" asked Ripley.

"Very much so."

"He fits," Ripley exclaimed. "He's in the demographic, he's a loner, he has a history of offenses. The scar on his head could be from defensive wounds when a potential victim fought back. Taxidermy requires manual skill and involves cutting up and reassembling. We need to investigate immediately."

Harris jumped out of his chair and summoned over four officers. "We've got a suspect," he announced. "Let's get ready to move. I want two cars, two guys in each. No time to waste, let's go."

Ripley turned to Ella. "We've got him," she said. "But believe me when I say guys like this never go down easy."

CHAPTER FOURTEEN

It wasn't signposted, but Ella could almost pinpoint the exact spot where the area known as Black Lake began. The trees became heavier and more overgrown, twisting into shapes that nature didn't usually create. They passed by a swamp, dark green in color and swimming with a host of predators. It was starting to get dark, and some of the more adventurous wildlife had come out to feast on weaker prey. On the dirt path from the town into the woodlands, their car violently shook as they entered territory which wasn't designed for vehicle access. Ella looked out the passenger window and watched shapes move in the darkness, making out the outline of an alligator marching through the swampland.

Their car struggled up a narrow path on a small hill, tree branches scratching the windows. Ella felt a sudden wave of claustrophobia. Her anxiety flared up, feeling like she was heading into the mouth of hell. Somewhere up ahead was the home of a possible serial killer. The options of how this could play out ran amok in her head, but she shook off the thoughts and told herself she needed to be in the moment.

The dirt track gave way to a sprawling, dead lawn with a beat-up truck abandoned in the middle of it. Behind a small, rickety fence was a farmhouse, impressive in size but hideous in condition. Its wooden exterior was being overtaken by nature, with several wooden panels on the verge of collapse. Any color had long since washed away, leaving a gray slab in place.

"Is he alone out here like this?" Ella asked.

"Looks like it. I haven't seen another house since we got into the woods," said Ripley. She picked up the car radio and spoke to Harris in the vehicle behind her. "Keep your guys back for now. We'll go ahead. We don't want to spook him. If he sees the cars, he might panic and run out the back. Have the other officers keep an eye on the other side of the house in case he flees."

The radio buzzed on. Harris's voice crackled through. "Understood."

Behind them, the squad cars turned off their lights and blended into the darkness. Ripley edged the car closer to the front of the house.

"You think he's already spotted us?" Ella asked. "Looks to me like he doesn't get many visitors."

"If I had to guess, I'd say he's watching us right now. With how quiet it is around here, you could hear a peen go soft."

Ella was too anxious to give a retort. If they managed to pull this off, it would cement her as a major player to the FBI big leagues. Only three days into an investigation and their perpetrator was within cuffing distance. Pulling this off could lead to the career she'd dreamt of for years.

She shook off the thought, and instead focused on what was most important to her. This was a real killer who'd taken four real lives. Shawn Kelly's parents no longer had a son. Christine Hartwell's brother no longer had a sister. Ella knew the grief all too well, and giving these people some closure was what mattered most of all.

All that stood in her way was an extremely violent, sadistic serial murderer with organization levels the FBI hadn't seen since Dennis Rader terrorized Wichita for almost three decades.

The farmhouse in front of her reminded her of a certain home which once stood in Plainfield, Wisconsin. Ed Gein's farmhouse. In 1957, once authorities gained access to Gein's home, they found some of the most morbid creations in history. A woman-suit made of human skin, dissected genitals, human skulls used as bowls. Maybe this guy had taken inspiration from Ed in more ways than one, Ella thought. In truth, she'd dreamt of seeing that old house in the flesh all her life. It was the nirvana for true crime obsessives; a dream and nightmare rolled into one.

"Ready?" Ripley asked, but didn't wait for an answer. "Let's go. He's probably already thinking about running."

Ella and Ripley jumped out of the car and scaled the hilly pathway to the farmhouse front door. "Want me to do the talking?" Ella asked. She was as anxious as she'd ever been in her life, but her confidence and adrenaline took center stage.

"Are you sure?"

"He'll be more likely to talk to a younger woman than—" Ella stopped herself.

"A frigid old witch. You're right."

Ella knocked, then stayed completely still, listening for movement. Ten seconds passed. Nothing. No signs of life, no barking dogs.

"Be inside, you bastard," Ripley said. "Come on."

From the other side of the door came a voice.

"What do you want?"

It stunned Ella and made her blood run cold. She hadn't heard any scuttling or any footsteps. It was as if whoever it was had been standing behind the door this whole time.

"Mr. Harmen? My name is Ella Dark and this is my partner Mia Ripley. We're working with local police. We'd like to ask you a few questions relating to an ongoing investigation, if you'd be willing."

There was a brief pause. "What investigation?" the voice asked. It was nasally, with a childlike cadence. He spoke with a heavy Louisiana accent.

Get the door open. Don't scare him away, Ella thought. "There have been a series of homicides in the area and we believe you may have some information which could be useful to us."

Another moment of silence, like he was thinking of the right thing to say.

"Is the sheriff there? I didn't steal the dog."

Ella and Ripley locked eyes. It was a question she didn't expect. "No. There's no one here but me and my partner. May we come in? It's very cold out here, and we don't want to get eaten by alligators. We assure you we won't keep you long."

The voice disappeared. Ella waited for what felt like hours, but was no more than ten seconds. Finally, the door began to rattle. She heard the sound of a creaky deadbolt being pulled aside.

Come on. Show yourself to me, Ella said to herself.

The door opened a few inches before coming to an abrupt stop. He'd left the chain lock on.

"Mr. Harmen, we can't come in if you keep the chain lock on, can we?"

"'Gators don't come this far out," he said. His face appeared between the cracks. Ella managed to get a clear view of his face. It was most certainly the same man from the mug shot, but with more cracked skin and long hair down to his shoulders. The scar on his forehead still hadn't healed, and judging by its depth, never would. Everything about him screamed misfit, or worse yet, deranged killer. Ella looked to her left and saw Ripley peering in the windows with a

95

flashlight. However, the dirt on them was so thick it was impossible to see through.

"You gonna need a warrant to get in here," he said.

Ella panicked. He was right, but she didn't want him to know that. "We only need a warrant if we suspect you might have been involved with the investigation we're pursuing. Right now, we just want to ask you some questions to clear your name. We know you have a prior history of offenses and we just want to rule you out."

Ella could see it in his eyes. There was no way that her words were going to break down his barriers. He knew that she was lying, and while that didn't bode well for his capture, it suggested that he was a proficient manipulator too. So far, he'd ticked off all of the criteria on her profile.

"You ain't coming in here. Get a warrant and come back, lady."

Ripley jumped in, passing her flashlight to Ella in the process. Ella took it from her and stumbled out of the way. Ripley stood right up against the small opening, getting as close to Clyde as she possibly could. "Buddy, we're investigating a very serious federal crime here and your name has cropped up, so I suggest you start talking pretty damn quickly. It's in your best interests to do so. One way or another we'll be talking to you within the next twenty-hour hours, so you may as well get it out of the way now. So, what's it going to be?" Ripley turned to Ella. "Shine that flashlight on him. I want to see who I'm talking to."

Ella turned the light into the small gap, illuminating Clyde Harmen's upper half. He was wearing an oversized black T-shirt and had washed-out tattoos on his forearms.

But behind him, something caught Ella's attention. She only saw a brief glimpse into his living quarters, but she spotted something that told her everything she needed to know: The man standing in front of her was the man responsible for these murders.

She turned the flashlight onto it to see it clearly. Both Clyde and Ripley followed its line of sight.

And without pause, Clyde fled into the depths of his house and disappeared into the darkness.

He knew his game was up, because sitting on his mantelpiece, like some kind of grim trophy, was a human skull. Ella shouted after him.

"What the hell is that?"

CHAPTER FIFTEEN

Instinct kicked in. Ella forced her boot into the door and felt it vibrate on its hinges. A little bit gave way, but not enough.

"Forget the warrant, the skull is probable cause enough," Ella shouted. If they didn't take this chance to arrest him, they night never get another one.

She stepped back and charged forward with another brutal kick, sending a shockwave of numbness through her right leg. After a third assault, the rickety door burst open, ripping the chain lock clean off its wooden panel. Ella rushed inside with Ripley in tow, hurling themselves into the unknown darkness of the strange farmhouse.

"You head left," Ripley shouted, running in the opposite direction. Ella saw Ripley pull out her pistol as she disappeared around the corner, and so Ella did the same. She hurried through a winding hallway, passing by a broken table and an old Victorian clock. The smell of mold and rot engulfed her senses. At the threshold between the hallway and the next room, her foot caught on something, almost sending her tripping to the ground.

She glanced down, and in the darkness she made out a pile of bones, but unlike the skull, they were small. Not fully developed. Childlike.

Oh my god, she thought. Her mind conjured up the worst possible scenario, but she pushed the thoughts aside to focus on the task at hand. She entered a vast room, high ceilings, with a decrepit chandelier hanging in the center. She shone her flashlight into the corners, praying that the suspect would jump out on her. It was preferable to the alternative—him escaping.

Familiar objects came into view. There was a grand piano, covered in dust and looking like it hadn't been touched in decades. There were cupboards, the doors of which were barely hanging on for life. But as she rotated the flashlight to the far end of the room, she recoiled in terror. She saw something that she'd never seen before, something ripped from the stills of a horror film.

Staring back at her was some kind of alien creature.

Attached to the wall, like a mounted stag head, was a bizarre creation made from mismatched body parts. It had alligator scales, but its head was that of a dog's. Its mouth was lodged open, and inside were enormous walrus fangs sticking out like wooden stakes.

Ella stopped in her tracks. She felt an icy shiver run down her spine. She turned the flashlight to the left of the beast, landing on another ominous sight.

A glass cabinet filled with jars. Every jar was filled to the brim with yellow liquid, and inside them were bat corpses, fully preserved and scarily lifelike.

What the hell is this place?

From a distant room, Ella heard Ripley's voice. "Clear. No sign."

Ella turned her flashlight from the cabinet to another corner of the room, but she heard a thunderous banging coming from a far cupboard. Suddenly, a swift flurry of footsteps rushed past her. Her peripheral vision made out the blurry outline of a figure in the darkness, black on black.

"Stop!" she screamed. He was heading in the direction they came, but his momentum halted as he had to stop and pull open the rickety kitchen door. Ella chased after him, reaching out to grab him and narrowly missing his black shirt. As he turned the corner into the hallway, Ella leapt toward him knee-first, colliding with his shoulder and sending him hurtling into the wall. He ricocheted off the wooden panels, bringing a layer of thick dust down from above onto them both. Ella locked her hand around his wrist, but that was when she realized something wasn't right.

The wrist was rock solid. Stone cold. She moved her hands up the arm, feeling further solidity. The thing beneath her was in the shape of a human, but it wasn't real.

She was holding a mannequin.

"What the hell?" She shone her flashlight down the hallway in the wake of a small thud, and she saw the front door flapping in the wind. Ripley's footsteps thundered through the hallway as she arrived from the other side of the house.

"What is it? What happened?" she shouted.

"Out the door," Ella said. "He's escaped."

Ripley turned and fled in the same direction. "Wait here," she called back.

Ella picked herself up off the ground, hearing Ripley disappear out into the wild. Between a crack in the door, she saw a few officers follow Ripley down the dirt path and out of sight.

She felt a crushing weight of disappointment once again. She cursed herself for not acting quicker, for not shooting instead of chasing. She wanted this guy alive, and because of that he was now on the run. She moved toward the door and peered out into the darkness but couldn't see beyond the driveway. She felt she'd let herself down, and those families she was desperate to provide closure to.

Wait here, Ripley had said. Ella wondered why she hadn't wanted her to follow. Had she let Ripley down too?

No, outside was treacherous. There was no point putting themselves both at the mercy of the wild nature. Ripley must have asked her to stay back so they could reconvene here, regardless of the outcome.

She decided to use the opportunity to scour the house for any potential evidence, so she retraced her steps back into the kitchen. She searched for a light switch by flashlight, but before she found anything, she heard something from another room.

There was a click. Then a metal clanging sound.

"Ripley?" Ella called out.

No response.

Ella pulled out her gun and held her flashlight beside it. She stealthily moved back into the hallway, noticing something different this time.

There was no light coming from the front door. It had been shut. The broken chain lock still dangled loosely, but the lock had been clicked in place.

Ella strafed toward it, pulling on the handle.

Nothing. The deadbolt lock had been turned.

For the first time, she felt the cold air prickle against her skin. She had a sudden awareness of this vast house, still lingering with musty and moldy scents of God knows what. Then she felt what others had called agent's intuition; a sudden and definite knowledge of something despite no evidence. But you knew it.

And Ella knew it.

She knew that she wasn't alone in here.

Then came the sound. A deafening whirring noise that was so close it felt like it was inside her ear canal. Instinct propelled her to protect herself by jumping back, and that was when she saw the same dark figure from before standing a few feet away from her. But this time, he had come prepared. He wielded something in his hands, but Ella couldn't quite make out what.

Ella pointed her gun and flashlight at him, but before she could even outstretch her arms to her shooting position, something collided with her hands. Both the gun and the flashlight flew to the floor, sending her staggering alongside them.

In a swift motion, she composed herself and kicked in the direction the figure had attacked from, but found only darkness. She couldn't make out anyone in front of her.

She turned her attention to the flashlight. She made a jump to grab it, but something came from nowhere and pushed down on her wrist. By the peripheral light from her flashlight, she made out Clyde Harmen standing above her. He was brandishing some kind of electrical saw in his hands. He lifted it up and perched it on his shoulder.

"I don't want to kill you, but I will if I have to," he said. He flicked a switch and the whirring noise started up again.

"You don't want to do this, Clyde," Ella screamed, struggling for breath. The terror had taken the wind out of her. She had a sudden flash of tomorrow's newspaper headlines. *BAYOU SERIAL KILLER KILLS FIVE. SERIAL KILLER CAPTURED; FBI ROOKIE MURDERED.*

"You're right, I don't," said Clyde. He brought down the saw, but Ella swept her legs around and managed to kick Clyde in the back of the knees. He reeled, dropping the saw almost fatally close to Ella's shoulder. She rolled to the side, jumped to her feet, and hurried into the room on the right-hand side of the hallway. It was too dark to fight. She weighed up the options in her head.

Either light up the room to give her a fighting chance, or buy time and wait for Ripley to come back.

She made her decision. Ella scrambled toward the walls, desperately hunting for a light switch. Footsteps came from the other room just as her hand found a pull cord. She yanked on it.

A bare bulbs hanging from a lengthy cord lit up above her, and she realized she was in the living room. In her bordering vision she saw more of Clyde's bizarre creatures, but she didn't have time to register them. She scanned the room for her exit points, but the living room led into a decrepit dining room piled high with rotting furniture. A table was overturned, and on top of it chairs were piled high. Beyond that, there was only a wall.

She had no way out. It was fight or die.

Ella rushed into the dining room to search for a weapon. She needed something to combat his saw to give her leverage. She leapt over a small sofa onto a pile of disused wood, coming across a discarded table leg. She grabbed it.

The light from the living room illuminated a small alcove in the dining, allowing Ella to see inside. Another one of Clyde's strange monsters guarded it, but this time, it was something colossal.

She spotted a taxidermied brown bear, eyeless and sprouting tentacles from its face. The bear was taller and stockier than she was. A quick idea formed. Ella pulled the bear slightly out from its alcove. To her surprise, it was reasonably light, about the same weight as a small sofa, she thought.

She rushed into her new hiding place. Then waited.

Clyde came hurtling round the corner, banging his saw against the wall as he navigated his living room. He was a different Clyde than what she saw ten minutes before. He was frightened, crazed, wretched.

"Come on out, little girl," he said.

Ella realized that the saw-wielding maniac a few yards away from her was a real-life serial killer hunting for his next body. She wondered what his game plan was. They knew his name, they knew where he lived. Would he kill her then run? Would he kill her then kill himself? Was this his going-out-with-a-bang finale before succumbing to prison life for the rest of his days?

Clyde reached the dining room. He tipped his saw onto his shoulder and eyeballed the bear. He laughed. "Come on out from behind there, sweetheart."

Ella clasped the wooden leg in both her palms, ran in from her hiding spot on the other side of the room, and crashed the piece of wood into the back of Clyde's head. She felt the recoil right from her fingertips down into her forearms. He toppled into his stuffed bear and they both fell against the wall. He swung around in haste and launched his saw out at Ella, but she blocked the blow with her own weapon. The saw blade stuck deep in the wood but didn't penetrate it. Ella saw her opportunity and took it.

She grabbed the wood with her hands at either end and yanked the saw from Clyde's loosened grip. She saw a glazed look in his eyes, clearly still reeling from her brutal head shot. Both weapons lodged together, she hurled them to the other side of the room.

Clyde swung at her with his fist, catching her in the jaw. A spurt of blood filled her mouth. A second fist came, but Ella blocked it with her forearm and clutched Clyde's wrist. She maneuvered around behind him, bending his arm with it and almost pulling it clean off his shoulder. Clyde cried out in pain. Ella felt the tension in his joints. Someone as skinny as him, she knew she could rip the bone in two if she wanted.

She pressed her knee into his spine and held him toward the floor, spitting a stream of blood out of her mouth.

"Fuck. Stop," Clyde shouted. "You're going to rip my fucking arm off."

"Got you," Ella said. "Game over." She pushed his cheek against the dusty floor, locking eyes with a man who'd taken four innocent lives in such cruel, unimaginable ways. It was her first moment coming face-to-face with a killer, and was as surreal as it was exhilarating.

Ella caught her breath as she kept him restrained. There was a sound at the front door. Heavy banging. *Please be Ripley,* Ella thought.

She heard the door burst into pieces and footsteps flood inside.

"In here," she shouted. The new arrivals followed the sound of her voice. It was Ripley, Harris, and two officers. They rushed across, relieving Ella of her duties and cuffing Clyde's hands behind his back.

Ella rolled off. Ripley leaned down to her. "Dark, are you okay? Shit, how did he get back here? If I'd have known…" She trailed off. She seemed genuinely sorry for making a mistake.

"It's fine," Ella said. Ripley helped her back to her feet. "It's my fault. I thought he left the house. He didn't. He must have hidden."

"Are you hurt? Your mouth is swollen. Let's get you to a hospital quick."

"No, I'm fine. Please. Let's get this guy out of here." She turned back to Clyde and saw Harris and the officers keeping Clyde subdued.

"Well, what a surprise this is. Clyde Harmen. I knew I'd be seein' you again," said Harris.

Clyde lifted his head up from the floor as much as Harris's grip allowed him to. He looked right at Ella, *through* her. He had the eyes of a true psychopath—small pupils, unexpressive, completely devoid of any positive emotions. There was only bitterness and fury in them. She saw pure evil; the face of a man who could take innocent lives so willingly and without remorse. Ella could see him pulling off all of these murders. She had no doubt.

Two more officers rushed inside and helped Harris bring Clyde to his feet. Clyde kept his gaze firmly on Ella, and she, out of some unexplainable urge, returned his gesture. While Harris read him his Miranda rights, Clyde kept completely silent. They always did. Gein went quietly and without issue, as did Dahmer. Kemper even handed himself in to police of his own accord. Once their game was up, they knew there was no point in fighting anymore. Besides, they had infamy to look forward to. Ella suspected that the man in front of her would be the same.

Ripley left the room and came back, handing Ella's pistol back to her. She took it and thanked her. In Ripley's other hand she gripped the same human skull that caused Clyde to flee. "You did amazing, Dark. Great work. Bujinkan again?"

Ella collected herself and then turned to face Ripley. "No, misdirection with a bear. And Muay Thai. Have you seen this place? It's a freak show."

"No? I couldn't see much in the dark."

"Well, look at that thing in your hands." She nodded toward the skull. "Should you really be touching that?"

But the look on Ripley's face told Ella that something wasn't quite right. She'd never felt her emotions flip so quickly from elation to disappointment.

"Bad news, Rookie," Ripley said. She tapped the skull with her knuckles. "The bones are hollow. This skull isn't real."

The officers took Clyde Harmen out of the door and into their squad car. Before he left, Clyde looked back at Ella and laughed.

***

Judging by what they'd seen so far, Clyde Harmen's house was like a museum for the grotesque.

Clyde was taken back to the precinct to await questioning. Meanwhile, Ella, Ripley, and Harris used the opportunity to scour his home from top to bottom.

"Fake?" Ella asked. "How can you tell?"

"The texture is completely different, and there's a hollow section where there should be solid bone. It's nowhere near heavy enough, either. When you've seen as many autopsies as I have, you know what a human skull looks like."

She didn't try to hide her frustration, but even with this revelation, Ella knew that it didn't mean Clyde Harmen was innocent. If he had a penchant for this kind of imagery, his capacity for morbid activity might go further still.

"So it's not the remains of a new victim," Ella conceded, "but he could still be our unsub, surely? He attacked me with a saw, for God's sake."

Ripley pursed her lips together as she fiddled around on the wall for a light switch. "Put it this way, this guy definitely has something to hide. What that is, I'm not sure yet, but chances are this house will tell us."

She found it. A dim orange glow was cast over the room, and what appeared was like something they'd never seen before. So far, they'd only seen Clyde's bizarre creations through the lens of darkness, but bathed in light, they took on a new life entirely.

"Well, I'll be dipped in shit," said Harris. "What in God's name is all of this?"

They were in the living room. The first thing Ella's eyes were drawn to was a squirrel standing on the table beside her, but it was by no means a normal squirrel. Bat wings had been sewn into its back and nails circled around his head like a crown of thorns. Up above her on a shelf was some kind of elongated vermin creature with ten legs, stitched together from the corpses of multiple rats. A giant tarantula sat beside it, but in place of its beady eyes was what looked like a single human eyeball.

"Taxidermy. Like you've never seen before," said Ripley.

Harris turned and spotted the stuffed tarantula. He jumped back in shock. "Jesus wept. Those things make me itch." He moved away from it. "I can't believe someone this insane lives in my town, but I have to say, all of this makes a pretty good case for this being our guy."

Ella picked up the tiny bones she accidentally stepped on before she found Clyde. She held a curved bone which resembled a human rib and took it back to Ripley and Harris.

"What do you make of this?"

Harris took it from her and inspected it. "Alligator bone. Looks like it's from a baby croc. They wash up on the shore all the time."

Ella was both relieved and disheartened at the same time, but if this house proved one thing it was that Clyde Harmen was severely disturbed. There was every possibility that experimentation with animal carcasses was a steppingstone to human slaughter. Not to mention he fit the psychological profile to a T.

Ella continued searching the ground floor, finding more and more uncanny constructions in every room she inspected. But it wasn't until she entered the kitchen that she heard a scuttling sound beneath her feet.

"Guys, get in here," she called. Ripley and Harris joined her. "Can you hear that?"

It took a few seconds, but there again was the unmistakable sound of something shuffling below them.

"I hear something," Ripley said. "Basement?"

"Let's check it. The entrance would be underneath the stairs," said Harris. They followed his lead to a small alcove in the hallway, but the entrance was barred by a solid metal door. Harris pushed it. "Locked up tight."

"Odd," Ripley said. "A steel door in an old house like this?"

"And no door handle to get in?" Ella added.

Ripley pushed on the door to no avail. "This door is brand new. And it's a fire-exit door. It only opens from the inside out. Whatever's behind here he doesn't want anyone to see."

"Can we get to the basement from the outside, Sheriff?" asked Ella.

Harris thought for a second, looking toward the windows. He shook his head. "No chance, this is a split-level house. Old-school housing style from the eighteen hundreds. Short of digging up the ground, the only way downstairs is through this here door."

"Then there's another way in," Ella said. "There must be."

"Well, you know this creep better than me," Harris said. "Where would a guy like this put a secret door?"

Ella surveyed the room. She thought back to when she was twelve years old, writing her diary entries each and every night by lamplight in her bedroom. She penned all her thoughts in there, however dark and however honest. She didn't know what she'd do if anyone found it, so she always hid it in a fake compartment in her drawer.

But on top of that fake compartment was another diary. A fake diary with counterfeit thoughts and feelings; the musings of a shy schoolgirl discussing boys and homework and nothing important. She knew that if, somehow, her aunt found this fake diary, her aunt's curiosity would be satisfied and she'd walk away, leaving Ella's genuine diary untouched.

This suspect, a somewhat infantile yet functional individual, would undergo the same tactic. "He'd put it somewhere nondescript, and he'd draw attention to it as a way to misdirect people from it." She hurried across the ground floor, back into the quasi-dining room. "Look for somewhere crammed with taxidermy creatures. Little ones, nothing too in-your-face." But then she stopped. "Wait."

"What?" Ripley asked.

Ella eyeballed the back door, equally as deteriorated as other parts of the house. However, blocking the door were several bags of large cement. "There's no way out of this house other than through the front door. And there's no upstairs. That's why he ran back toward it when we closed in on him." Ella looked at Ripley. It took her a few seconds to catch on.

"So in a panicked state, he would have headed for the only place where he might avoid us," Ripley said.

"I would have, wouldn't you?"

"Most definitely. Where was it?"

Ella retraced her steps, standing in front of the cabinet with the bat jars. "Then he appeared over there," she pointed. She moved to a large wooden cabinet indented into the wall. She pulled it open. It was around six feet tall and four feet wide.

"Damn, I should have known," Harris said. "Split-level houses like this have their baths and toilets separated. This here is what used to be the toilet."

But inside looked like a regular cupboard. There were three shelves of monstrous taxidermies, with a two-headed fox guarding the bottom half.

Ripley jumped in. She picked up the fox and threw it out into the dining room. She reached down and pulled up the bottom panel, revealing a rough hole cut into the floor.

"Holy hell," said Harris. "Would you look at that?"

"This is it. He ran toward here because he thought it was his only chance to escape. But when he realized we'd find him eventually, he tried to run back out the front door." Ella shone her flashlight down into the darkness. A horde of cries and unrecognizable sounds came from below, as though they'd disturbed a distant alien colony.

"Something's alive down there," said Ripley. She inspected the hole. It was amateur in creation; jagged with uneven cuts. Ella shone her flashlight down but couldn't make out anything solid. The three exchanged glances.

"Who's going down first?" Ripley asked.

Ella showed no hesitation in climbing through the hole, at least on the surface. She'd caught this suspect and the adrenaline was coursing through her like a heavy drug. There was definitely fear in her heart, but something prevented her from showing it. Inside, she was screaming, but determination overrode every emotion.

There was no ladder or staircase, only a short drop from ceiling to floor. She landed on a concrete surface, the cold, musty air hitting her hard. The cries came louder, almost frenzied, but didn't get any closer. She reached around the wall looking for a light switch, finally landing on a pull cord.

Her heart pounded as an orb of light appeared in the center of the room. It wasn't much, but it was enough to bring the basement's horrors into view.

"Oh my god," Ella said.

***

Trapped in cages in the far end of the basement were living creatures crying out to be saved. A baby alligator paced up and down its small prison, clawing at the steel bars in a desperate bid to escape. Beside it, two dogs lay down together, limp and frail, possibly waiting for death to free them from their suffering. Sitting along the wall to her right was a long rectangular box. She peered inside, finding a mass grave of dead birds. One or two were still alive, still fluttering. Almost every inch of the room bore remains of some kind; snapped bones, animal hides, scales, feathers, dog heads.

Ripley and Harris descended from above down into the chamber of horrors, sharing the same reaction as Ella.

"Jesus in heaven. I knew he was a wacko but... I never expected this." Harris's voice from behind.

Ella turned to basement's opposite end, seeing the staircase which led back up to the hallway. Dead beasts and decaying carcasses lay at her feet. Tufts of hair, torn limbs, and the skeletal remains of a dog decorated a large operating table which spanned the entire width of the basement wall. It seemed that the dog was next in line for Clyde's amateur surgery.

"This has to be our guy," Ella said. "Look at this. This is pure sadism and experimentation. Between kills he must experiment on animals to satisfy his urges."

Ella was convinced, but Ripley's face told her a different story. She watched Ripley study the room with that expert eye. Behind her, Harris's phone rang. He answered it as he gazed at the withered dog remains on Clyde's worktable. He stared at it in disbelief. "Okay, I'll tell her," he said. He hung up.

Before Ripley could chime in with her thoughts, Harris spoke up.

"Clyde is back at the precinct, and there's good news and bad news," he said. "The bad news is that he's not saying a word to my guys."

"And the good news?" Ripley asked.

"The good news is that he's willing to talk, but only to Miss Dark."

CHAPTER SIXTEEN

Ella, Ripley, and Sheriff Harris stood outside the door to Interrogation Room 3A. Through the one-way glass, Clyde Harmen looked a lot less intimidating than he did in the shadows. But then again, they all did. Ella thought back to the pictures from 1957. For all of Ed Gein's grisly exploits, he looked like nothing more than a frail old man once the handcuffs were snapped on.

"Are you sure you want to go in there alone?" asked Ripley.

Ella had profiled this guy down to the last detail. She'd been the one to apprehend him. It was only fitting that she extracted the truth from him too.

"Yes. I can do this," she said, not taking her eyes off him through the glass. "I know how to get a guy like him talking. I'm convinced he's our guy. It's in my gut."

"Last time he was in here, he was a perv with a capital P," Harris said. "A young gunslinger like you, he's going to talk some serious flash to get you riled up. Be ready."

Ella acknowledged it, took it on board. It was fine, she thought. That was something she was used to.

"Little bit of advice," Ripley started. "With a creep like this, being tough won't get you anywhere. He won't confess no matter aggressively you ask him. You need to get under his skin. Make him uncomfortable. Get down to his level and outsmart him, okay?"

Ella felt the nervousness settle in her stomach. She thought back to how the authorities had gotten Charles Manson and David Berkowitz to talk. In short, they'd told them to cut the bullshit and get to the facts. It was a trick that worked assuming that the killer knew that *you knew* they were guilty. Given that Ella and Clyde had been in an almost fatal battle less than two hours ago, there was already an I-hate-you-and-you-hate-me relationship in place. She couldn't play to his ego, like they did with John Gacy and Richard Speck. It wouldn't work, since she'd already bested him. She had to be the authority.

She entered the interrogation room, again realizing why they called it the ice room. She ignored the discomfort and kept her attention on Clyde.

It was her first face-to-face conversation with a potential serial killer. She'd dreamed of a moment like this for years, in the same way she'd morbidly dreamed of scouring a real-life house of horrors in the flesh. Never in a million years did she imagine she'd do both on the same day, and neither did she imagine that such sights and events would leave a mental scar she might never recover from. When she looked back on this day, she knew that she wouldn't remember them with fondness. It had been a harrowing experience, and if she knew back then what she knew now, she might have forgone this horror house fantasy in favor of something less traumatic.

"Where do you want to start?" Ella said. She pulled out the chair and sat opposite Clyde, ensuring her posture indicated confidence. Standing up and walking around would give off that an aura of pseudo-dominance, which she knew wouldn't fly with a personality like Clyde's. He needed to know she was in charge but not so domineering that he'd begin to oppose her authority.

Clyde rested his shackled hands on the table between them and watched her closely as she took her seat. The fetters locking his feet in place jangled as he quivered his knees in an unconscious display of nervousness. Ella saw the goose bumps pop up along his exposed forearms.

"Who are you, the secretary?" he asked.

Ella let the moment hang in the air. "Yes, I'm the secretary who kicked the shit out of you about an hour ago."

That's something Ripley would say, she thought.

Clyde ignored the comment. He coughed what was obviously a fake cough. "Why would a pretty girl like you become a police officer?" he asked. "Seems a waste if you ask me."

"FBI agent, actually," she said with a hint of venom. It felt good to put him in his place.

Clyde smiled. "Wow. You must have slept with some very powerful men to get that job."

Don't rise to it, Ella thought. *If you acknowledge his little digs, he'll know he can get under your skin by making more of them.* "Sure did. So tell me, why did you only want to speak to me?"

"An FBI agent can't figure that out?"

110

"Apparently not."

"Try harder."

"Come on, Mr. Harmen, we're not here to play games" said Ella.

"Sounds to me like you don't know."

She decided to hit him with some harsh truths. Knock him down a peg and show him that she was the one in charge. She wasn't going to let this guy get one over on her.

"Mr. Harmen, I found you based on extensive behavioral analysis, psychological profiling, and inductive reasoning. You think I don't already know everything about you?"

"There are a lot of things you don't know about me."

"Like?"

"Fine, I'll tell you. But you have to answer my question. What's got two thumbs and prefers young bitches over miserable old sheriffs? Clue, it's not the dead monkey in my basement."

Ella took a mental step back. She hadn't expected Clyde to be like this at all. She anticipated a shy, withdrawn man who wasn't comfortable around women. She expected silence and anxiety from him, not defiance, and certainly not jokes.

Ella shook her head. "A two thumbs joke? Is it 2002 again?"

"Oh, come on. A girl like you should laugh more."

"Speaking of your basement," Ella began, "want to tell me what that's all about?" She watched a wry smile spread across his face. She could tell that he'd been waiting a long time to tell someone about the horrors inside his basement.

Clyde sat back in his chair and rattled the chains around his wrists. "I run a taxidermy business," he said. "Can't do taxidermy without animals, can you?"

"Do they need to be locked up in cages, on the verge of death? Tortured? Starved?" she said, feeling the anger gradually build. She had a low tolerance for animal abusers. They were the weakest of the weak. Some of the most heart-wrenching cases she worked on during her time with the Virginia state police involved animal neglect. She'd tried for many years to brush them from her memory.

"No," Clyde laughed. "That's a personal choice."

Ella felt a sudden rush of sickness. She was rarely confrontational, but if she was anywhere but here she would have leaned across the table and elbowed Clyde in the mouth. "You can laugh all you want, but you're on the hook for some serious offenses. Animal cruelty, neglect, abandonment, unlicensed hunting,

111

livestock theft. Not to mention gross bodily harm to a special agent. We can also have you for intent to murder, and that alone can be twenty years. That's just the beginning, too. Mind telling me where you were last night at around eleven p.m.?"

"Why?" asked Clyde.

"Because a local man was murdered, and something tells me I'm looking at the person who did it."

Clyde's body tensed up. Something changed. "Me? Murder? Are you out of your fucking mind?"

Ella saw a crack begin to form, a chink in his armor. "Mr. Harmen, do you recall the events of this evening? When you attacked me with a saw? Or do you have the memory span of a goldfish?"

"I was fooling around. You came into my home. I'm allowed to defend myself."

"We informed you beforehand that we were agents. That excuse won't fly."

"Whatever. I'm not a murderer."

"Mr. Harmen, when I see a house filled with dead animals, sideshow gaffs, and cheap Frankenstein rip-offs, it tells me that whoever lives there might be a sociopath. It tells me that whoever lives there suffers some disturbing thoughts. It tells me he's a sadist, an experimenter who has to take out his frustrations on things weaker than him, things he can control. It suggests to me that animals might not be the *only* thing he's torturing. You see where I'm going with this?"

"I didn't kill anyone. I've never killed anyone."

"So, where were you last night?"

Clyde adjusted himself in his seat. Underneath the heavy lights, beads of sweat collected on his forehead. He flicked his hair back behind his shoulders.

"I was at home."

"Convenient," said Ella. "That's all?"

"What do you want me to say?"

"Can anyone confirm that?"

"Not unless alligators can talk."

"What about last Friday night?" Ella asked.

Clyde thought for a few seconds, then smiled mockingly. "Same again. In fact, I haven't left the house for a couple of weeks now. Been too busy with my projects, if you know what I mean." Clyde's slimy tone sent a sudden rush of frustration through her, the same way an unexpected loud noise brings up a feeling of irritation and adrenaline at the same time.

"When you put on that fake machismo nonsense, you know it just makes you look more like a guilty man, don't you? I'd drop it, if I were you. When we catch the person responsible, he's going to prison for about four hundred years. Possibly execution."

Clyde ignored her threat, but Ella decided to let the idea hang in the air. Finally, it was Clyde who broke the silence.

"Did you have a pet as a kid?" he asked.

Ella decided to humor him. The more he talked, regardless of the subject, gave an insight into his demeanor. "Yes. A dog."

"Me too. Had him for twelve years. But then he got too old and I had to put him out of his misery. He was my *first*, if you know what I mean."

He was trying to make her uncomfortable, she thought. He'd noticed how she reacted when he mentioned torturing animals and was doing the same again. She played the same game back.

"And since then you've gone through every species, culminating in humans," said Ella.

"Wrong."

Get under his skin, she thought. *Get down to his level.*

"All because daddy didn't give you enough love when you were a kid?" she said. "Or was it the opposite? Was it *too much* love?"

Clyde snapped back in his seat, scraping the chair against the hardwood floor.

"How about you shut the fuck up, secretary?"

"Yeah, I read your police report before I came in here. Every night when daddy would come into your room, you'd pretend to be asleep, wouldn't you? You'd hope that just for tonight he'd spare you. But he never gave you a night off, and they only got more brutal as you... loosened up, shall we say? You'd cry into the pillow until it was over, and the next day you'd go out and find a small animal to kill to claw back some kind of power in your own life. Wasn't that how it went?"

Clyde's eyes dropped to the table. He shook his head repeatedly.

"And poor old Clyde never quite came to terms with it, did he? That's why he's still out there now, even at his age, creating weird sideshow gaffs and taking his frustrations out on those people much more adjusted than he is."

113

"*Enough,*" Clyde screamed, crashing his wrists against the table. A shrill clanging sound startled them both. "I don't kill *people*, do you understand? I kill *animals*. I completely stay away from people. I try my hardest to be alone, because I know that I'm not fit to live amongst you types. Do you hear me? Why do you think I live like a fucking hermit? Because I want to?"

And through his rage, Ella saw something which she feared more than anything she'd seen so far. She saw the truth spilling out. Raw, primal truth being channeled via anger.

"Oh, and they're not sideshow *gaffs*," Clyde said through gritted teeth. "Gaff means fake. Mine are *real*. Don't talk about things you don't have any knowledge about."

Ella let the room quiet down for a second. She let him calm, and almost conceded defeat. But then, an idea formed.

"If you're not our perpetrator, then you won't mind us showing you these photos?" Ella said. She dropped a folder onto the table and pulled it open. The photo on the top was of Shawn Kelly's corpse draped on his sofa. "What do you think of this?"

Clyde peered at it, then looked away. "Disgusting. I don't want to see that shit."

"You have animals from Satan's zoo in your house and you think this is disgusting?"

"I don't like seeing dead bodies."

"We think he's copied Jeffrey Dahmer at this crime scene. You know who Dahmer is, right? The cannibal from," Ella paused and pretended to think. "Iowa, I think. I dunno. Who cares, though? He killed gay black men. A massive coward, really, just like whoever did this."

Ella knew Ripley was watching, but she also knew that Ripley would recognize the mind games Ella was playing. Ella concluded that Clyde was a loner with very few connections to the outside world. He couldn't exactly spread the word around, and even if he did, who'd believe a guy like him?

"Sure, I remember him. Was this victim gay too?"

"Sure was."

"Maybe he got what he deserved then."

She let the remark pass, then pulled out the next photo. "See this? This is a local woman named Christine Hartwell. Familiar with her?"

"No."

"Well, we think he was mimicking another serial killer here too, except the scene was so amateur we couldn't really tell who. To us it just looked like one big mess. Maybe Dennis Nilsen, the gay guy from England? We're not sure."

Clyde shrugged and turned away. "No idea who that is."

Next up was the crime scene photo of Winnie Barker, left bleeding in her bed. "What about Ms. Barker? In her eighties. Stabbed while she slept. Kind of a spineless move, don't you think?"

Clyde examined the photo while Ella watched for any sign of guilt or remorse or delight behind Clyde's dead stare. There was no emotion, just detached curiosity.

"Still alive in her eighties? Guess this guy did her a favor."

"He was copycatting another criminal this time. Aileen Wuornos, the female serial killer from Florida. He didn't pull it off quite as well as she did though. Sometimes you need a woman to get things done right, you know?" She was purposely giving Clyde erroneous information, trying to trip him into correcting her.

Clyde waved his hand at Ella. "Look, you're talking at me like I know these people. I've told you once already, I didn't do this. I don't know who did this, and I don't know the names of these people you're throwing at me. That's all I've got to say on the matter."

Ella felt defeated, exhausted. She had to use all of her willpower to not reach across the table, grab Clyde by his dirty black shirt, and scream *I know you did this, you son of a bitch.*

The interrogation room door swung open, making Ella almost jump back in fright. Ripley entered with an intense look on her face. Ella had seen it before.

"Ms. Dark," she said, "I need to speak you with you urgently."

CHAPTER SEVENTEEN

Alex had never really driven his Ford Focus outside of town before, but he'd drive it to the moon if it meant he could sell it.

The car was a wreck, serving only as an intermediary while he familiarized himself with the rules of the road. A year since its purchase, without a scratch or a dent to its name, Alex had decided to upgrade to something which might net him more street cred.

So when the anonymous bidder had told him he'd happily take the car off his hands, providing he could drive it to his house, Alex had jumped at the chance without a second thought. A quick search of the man's address told Alex that he lived somewhere out in the sticks, and on the screen, things didn't seem so treacherous. But out in the boonies, as the locals called it, Alex's beat-up Ford struggled to cross the rickety ground into the bayou's heartland. Houses were rare, and human life rarer still. Trees faded from green to yellow and the wildlife increased in size and hostility. He was still a mile away from his destination when his sat-nav told him it didn't recognize the region he was in.

But Alex continued on, eventually entering the small town of Starksville. He felt the relief. Houses were scattered across the greenery in no particular pattern, so it took him a few minutes to find number eleven.

He knocked on the door. A flurry of footsteps sounded against a wooden floor inside. The door opened and Alex found himself starting at a man, mid-thirties, with jet black hair and a wry smile on his lips.

"Hey. I'm Alex, the car guy," he said. For a second, the man hiding behind the door looked like he was staring at a ghost. He measured Alex up and down for a few seconds, the awkwardness not lost on either of them. Then the man's demeanor quickly changed.

"Alex! Of course. Sorry, I forgot you were coming. Please come in."

Alex stepped inside a home that was surprisingly modest, despite it being at least a mile away from civilization. "Wow, most of the homes around here are basically shacks. You've got a nice place here," Alex said as he traversed the hallway into the living room.

"Thank you," the man said. "Built it myself, actually. I like the solitude out here."

"You're lucky," Alex said. "You must have some money."

His living room was spacious, decorated in a sleek white finish to contrast against the home's traditional wooden foundations. An oversized television took up one corner of the room. Beside them were some framed photographs of two young children.

"I've got enough," the man said. "By the way, call me John. Can I get you a drink?"

"Oh, no thank you," said Alex. "I can't stay too long. My dad's waiting for me to call him to pick me up, if you decide to buy the car."

"Sure? I've got coffee, soda, maybe a beer if you want?"

"I'm good. Besides, I'm not old enough to drink beer," Alex laughed. "I'm only nineteen."

John's face twisted into a snarl. "Well, you know it's rude to turn down a drink, especially booze. That's something they don't teach you at school, I bet."

The comment caught Alex off guard. "Sorry, I didn't mean to offend. I'm sure your beer is delicious."

John took a seat on the other side of the room. He stared at the TV even though it was just a black screen. Alex felt the mood suddenly change.

"Anyway, the car," he began. "It's yours if you want it."

"Great, thanks. I'll need to test drive it first."

"Sure."

"Alone," John added. "I don't want you trying to hide anything from me." It was worded like a joke, but all the necessary tonality was missing from his delivery.

Alex hesitated. "All right... Here's the keys." Alex pulled them from his pocket, and John reached over and grabbed the whole bunch in the blink of an eye. Alex began to feel a little uncomfortable. "Umm… you want me to just wait here?"

"Yes."

Alex remained seated while John left the house outside. Through the living room window, he saw John jump into the Ford Focus without really looking at it much. The engine started up, but the car didn't move.

All fell quiet. Alex used the time to casually inspect John's home from his seat. John be incredibly trusting, Alex thought, leaving a stranger alone in his house. But what did it matter as long as he was able to shed that rusty old vehicle that barely drove a mile before a warning light clicked on.

Alex turned and looked into the kitchen. It was attached to the living room but separated by a makeshift bar, complete with whiskey bottles, tumblers, and Guinness pint glasses. Outside, he saw the car move for the first time.

Alex stood up to stretch his legs and idly inspected the kitchen. He came across a large glass patio doorway which led out into John's backyard, although it was less of a backyard and more of a football field. The nearest house, a small single-room hut, was a mere blip in the distance. Alex saw that John already had two cars sitting inside a shack-turned-garage adjacent to his house. He couldn't make out the models, but they had brand new plates. The question of why John would want to buy a beat-up old Ford ran through his head, but it was none of his business, he thought.

On the kitchen wall, Alex spotted a photo calendar. It was a family of four. Mom, dad, and two young girls. It was one of those personalized ones, Alex thought, casually flipping from November to December and back. A whole calendar of family pictures. How sweet. He remembered having one as a kid, back before his mom passed away.

But then Alex noticed something.

The man in the pictures wasn't John.

He had no time to ponder the mystery as John came speeding back into view, parking the car in his backyard at a crooked angle between the house and garage. He hadn't been long. Thirty seconds at most. Alex rushed back into the living room and took his original seat to give the impression he hadn't moved. John came bursting in through the back patio door.

"She drives good," he said. "I'll give you a thousand in cash. How's that sound?"

Relief filled him. Finally, someone wanted to buy his junk. "Deal," Alex said. "Thank you."

"My pleasure."

"What are your plans with it?" Alex asked, making small talk while John disappeared into an adjoining room. "I see you've already got two newish cars."

"Yeah. It's for my son," John shouted back.

Alex looked back toward the pictures on the TV stand, the calendar. He was no expert, but the children in the photos looked like girls to him. He thought best not to inquire.

"Oh, well, I hope he likes it."

"I'm sure he will," John said, returning to the lounge. Alex saw he had something gripped in his palm, but it didn't look like money. "Listen, while you're here, do you think I could try something?"

Alex froze up. "Like what? Something to do with the car?"

"No, not that. This might sound a little weird, but I'm actually an entertainer by trade. The wife and kids have been at the lake all week, and I've got a new routine I've been desperate to try."

"You? An entertainer?" Alex asked.

"Yes, me. Why is that a shock?"

"Sorry, I didn't mean it like that. You just didn't strike me as the type. What type of entertainer?"

"A magician."

"Wow, that's cool. You don't want to saw me in half, do you?"

"Not exactly," said John. "Look, I'm doing a show tomorrow night and I really want to include this new piece, but I haven't been able to practice it with anyone. Can you spare five minutes before you head home? I know it's a strange request, but you can probably see that I can't just call my neighbor over."

This was the last thing Alex expected, but it would be a funny story to tell his friends. Besides, who was this guy? He wasn't Criss Angel, but he might be a famous magician he'd never heard of. "Sure thing. What is it, a card trick?"

John opened up his hand and a pair of handcuffs fell out. Alex felt a twinge of discomfort. "Uh, what the hell is this? Why do you want to handcuff me?"

"Not you," John said. "Me. I'll do the whole thing. Look, inspect them." John held up his hands to show they were empty. "Nothing in the hands, and perfectly normal cuffs, right?"

Alex picked up the cuffs and looked them over. He wasn't really sure what was considered normal and what wasn't, but he played along anyway.

"They look fine to me."

"Good. Now cuff me." John turned around and stuck his hands behind back. "Go on. Slap them on me and pull them tight."

119

Alex stood up from the sofa, fiddled around with the handcuffs until he figured out how they operated, and then attached them in place. He squeezed them so the metal was flush against John's wrists.

"Done, I think."

"Good. Now watch this." John turned around to face him and began to wriggle his arms around behind his back. John creased his face, closed his eyes, and reopened them when he heard a clink. Slowly, he pulled one arm free. Another clink, and the handcuffs fell to the ground beside John.

"Ta-da."

Alex thought it best to feign interest. The trick was hardly groundbreaking. He expected something with a much more satisfying payoff. There was something weird about this guy and Alex didn't want to stick around to find out any more about him. "Wow. Did you pick the locks or something?"

John reached down and picked up the cuffs. "No, nothing like that. A magician shouldn't reveal his secrets, but honestly, this trick is so simple it doesn't really matter. Anyone can do it."

"Oh right. Well, let me know where you're performing and I might come see you." Alex said, not even trying to hide his desire to get out of the house. There was something about middle-aged men doing basic magic tricks that was universally unsettling.

"Here, let me show you." John launched toward him and maneuvered behind him. Alex resisted as he pulled his arms back, but John held onto them with an iron grip.

"No, it's fine. I really need to be heading back."

"It will only take a second. Look." Before Alex could move away John had snapped one cuff on Alex's wrist. Alex tried to shake it off, but before he could, the second cuff was on. The sudden lack of mobility in his arms sent a violent wave of panic through his nerve endings. He jigged his wrists around ferociously to try and free himself.

"This isn't funny," he shouted. "I don't want to do this."

"Relax," John said with a smile. "Here, I'll show you the trick. It's easy."

Alex felt John's breath on the back of his head. Close up, he smelled like dirt. "How do I get out? What's the trick?"

Alex felt John's hand caress his scalp. Alex froze in a state of confusion. Maybe this was part of the trick, he thought.

But then John's hand squeezed together, grabbing Alex forcefully by the hair with an impermeable grip. An intense stabbing pain ran across his scalp. John pulled his head backward as he kicked Alex in the back of the knees, dropping him down to the ground.

"The trick is to have the key," John screamed, holding a solid, silver key up against Alex's face. John threw the key to the floor as Alex lost all balance and collapsed on his back. He felt John's hands tightly grip his neck, sending him into a frenzy of kicking and flailing. He couldn't displace the tension in any way. There wasn't enough space between him and John to build up any force, and all his feet were finding was the base of the brown leather sofa he'd just been sitting on.

He began to choke and splutter as John's thumbs pressed against his windpipe. He tried breathing through his nose, but any oxygen intake was cut off at the neck.

Adrenaline forced him to pull on the handcuffs with every ounce of energy he had. Severe burning pains overtook his wrists, but in his right hand, he felt the pain extending upward. To his thumb. To his knuckles.

The right cuff was loose.

Through one last agonizing heave, Alex broke his right hand free of the cuff, tearing layers of flesh and tissue along with it. He instinctively tried to alleviate John's grip around his neck to allow some airflow into his lungs, but John was too strong, too overbearing. Alex reached out to claw John's face, but John jerked his head out of the way so the distance was too great.

Blurriness set in. Suddenly, the excruciating pain began to subside, being replaced by a kind of hallucination and fuzziness. His vision slowly faded to white as his right arm fell to his side.

Then he felt something against his fingertips. Something metal. He frantically pulled it between his fingers and felt that it was around an inch long with a jagged end.

The handcuff key.

Alex prayed that blind luck was on his side. He summoned the strength to jam the key into his attacker's face, hoping that he'd do enough to disorient him.

"Fuck!" John screamed.

Air seeped into Alex's lungs. Vision came back and reenergized him. On top of him, John was covering one side of his face with his

121

hands, bleeding through the cracks in his fingers. Alex had stabbed him in the eye.

Alex did the same again. Repeatedly. He shoved his improvised weapon into John's face, his temple, and his free eye in quick succession, doing enough to make him lose his balance. Alex kicked himself free, jumped to his feet, and propelled himself toward the front door. His blurry state made him collide with it with a thunderous crash shoulder-first. He pulled on the handle. Furiously messed with the catch. "Open, you fucking thing," he screamed. "Open!"

But it didn't. Dimly he noticed it had one of those deadbolts that needed a key. John must have locked it when he came in.

The back door.

Alex turned back to the living room, where John had risen to his feet. Alex picked up a vase off a windowsill and threw it at John. The impact staggered him, and John landed in the entranceway to the kitchen. Alex hurled himself toward the bar and leapt over it, smashing a variety of alcohol bottles as he did. He reached the patio door and yanked on the handle.

The door slid open.

John's footsteps thundered behind him, but Alex was out into the open. He ran as fast as his legs would carry him, covering what seemed to be a quarter mile of muddy grass in less than a minute. He reached a small road, then stopped and checked his surroundings. There was still an agonizing burning sensation in his neck and throat. A pair of handcuffs still dangled from his left wrist, while a ruthless, sharp sensation ran up and down both hands. The winter mist combined with his blurry vision made detection of anything, living or not, difficult.

He surveyed every direction, praying that he'd outrun the man who called himself John. He saw nothing but a pair of lights in the distance. They came toward him fast.

Alex ran toward the vehicle. "Stop," he shouted. "Please stop." Alex fell to the ground in the middle of the road. The pressure in his ankles caused him to collapse where he stood.

A small, silver Volkswagen appeared and abruptly stopped in front of him. A young woman jumped out of the driver's seat but stood behind her open door for protection.

"Please. My name's Alex Bauer. I've been attacked," Alex blurted out before the woman could say anything.

"Oh my God, are you okay?" she said in a frenzy.

"No. He strangled me. I can't breathe properly. Please get me out of here. He might still be looking for me."

The woman opened the back door and helped Alex inside. She rushed back into the driver's side and locked all of the doors.

As the car rumbled back into life, Alex was sure he saw a figure in the distance. A small dot on a green field.

Growing in size.

Getting closer.

He saw the same face again. The same blood-covered clothes. He was still in pursuit, staggering across the grass.

"Drive!" Alex shouted. "Please God, get out of here."

The rumbling engine spluttered. A plume of black smoke appeared at the back windshield. Alex knew that sound, knew that smoke. His own car had produced the same thing many times.

"Shit," the woman said, pushing the accelerator down as far as it would go. Alex heard her foot smack the floor of the car. "It won't start up again!"

And Alex felt the worst fear he'd ever felt in his life.

CHAPTER EIGHTEEN

Ella dropped her head back in her chair. She pushed her hair off her shoulders. The familiar pang of frustration came back, the same one she felt when Ripley told her the human skull was fake. Victory felt within arms' reach, but at the same time was blocked off by some invisible, impenetrable barrier.

Ella jumped out of her chair and made her way to the door. Ripley held it open for her as she left. They met Harris, who was watching through the two-way glass.

"Leave it," Ripley said. "It's not going to happen."

Ella felt the disappointment creep up on her. Hearing Ripley speak in an equally dejected tone filled her with a sense of defeat. She felt like she'd just stepped out of a boxing ring after being pummeled for ten rounds.

"Sorry," Ella said. "I tried to get him to slip up any way I could."

"You did everything you could, Dark," said Ripley. "Sometimes you can't get through to them no matter what you try. It was a great idea, purposely getting the information wrong to see if he reacted, but he didn't go for it."

"Is that what that was?" Harris asked.

Ella nodded. "Yes. When he got upset that I called his taxidermies fake, I thought I'd try the same approach with the crime scenes. If he idolizes those serial killers as much as we think he does, he would have been irate that we got the important details wrong. But it didn't seem to faze him at all." Ella hated having to say the words. She could barely stand to look at Ripley, knowing that she wasn't able to get the job done.

"Right," said Harris. "So what now?"

"I think Clyde Harmen is a lot of things," Ripley began. "Sexist, homophobic, deeply disturbed, sexually incompetent. But I don't think he's a serial murderer."

"There's still a possibility, right?" Ella asked, almost pleading. "There must be. Just because he hasn't admitted it doesn't mean it's a lost cause. He has no alibi for the Hartwell and Kelly murders. He has a history of sexual deviancy and animal cruelty."

"Sorry, Rookie, but my gut is telling me that the guy in front of us couldn't pull off any of the scenes we've seen so far. Look at him. Weak, skinny, childish, dressed like a skater from the nineties. I can see him selling weed outside Walmart. I can't see him pulling off organized, complex homicides without leaving behind a single trace. Did you see how he reacted when you accused him? Raw emotion, like killing a human is the last thing he'd ever do."

Ella stared at Clyde through the glass. He sat with his back toward them gazing at the far wall. He hadn't turned to face the crime scene photos once since Ella left the room.

"We'll keep him here for a while anyway," said Harris. "We've got the local wildlife commission emptying his house as we speak. At the very least we can charge this sicko with animal cruelty, not to mention his attack on Miss Dark. A prison sentence wouldn't be out of the question, either."

"I wanted it so badly to be him. More than anything," said Ella, still looking through the glass.

"So did I, but look, we caught this guy and stopped him doing some grim things. That's a victory. If you can find this guy using just your profiling abilities, you can also find the real killer, right?" said Ripley.

"I'm still not convinced. Everything matched up so perfectly. Let me go in there again. I'll try a different approach," Ella said, almost trying to convince herself rather than Ripley. The feeling of envy came surging back. Ripley could just *see* it. See beyond the fleshy exterior, the bullshit, the grandiosity. But Ella couldn't. It was almost overwhelming, this realization that the visceral reality was a different beast entirely from reading books and memorizing historical events.

"Dark, I'm not saying we shouldn't keep interviewing this guy, but you going back in there isn't going to achieve much."

Ella sighed. She knew it, but struggled to accept it. "Can I just try?"

"Look, your knowledge caught this guy, and that's an incredible achievement. But being able to see into someone's core, extract the truth from them? It's not something you learn in forty-eight hours. It takes years of practice, trial and error. You can't do it. Not many people can. Don't feel bad about it, Dark."

It was a tough understanding for her. Ella had always assumed that if she studied enough, she could do anything. For most areas of her life, it had worked. But this was something that needed experience, that no textbooks could teach you. She felt a little dejected as she realized she had a long way to go before reaching the levels of capability she desired.

Ella moved toward the interrogation room door but Ripley held up her hand to stop her. As she did, her phone began to ring in her pocket. Ripley pulled it out, checked the number, and answered. "Hello?"

Within seconds, Ella watched Ripley's face as it turned into an expression she'd seen once before. That very morning, in fact.

"We'll be right there," Ripley said. She hung up the phone.

"What's happened?"

"Clyde isn't our man."

"How do you know?"

"We need to get to the local hospital. You're not going to believe this."

***

Harris drove them from the precinct to Saint Mary's Hospital on the edge of town. It was the only hospital within an eight-mile radius. Heavy winter rain bouncing off the car windows provided the soundtrack for their journey. It was a bleak night on all accounts.

"What did they say exactly?" asked Ella from the backseat.

"Not much. They just said a young kid arrived at the hospital, could barely talk after being strangled. His story was that he was attacked by a man living in isolation out in Starksville."

"Boy, it's barren out there, let me tell you," Harris said. "Quieter than a graveyard. Starksville's about a mile deep and there's about five people living there. It's where the rich retirees go."

They pulled into the Saint Mary's Hospital parking lot and Harris parked in one of the spaces at the front designated for emergency service vehicles. The three of them got out and made their way through the hospital's double doors. Ella took her glasses off to shield the lenses from the rain.

"We don't even know if it's connected so let's not get ahead of ourselves," Ripley said as they stepped into the hospital and navigated the hallways. They followed Harris's lead. The hospital was eerily empty, with nothing but a long white corridor stretching forever onward in front of them. A pregnant woman in pajamas suddenly appeared from one of the corners. An orderly helped her along. Harris nodded to them both.

"Here." They reached corridor 43. Inside were the beds for ER patients. At the reception desk, the assistant pointed them to the bed of Alex Bauer. There were only three other patients in the room. Two were sleeping, and one was keeping an intrigued watch on the officers.

Ella, Ripley, and Harris approached Alex's bed. He was awake, sitting upright and scrolling through his phone with his left hand. He had a bandage around his neck and his right arm was bandaged from the hand to the forearm. He looked at the three new arrivals with panicked suspicion.

"Mr. Bauer?" asked Ripley.

The boy nodded. His wounds were apparent, more noticeable than his youthful good looks, Ella thought. A redness enveloped the bottom half of his face, presumably traveling underneath his bandage and staining his back too.

"My name's Agent Ripley and this is Agent Dark and Sheriff Harris. We understand you've been through a lot in the past few hours, but do you mind if we ask you some questions about the incident?"

Ella thought that Alex looked like a good kid, with his mop of blond hair and jock-like appearance. He would no doubt go on to be an attractive man once true adulthood kicked in, but she couldn't help but wonder how such a traumatic experience might affect his later life.

Alex opened his mouth to speak but only growls came out. He tried again, but then stopped and shook his head. A nurse, clad in loose blue scrubs, rushed across from the bed of the observing patient.

"No, no, no. Officers, I'm sorry, but Alex has suffered severe trauma to his cervical spine. The blood vessels around his esophagus have gradually swelled up since his injury occurred, which makes talking difficult and painful. I'm sorry, but you can't speak with him."

Ella saw the frustration on Alex's face. He shrugged, then went back to tapping away on his phone.

"Understood," said Ripley. "Alex, we'll come back when you're healed so we can talk to you properly."

But Alex turned back to the officers and held his phone out to them. On the screen he'd written *I can talk through here.*

Ella and Ripley exchanged a look of confirmation. "Are you sure?" Ella asked.

Alex nodded a hearty yes.

"Well, thank you for being so cooperative," said Ripley. "Can you talk, or type, us through what happened?"

There was a brief silence while Alex tapped away. Ella had already scoured the depths of her brain for serial killers who targeted young boys, and the list was too exhaustive to acknowledge just yet. If there was something else that would help narrow it down, it would soon make itself known.

Alex presented his phone after around thirty seconds. *I advertised my car on Auto Trader. I got a call out of the blue from a withheld number. It was some guy who said he'd buy my car if I could get out to his house today.*

"What did he look like? Was there anything identifiable about him? Birthmarks, tattoos, scars?" Ripley asked.

Another short wait. *Not really. He looked like a normal guy. He had black hair and brown eyes and was a bit taller than me. About five-eleven. Not young, not old. He said his name was John. He acted a bit weird at first.*

"Weird how? Talk us through it."

Alex furiously typed away. *He offered me a drink and got pissed at me when I said no. Then he took my car out for a drive and parked it in his backyard. When he got back, some shit went down and he had me in handcuffs. I fought like crazy and hauled ass out of there. He came after me. Chased me until I got in someone's car. He nearly caught me but we managed to speed off just in time.*

"Handcuffs?" Ripley asked. "How did he bring them into the conversation?"

Another spark, another connection. But Ella kept her mouth shut. She didn't want to give away any hints to Alex. Exposing theories to medical staff was one thing, but giving them to a teenager would be the kiss of death when it came to keeping things under wraps. The nurse came back and popped her head in between them.

"Sorry to interrupt, Officers, but we need to treat Alex's swelling. It's inflamed since we last checked so we need to be cautious. If you could hold on for half an hour we'll have him back to you?"

"Of course, treat him," Ripley said. "We need to head out now anyway."

"I'll stay," Harris said. He pulled out his car keys and threw them to Ripley. "Check out the house. Starksville's about seven miles away. I'll stay and talk to the kid when he's ready and I'll call in two squad cars to meet you there. I'll get an ID on the homeowner too."

Ripley nodded a confirmation. She turned to Alex. "If you could provide us the address, we'll head there right away." Alex wrote the address on his phone and showed it to the agents. Ripley made a note of it.

They made their way out of the hospital and back into the car, leaving Harris behind to finish the interview. If Ella didn't have to leave, she'd have stayed with Alex for longer, she thought. Seeing this poor kid in his condition, especially in the prime of his life, felt like a knife in her gut. Seeing a dead victim was one thing, but seeing an alive one was worse, in a way. She knew he'd be rife with trauma and flashbacks for the rest of his life, something she knew all too well herself.

"This our guy, you think? Does it fit?" Ripley asked, unlocking the squad car doors.

If this was indeed their perpetrator, Alex had painted a picture of an impulsive, fantasy-driven offender who would go to great lengths to achieve his goals. This murder attempt was different from the rest, she thought. She wasn't certain it was him, but the signs so far all told her that it was.

"I don't know what to think. I thought our guy was locked up at the station. Time to find out."

CHAPTER NINETEEN

Ella and Ripley arrived at the address just before midnight. It took longer than expected to reach Starksville, since the heavy rain and lightless country lanes made for difficult navigation. Under other circumstances, the boundless greenery and secluded houses would have made for pleasant daydreaming of a less hectic life, but Ella had no time for such trivialities.

A cobblestone path led to the home's front door. Ella banged on it. Ripley kept her hand firmly around her Glock 17 pistol as they waited for an answer.

Thirty seconds passed without a response. Ripley's phone vibrated in her pocket. She picked it up.

"Harris. Go. We're at the suspect's home. Looks like it's empty." She turned on speaker phone.

"It would be," Harris's voice crackled through. "The house belongs to a couple named Jared and Chloe Green, but here's the thing, they've been on vacation in Europe since last Friday. I just got through to Chloe and she assured me there should be no one in their house. They locked it all up when they left."

"Then someone's using their home to attack young kids. We're going in," Ripley said. Ella took the initiative and began to shoulder the front door, but it was too rigid to budge.

Harris's crackly voice again. "The other officers are on their way. The GPS gets all screwed up out in the sticks."

"Understood," Ripley said, placing the phone in her pocket. "Back door. Let's go."

Ripley and Ella made their way along the side of the home, past a handful of windows, all of which were locked shut. Inside was shrouded in darkness too. There was no fence separating the home's backyard from the region's grassy surroundings, only an open garage which signaled the rough area where the home's outdoor territory ended. Ella spotted three cars.

"Two Audis and a Ford Focus," Ripley said. "One of those isn't like the others."

"The Ford must be Alex's. He said the guy took it for a test drive. Look how he's parked it."

"Jammed between the garage and the back door, so Alex couldn't make a quick escape in it if he got free."

Ella put herself in Alex's position. If he'd have managed to get in the car, it would have taken some serious maneuvering to get it out of the angle it had been locked in at. She felt a sensation of helplessness as she imagined Alex trying to escape his captor, realizing he'd have to escape on foot.

They approached the back patio area. Two sliding glass doors gave a glimpse into a kitchen area. Ella pulled on one of the handles and the door opened the first time. She looked back at Ripley.

"He escaped through here and didn't have any way to lock it," Ripley said. She pulled out her flashlight and shone it inside, finding a light switch to her right. She flicked it on. The kitchen area lit up. A pile of smashed glass lined both the kitchen surface and the floor. Ella moved forward and found the light switch for the living room.

"Jesus wept," said Ripley, scrutinizing the pile of blood which had dried into the gray carpet. "Alex must have caught him good." Beside it was a white and gold vase, with a large chunk missing from its side.

"Any thoughts, Dark? I'm not seeing any reason why this might be connected to the four other murders. Breaking into a home eight miles from his last murder site? A ruse about selling a car? Handcuffs? Why would he go to these lengths? If I was looking at this through the lens of an isolated murder case, I'd argue that sexual gratification was the prime motivator here, something which the other murders lacked."

"No, our unsub did this. I'm sure of it." Ella knelt down beside the blood pool and recreated the scene in her mind. She visualized Alex's entering and making small talk with the killer. She saw the killer eyeing him up from behind, ensuring that he was a suitable victim type. When he approved, he poured a drink and offered it him. Alex said no. Then she saw the rage and frustration overcome the killer. She saw him panic and reconvene his plan. Then came the recreation of historical events. Ella pictured the killer using the references in her memory bank. He was a stocky man, physically adept.

A clown.

This scene was indeed different from the rest, but also similar in one very crucial way. Things fell into place almost seamlessly. When she was sure she had the events in linear order, she ran it by Ripley.

"Alex came in and sat down here. Remember how he said this *John* got upset when he refused his offer of a drink?"

"Yes."

"That's because he was trying to pry him with alcohol, or possibly drugs to loosen him up, to make him an easier victim. We know this guy isn't confident in his physical abilities. He always blitz attacks when his victims least expect it. He had to use drugs to sedate Shawn Kelly because he posed a physical threat, and Alex did too. He needed him weakened before he was comfortable enough to strike."

"I agree, he does," Ripley said. "But that's pretty common in murder cases the world over."

Ella looked out toward Alex's car abandoned in the yard. She pulled up the visualization again in her mind and went through it step by step. "He was banking on Alex taking the drink, but when that approach didn't work he had to think of another way to make Alex's escape more difficult."

Ella pictured the killer doing his best to keep calm, but fretting on the inside. She saw him wanting to blitz-attack Alex like he had done with the others, but he knew that he couldn't. She could almost see the look on his face as he fought that internal battle with himself. Get the kill, or pay the correct tribute?

"Alex was sober, so he had to remove the car from the equation. That was when he came up with the test drive story. He was able to take the keys off Alex and park the car somewhere where it was more difficult to escape in. If Alex did manage to get the key somehow, or if he had a spare key in his pocket, he'd need to maneuver the car quite significantly to get out of that position."

Ripley listened with interest, following Ella's pattern of thinking. "I suppose you could be right. If Alex did fight back, the only escape would be to run through the fields, giving the unsub a better chance of recapturing him."

Ella picked herself up off the blood-soaked floor. "Is Harris still on the line?"

Ripley held up her phone. "He is."

"Tell him to ask Alex something. Ask him if this John person tried to show him a magic trick with the handcuffs."

Ripley did, then thanked Harris and hung up. "Ten out of ten, Rookie. What do you know that I don't?"

Ella didn't yet respond. "The handcuffs approach wasn't a deviation from his intentions. He had planned to do it, only he planned on Alex being intoxicated at the time. But because he couldn't follow his plan to the letter, like he did with all the others, he slipped up."

"He panicked. That tells us he's not good at thinking on his feet. Maybe he's not as organized as we thought."

"There's one thing I'm missing, though," Ella continued. "Why here? He chose Alex because he fit the profile he needed, but the location is strange."

"He might have easy access to this place. He might be a friend or relative of the owners. He might have just chosen it at random. He might have tried a hundred houses before landing on this one."

"Do you think this guy would do that?" Ella asked. "All of his other scenes have been calculated and controlled to the letter."

"You tell me. In your profile of the unsub, you said that location was as important as victimology and signature."

Ella thought about it. "He wouldn't just choose this place at random. He doesn't do randomness, or convenience. Staging is everything to him. He needed to kill Alex in this house because it was part of the signature. Everything else matches up, except—" Ella stopped mid-sentence. She was browsing the window ledge which overlooked the front lawn.

"What is it?" Ripley asked, seemingly picking up on her thoughts telekinetically. "Out with it."

On the shelf was a row of three trophies. Each one depicted a golfer in a different stance. Ella lowered herself to read the plaques on them all.

The first one, UNITED STATES GOLF ASSOCIATION— JARED GREEN.

The next, LOUISIANA GOLF SOCIETY SILVER AWARD— JARED GREEN.

But it was the third one that made the sparks connect.

Ella picked up the trophy and pointed to the engraving. It simply said *J.G.*

"What about it?" Ripley asked. "So he's a golfer."

133

"No, look at the initials. The guy who owns this house is Jared Green. *J.G.* This whole scene is a tribute to John Gacy."

Ripley considered it for a moment. "Shit, I think you're right."

"Between 1972 and 1978, John Wayne Gacy was responsible for the deaths of at least thirty-three young men and boys throughout the Chicago area. His victim count made him one of the most prolific serial killers in modern history. In his personal time, Gacy doubled as a children's entertainer—a clown."

"It makes sense," Ripley agreed. "This house a makes a great location for him. It's in the middle of nowhere so it gives him privacy. It's lavish, so people are going to be more inclined to come inside. It's all here."

"It really is. Gacy preyed on young boys, the average age around nineteen. He used a number of ploys to get them back to his house, then he'd pump them full of alcohol until they were in no fit state to fight back. I'm just struggling to understand how he found a house not only with the homeowner's initials being J.G., but who would also be out of town."

"There's probably a million homeowners with those initials. Or he could have found one just named John, or Wayne. It's called multiple outs. There were different ways he could have referenced the name, and finally, when he realized these guys would be in Europe, that cemented the decision."

Ella thought on it, then agreed. "I guess. After Gacy was done plying them with alcohol, he'd use the handcuff trick."

"Then strangle them and leave them under the floorboards," Ripley finished.

"And that was probably his intention here, but he failed," Ella said. They exchanged a look.

"In my experience, when serial killers fail, things tend to get more difficult for the investigators."

"How so?"

"Serial killers lash out if they don't manage to appease their fantasies, like if they get interrupted during the kill. It's like someone slapping you in the face when you're about to orgasm."

Ella's mind jumped to Jack the Ripper, who had killed two women in one night because he didn't manage to mutilate the first.

"Some people like that," Ella said.

"True, and just like those people, I can feel things getting rough. If this is the first time his plans have been thwarted, his next attack could be completely unpredictable. It could be a random stabbing in the street, or an impulsive home invasion."

Ella ran through the possible scenarios in her head. Given his failure here, would he redo the Gacy murder? Would he find another victim, another home? Or would he go back for Alex again?

"We'll get forensics over here to comb through this place. We've got enough DNA samples here to get a perfect match if he's on the database."

The other possibility was that he'd accept his failure and move on, but if so, to what?

The only certainty she had was that the man in the holding cells back at the precinct was not the person responsible for these murders.

"We need to get back to the precinct and revisit the profile," Ella said. "There must be something we've missed."

"No sleep for us tonight," said Ripley as they made their way out. "We need to solve this thing now."

CHAPTER TWENTY

When Ella arrived at the precinct the next morning, her mind was a deadfall of questions. There was a new determination in her, because during all of yesterday's chaos, Ella had overlooked something.

She had been right.

She locked herself in the office and began scrawling away on a whiteboard. She was quickly consumed by her thoughts, but a knock on the door pulled her back to reality. Ripley walked in with a steaming coffee in her hands.

"You're early," Ripley said.

Ella prayed that the red circles around her eyes had disappeared. She prayed Ripley wouldn't notice the signs of tiredness on her face and skin.

"Couldn't sleep," Ella said.

"Those blotches give you away. You're exhausted, and I'm not surprised."

Ella slumped herself down in her chair and stared up at her work. She'd drawn a table listing all of the serial killers the unsub had mimicked so far, listing victim counts, locations, times, dates, number of escapees, murder weapons, victim characteristics, specific rituals and M.O.s. In her hand she held a printout of her psychological profile. She ran her pen up and down the page, feeling a surge of overwhelming anxiety jolt her in the stomach. There was too much information for her to break down, too many factors, too much complexity. She had all this information as a baseline, but what if it was completely wrong? More people would die, and it would be her fault for taking the profile in the wrong direction. That was a burden she couldn't handle. Despite what they found at Clyde's home, she couldn't help but feel that the whole endeavor had been a waste of precious time—and it was all her fault because of her profile. While they were looking in one direction, the real killer was striking in the other. The guilt plagued her; one of the reasons why she barely managed four hours of sleep last night.

"Dark, talk to me. What's on your mind?"

Ella looked down at the paper in her hand.

It would be safe to assume he would emulate similar lust killers, such as John Wayne Gacy, Gary Ridgway, Dennis Rader. If he was to emulate John Wayne Gacy, he would choose a young adult male or teenage boy.

"I predicted he would only copy lust killers, and that Gacy might be one of them."

"And he did exactly that."

"So, I think I know how he might strike next, but I can't be sure."

"Go on."

"With every kill there's been an escalation of some form, correct? If you were looking at these outside of my theory, how you would view it?" Ella asked.

Ripley took a gulp of her coffee and pointed to the first name on the list. "Well, the unsub's first kill of Julia Reynolds was simple and straightforward. He dispatched her quickly, disposed of her immediately, and didn't spend considerable time with the body, nor did he pose her or stage the scene in any way. "

Ripley moved to the next name. "His second kill, Winnie Barker, was similar, but there was also a change in M.O. He killed her quickly and didn't spend any time with her while she was conscious, but this time he left a small message in lipstick. This was where he really put the stamp on his kill. If he hadn't done this, we might, or rather, *you* might never have suspected he was mimicking Richard Ramirez."

"And Christine Hartwell?"

"That's where he began to really hone his operation. He perfected this scene down to the last detail, even spending considerable time with her corpse postmortem. Here, he included things he hadn't done before, copying Gein's actions right down to minor things like restraint equipment. The whole thing was staged to obsessive levels."

"Would you see Shawn Kelly's murder as a de-escalation, considering the staging was less dramatic?"

Ripley thought for a second. She pushed back her auburn hair and held it in a ponytail. "No, I wouldn't say that at all," she said. "Just because the postmortem brutality wasn't quite as extreme, it doesn't mean there wasn't an acceleration in his psychopathology.

Escalation can mean different things in the confines of a crime scene and psychoanalysis. It isn't restricted to displays of violence."

Ella considered the idea. She'd been agitated by the fact that Shawn Kelly's murder was less theatrical, less systematic than Christine Hartwell's. "Like how?"

"Well, tell me how Jeffrey Dahmer approached his victims."

"He befriended them in gay clubs around Milwaukee and invited them back to his apartment. He promised them booze, drugs, and sex, then once they were alone, he'd get them inebriated and then attack them."

"And how does that differ from the others? Kemper, Ramirez, Gein?" Ripley asked.

"They all attacked on sight. Kemper spent a little time with his victims, but that was just to get them out in the open. Ramirez and Gein didn't gain their victims' trust at all."

"Right, well in that case, that's the escalation here. Our unsub engaged in conversation with Shawn Kelly before subduing him. At least, to levels he hadn't done before. Personalizing the victim is a common acceleration in serial killers since it makes the murder that much more satisfying when they do go through with it. They get off on the deception, and then again during the kill."

"Okay, and would you argue this escalation continued on to his Gacy kill?" Ella asked.

Ella warmed her hands on her coffee, then rubbed them together. "Without a doubt. He went to the trouble of locating an empty house, arranging his victim to come *to him*, plying him with alcohol right there and then, *and then* went through the whole ordeal with the handcuffs? That's a big jump from just drugging someone and waiting for the intoxication to take hold. Not to mention, we don't know exactly what he would have done if the victim hadn't escaped."

"I also think he's escalating in terms of serial killer notoriety too," Ella said. "The crime scenes aren't just paying tribute to these people, they're reflective of each killer's presence in modern culture. Ask a random person on the street if they've heard of Edmund Kemper or Richard Ramirez, and they'll probably say no. Ask them about Ed Gein, maybe one in ten people would say yes."

"But ask them about Dahmer and Gacy, and most people would recognize their names," Ripley added.

"Exactly. And now he's reached Gacy, where do you go from there?" Ella asked. "Highest victim count of any modern serial killer in the US, one of the most prolific murderers of all time."

"You tell me."

Ella cleared her throat. "We excluded overseas killers like Jack the Ripper and Harold Shipman. We excluded historical killers like Albert Fish and H.H. Holmes. We excluded female killers like Aileen Wuornos. So, there's really only one other notorious serial killer who could possibly come next."

"Who?"

"Ted Bundy," she said.

Ripley bit her lip as the idea lingered between them. She looked back toward the whiteboard as though it was an idea she didn't want the burden of confirming.

"It can't be anyone else. It has to be Bundy," she continued.

Ella went over the possibility again in her mind. Ted Bundy was the gold standard of evil, the serial killer to end all serial killers. Even decades after his death, his claws were still firmly dug into the fabric of American culture. Ted Bundy was as iconic as Monroe or Lincoln. If this unsub was going to escalate from Dahmer and Gacy, the only possible subject could be Ted Bundy.

"Bundy. Of course. I've tried my best to forget about that asshole. We were interviewing him when I first joined the Bureau. He was all I heard about for the first few years of my career."

"Do you think I'm right?" Ella asked. She returned to the whiteboard and began frantically jotting down details of Bundy's crimes from memory.

"Rookie, I don't know. I wish I did."

Ella ran a hand through her hair. She began shaking her head. A shortness of breath overcame her, along with a mild choking sensation in her throat. She looked toward the ceiling. She breathed heavily, then spoke in tones that wouldn't sound out of place in a in priest confessional booth.

"What if I'm wrong, Ripley? What if I'm completely wrong, and we wind up with another dead body in our laps tonight? It would be my fault for not predicting his behavior effectively. I'll have gotten another person killed because I couldn't out-think this guy. And then what? He goes into hiding and we never hear from him again? Then every time I hear the word murder, death, serial killer, I'm reminded of the blood on my hands." Ella leaned her head against the whiteboard. "I couldn't live like that. I don't know how any of you agents live like that."

"Dark, we're playing a game that we can never win. Tragedy comes with the territory. It's not a failure if you don't catch every unsub you're assigned to. We miss a lot more than we hit, believe me."

"But it's more than that. I don't care if I let myself down. I've failed myself before and I'll fail myself again. But if I get this wrong, more people will die and it'll be on my head. I'm not just failing myself here, I'm letting everybody down."

"Rookie, listen to me." Ripley jumped out of her seat, snatched the pen out of Ella's hand, and turned her around to face her. She put her hands on Ella's shoulders and looked her dead in the eye. "You're going to have to trust your intuition on this one. I know I didn't believe your theory at first, but that was because I didn't want to. You had this right from the beginning, okay? Do you know how many profiles I've put together that didn't yield anything? A lot. Meanwhile, yours leads us to an arrest in a single day. Out of everyone the FBI has to offer, why do you think I picked you to come out here?"

"What? You?"

"Edis showed me some suitable candidates and there was only one person on the list who I felt could handle it out in the field. That was you."

Ella fell completely mute with shock. Up until now, she thought everything had been Director Edis's doing.

"Oh. I had no idea you were involved."

"Of course I was involved. You think I'd let them pair me with just anybody? I saw your previous work and I saw you at the shooting range and the gym more times than I can count. Honestly, when you got out here, I expected you to survive and nothing more. I didn't expect you to thrive. But with how you took down Rick and Clyde, and how you've pieced this case together based on memory, I'd put my life in your hands, and that's more than I can say about my previous partners."

Ella nodded her head, unsure how to respond. She felt gratitude like she'd never felt in her life. "Well, thank you. I appreciate it."

"You've got the talent, but talent is cheaper than table salt. What separates the successes from the failures is hard work. You scratched the surface of this guy with your profile, now you have to dig deep. You know the serial killers he's copying, and you have an idea what's going to come next. I wish I could offer my own advice but I don't know these historical killers half as well as you do. I remember the basics but you remember the fine details. That's how we're going to catch him, okay?"

Ella took it all on board. "Let's do it." She grabbed her papers with a renewed sense of determination. She rushed over to her files, pulled out a pile of new folders, and slammed them on the desk.

CHAPTER TWENTY ONE

Coffee and crisp morning air helped clear Ella's mental fog, and upon returning to the office now designated the War Room, her mind turned to the recent failed murder of Alex Bauer.

She stood before a map of the local area pinned to the precinct wall. Five dots indicated five murders, arranged in a distorted V-shape. Along the left-hand side of the V was where the precinct was located. Ella thought back to how many serial killers had been caught with the triangular technique. That was, pinpointing all of the murder scenes on the map often created a triangle shape. The person responsible then most likely lived near the center of the shape.

Harris and his team had scoured the Starksville area for footprints or tire tracks; anything that might indicate how this mysterious *John* arrived at the residence he had attacked Alex in. Their report indicated that the only tracks were from Alex's Ford Focus, suggesting John must have arrived by cab, or taken a bus to the nearest station around a mile away, and walked. The deep grass made footprints difficult to unearth, but a specialist team was still working away.

Neighbors had reported no sightings of any strangers, but given the distance between the houses, Ella wasn't surprised.

Forensics had provided a report of their sweep of the crime scene, and while there were no full fingerprint matches or DNA matches as of yet, one item on the manifest caught Ella's attention.

Car key for Ford Focus 2009 Zetec-S model inc. metal split ring.

Or rather, what was missing from the manifest.

Ella pulled up a printout of the transcription of Harris's interview with the escapee victim. Once the swelling in Alex's neck had subsided a few hours after being taken to the hospital, he was able to communicate vocally again without discomfort, so Harris was able to extract much more information from him about the incident.

Ella speed-read the piece until she found the section she needed.

S. Harris: *So you entered his house, refused his offer of alcohol, and sat down. Can you explain what happened next?*

A. Bauer: *He asked me about the car specs and I answered as best I could. Then he said he wanted to test drive the car, so I thought sure, why not?*

S. Harris: *And you passed the keys to him?*

A. Bauer: *Sort of. He grabbed them from me, really. I didn't even have time to remove my key ring. It was a little metal thing with my name engraved on it. He just took the whole bunch.*

Ella had double-checked with the forensic technicians and no key ring was found anywhere at the scene or in the grassy areas surrounding the home, despite the car key and split-ring being discarded in the home's backyard.

This could only mean one thing: The unsub purposely took Alex's key ring with him.

So far, Ella had been so focused on the fact that the killer brought things *with* him to the crime scene that she'd overlooked the things he might have taken away from them. The cogs began to whir and she turned her attention back to the whiteboard. She added a new row at the bottom of her table entitled *Trophies*. She began to jot down the thoughts as they infiltrated her head.

Edmund Kemper had kept ID cards and trinkets from the girls he killed.

Richard Ramirez kept various items he took from his victims' houses.

Ed Gein was more known for the grisly trophies he kept than anything else.

Jeffrey Dahmer preserved various body parts in fluid.

And John Wayne Gacy went as far as keeping entire dead bodies in his home.

Ted Bundy, on the other hand, did something rather unique. While he also kept various trinkets belonging to his victims, one of his twisted perversions was to give jewelry from his victims to the women in his life. He got a thrill from seeing his victims' possessions around the necks and on the fingers of living women, with them obviously being unaware of the objects' origins.

Ella's thought process was that if any jewelry had been taken from the previous victims, they could perhaps try and locate it adorning the figures of others. Alternatively, they could check any pawn shops in the area for recent jewelry bulks.

Therefore, her first step was the morgue. If she could determine that something was pulled off a body, that would be a decent enough starting point.

Ella looked through her notes and found the number for the coroner's office. A receptionist picked up after three rings. Her voice was soft, with a North Carolina twang.

"Can I speak with Dr. Richards, please?" she asked. "The coroner."

"I'm afraid not, sweetie. Dr. Richards left at eleven this morning. Said he was celebrating a birthday. Is there anyone else who could help you?"

"My name's Agent Dark, and I'm working with the local police. I need to get over there and inspect some recent arrivals to your morgue. Would that be okay?"

"Unfortunately, we can't let you in without an on-site coroner present. Dr. Richards will be back in the morning, if that's any use to you?"

"No, it's fine. Tell Dr. Richards happy birthday," she said snappily.

"Oh, it's not his own birthday. Someone close to him, he said. But I'll leave him a message to let him know you called."

Ella gave an abrupt thanks and hung up, then dropped her phone on the table in frustration. She needed to make progress immediately, or, given the extreme frequency this unsub was operating at, there would be another victim within the next twenty-four hours.

She opened up the case file on her desk and pulled out some of the autopsy pictures. If she couldn't get there in person, photographs would be the next best thing. She laid them out and scrutinized every visible detail, looking for perhaps a faint mark where a ring or a bracelet or an earring used to be.

But as she held a photo of the first victim up to eye level, she notice something strange. In the background of the photo, she could make out the profile of Dr. Richards. Even in near blurriness, she could his attractiveness. He had a boy-next-door thing about him, something that Ella always found much more appealing than muscular physiques or defined jawlines.

In the few days since she'd seen Richards, she'd been so overwhelmed with everything that she'd forgotten what he looked like. When she thought about her few minutes with him, she remembered that he'd known about an obscure Mexican serial killer from the fifties.

But then something hit her.

She pulled out the transcript of Alex's conversation again and frenziedly scanned it up and down. What had Alex said that *John* looked like?

He looked like a normal guy. He had black hair and brown eyes and was about five-eleven. Not young, not old.

The man in the backdrop of the autopsy photo fit this description exactly.

Ella considered the idea for a moment. Sure, it was a vague description, and these were all very common characteristics, but right now she needed something to cling on to.

Dr. Richards had recognized the names of the serial killers she'd mentioned, and what did he say about the cuts to the victims' limbs?

These mutilations were carried out with almost surgical accuracy. I've been doing this fifteen years and I've never seen any kind of cuts like this before. Let me tell you, there's not many folks in this neck of the woods who could pull off something like this.

But the more she thought, the more doubt crept in. Aside from looking similar and having surgical knowledge, almost nothing about Dr. Richards fit the profile. He was a medical professional, with no history or prior offenses. He was alarmingly good-looking, a stark contrast to the physical repulsiveness of the men this killer was emulating.

Kemper, Ramirez, Gein, Dahmer, Gacy. Physically hideous, sexually incompetent, zero charm, shunned by the opposite sex.

But then there was Bundy. Charming, alluring, confident, a lady's man in every sense.

Suddenly, something she'd overlooked came to the forefront of her brain. It took a few milliseconds for her subconscious to make the connection, and when it did, it was like the last piece of a jigsaw had fallen perfectly into place.

Nervousness bolted into her stomach and sent her light-headed. There was a rush and a moment of clarity. This was it, this *had* to be it.

She knew who the killer was.

***

"Holy *shit*," she said, jumping out of her chair. She rushed to the door, burst through it, and let it shut behind her with a deafening slam.

"Ripley," Ella shouted, drawing the attention of almost every officer in the precinct's main office. Ella ignored them. Ripley was furiously typing away on her laptop in the corner.

"What is it?"

"It's Dr. Richards. Our killer is Dr. Richards."

Ripley stood up and narrowed her eyes at Ella. "What? Are you sure?" She called Harris to join them at her desk, then the three of them moved into an office away from the prying ears of the other police workers. Harris shut the door behind them.

"It's Dr. Scott Richards from the coroner's office. It has to be."

Ella's eyes darted between them both. Ripley clasped her hands together as if to say *continue.* Harris squinted and scratched his head.

"Richards?" Harris asked. "I've worked with him for years. I really don't think he'd do anything like this."

"Look at the evidence. What did Alex say the killer looked like? Black hair, brown eyes, five-foot-eleven, a little bit weird. Remind of you anyone?"

"Miss Dark, that description applies to a lot of people. Hell, half my police squad could be the killer if we're going off that."

"No, there's more. You remember how he knew about the serial killers I mentioned? He even knew that obscure one. And he said there weren't many people who could pull off cuts like the one in the victims. That was his way of boasting to our faces. It was his way of showing he was one step ahead of us."

Ripley and Harris exchanged a look that said the same thing. "It's pretty common for a serial killer to insert themselves into the investigation somehow. And when they do, some of the more confident ones like to push the boundaries and see what they can get away with," Ripley added.

"But that's not all," Ella said. "I called up the coroner's office to see if I could see the bodies again, and the receptionist told me that Dr. Richards had already left for the day. He said he was celebrating the birthday of someone close to him."

"So?"

"What date is it today?"

Harris checked his watch. "The twenty-fourth of November."

"Exactly. Today is Ted Bundy's birthday."

CHAPTER TWENTY TWO

Ella had watched the atmosphere in the precinct go from reasonable chaos to calm in a matter of seconds, like she'd lit a fire under a wasp nest.

"We've got all our available officers on the hunt for him," said Harris. "We've got his details from the coroner's office and we're checking every avenue. We know his license plate and his home address and we've got watchers on both."

"Good. Keep an eye on the house from afar. Knock on the door, but if no one answers, don't break in. Staking his house is the best chance we have of catching him. If he gets back and sees a broken door, he's going to run a mile," Ripley said. "What about his cell phone?"

"Switched off. But we're gonna keep trying."

"It's useless," said Ripley. "If he's planning another attack, there's no way he'd switch it on before he's committed the crime. We need to find him another way. Keep the hunt on for him all night."

"We've grilled his secretary on his whereabouts and she's got nothing. She said all she knew was that Richards said something about a birthday. Nothing more," said Harris. "We're doing everything we can, Agents. If we want eyes on every inch of this town, we're going to have to call over some officers from another precinct."

"Do it," Ripley said. "Get your guys onto his colleagues, his family. Look into his bank accounts. See when he last used his debit card and follow the trail. This guy is somewhere in this town right now."

"We have about twelve hours before he probably kills again. Call in every reinforcement you have to track this son of a bitch down." Ripley turned to Ella and put her hands on her shoulders. "Rookie, I know I doubted you before but I think you're dead right with this one. It matches up too well for it to be a coincidence."

Ella had a feeling there was something else coming. A request. Ripley took a deep breath and continued.

"But knowing his identity is half the fight. When he switches his phone on and sees that a bunch of different numbers have tried to call him, he's going to get suspicious. He's probably going to know that we're onto him, and then he's going to hide."

Ella's face fell flat. "I know. We can hope that he just assumes it's related to the autopsies of the new victims, right?"

"No. His suspicions will already be heightened. If he's planning a murder, his emotions will be chaotic and uncontrollable. Paranoia will be rife. And besides, by that point he might have already claimed a new victim. Given how rapidly he's racking up the bodies, we can't wait around. We need to hunt him down before he can strike."

Before Ripley said another word, Ella already knew what was coming. It was on her to predict his whereabouts, on her to walk a mile in this stranger's shoes.

"You've come this far," Ripley carried on, "now it's time to get into this guy's head and work out where he's going, what he's doing, what his plans are. Everything you need to know is in your head, you just need to extract it."

Ella felt an invisible weight crush her from above. It was the weight of burden, with real human lives as the price. Ripley hushed her tone so no one else could hear. "Our best chance of catching Dr. Richards is with you. We've got twenty officers patrolling eight miles of land looking for a nondescript guy who could be anywhere. I don't like those odds. Unless Richards goes back to his house, we're not gonna find him."

"So what do I do?" Ella asked. "You said it yourself, there's eight miles' worth of places he could be. I was wrong about Clyde Harmen and I could be wrong about this. What if I send the entire police force to the wrong place? This is a responsibility I can't live with if it goes wrong."

"The truth, Rookie, is that you have two choices. Either we can run around this town and hope that blind luck is in our favor, or we can apply the techniques that you and I have spent years mastering and increase our chances of finding him tenfold. Taking a shot and missing isn't the biggest mistake you'll make, but not taking the shot at all is. What's it going to be?"

Ella shut her eyes and thought of everything that had happened over the past few days. Her old life, sitting behind a desk in the Intelligence department, seemed like a world away. She felt a sudden homesickness for that life, and even for all its stresses and its mental exhaustion, it seemed like heaven compared to where she found herself now.

"I can do this," Ella said. "Let's take the shot."

***

Back in the War Room, Ella laid out the pages of her psychological profile and the crime scene photographs of all five victims. She turned to Ripley beside her. "Where do we start?"

"Start with your intuition and work backwards. Somewhere out there, our killer is planning an homage to Ted Bundy. It's going to incorporate major elements of Bundy's most infamous murders, and perhaps other aspects of Bundy's M.O. too. It will be something specific, something obvious. What does your gut say?"

Ella reflected on everything she knew. She thought to the most important aspect of the killer's modus operandi, victimology, and transposed it to Bundy's life and crimes.

"Bundy killed over thirty people, from twelve-year-old girls to women in their early twenties," she said, feeling the panic set in. Only on reflection did she realize how vast and sporadic Bundy's crimes were. "How can we possibly know what age he's going to target?"

"Stop right there," Ripley said. "So, unlike his last two kills, we can safely say he's going to target a female, yes?"

"Well, yes. Without a doubt."

"Then that's the first characteristic of the profile. Given what we've seen in his other murders, what possible references might he make to Bundy? Outside of victimology, how did our killer ensure that *we knew* he was paying tribute to Kemper, Ramirez, Gein, Dahmer, and Gacy?"

Ella scanned the crime scene photos, relaying the details once again. "In his first murder, it was only the dismemberment and the body disposal that referenced Edmund Kemper."

"You have to remember that if that was indeed his first murder, then his confidence levels would have been much lower than his later kills. Back then, he was still playing the part of a serial killer rather than actually being one. He wouldn't have planned too intensively on his first kill because he wasn't aware of his own

150

capabilities at that point. He didn't *become* a serial killer until his third or fourth kill."

Ella looked at the photo of the unsub's second victim, lifeless in her bed. There was a close-up of the pentagram on her leg.

"His Ramirez kill was nondescript too, but the pentagram was his way of linking this kill with his first. This was the beginning of his personal ritual, correct?"

"No, this unsub exhibits no ritualistic behavior of any kind. There are no repeat patterns. Everything is different every single time. What you're talking about is his signature. The signature is the components of the crime which take place outside of the murder; the components which aren't necessary but he does anyway. In the case of his Ramirez kill, it was the pentagram."

"In the Gein kill, it was the butchery and staging," Ella finished.

"Correct. And it was the same in his Dahmer kill and Gacy attempt. They all took place indoors where he could exert full control over the staging and where someone was guaranteed to find the bodies."

"Bundy dumped most of his bodies in rivers and mountains," Ella said. "So, chances are he *won't* do that, right? He wants us to see his handiwork in all its glory. He wants us to feel like we're walking right into a real-life Bundy crime scene."

"Exactly," Ripley said. "So, in keeping in line with this signature, the crime he's going to commit will have parallels with Bundy's actions which are indisputable and easily identifiable. Bundy killed women, but so did thousands of other people, so ignore that component. Tell me what Bundy did that no one else has done.
"

"Shit, he did so much. I mean, where do I start? Hid corpses in the woods and paid regular visits to them?"

"No. That's post-crime methodology. Something else."

Ella ran through Bundy's timeline in her head. She blurted out the facts as they came to her. "His first murders throughout 1974 were unremarkable. Abduction, bludgeoning, and disposal in woods and mountains. There's nothing there that stands out at all."

"Keep going. Think harder."

"His murders in 1975 were almost exactly the same, and nearly all of the bodies of the victims he killed that year were never discovered. And then... wait a second," Ella said. "You said our unsub didn't really *become* a serial killer until his third or fourth kill?"

Ella felt that spark again; the pieces coming together and forming a full, identifiable pattern. Bouncing her thoughts off Ripley had opened up new avenues in her mind. She was making connections she wouldn't have made by sitting alone and ruminating on them. Things began to take shape, and then a feeling of elation rose through her.

"Yes, both in terms of the legal definition and in the unsub's mindset. That was when he fully evolved both psychologically and emotionally to accept his nature as a multi-murderer. It's not something you can accept immediately. Even a psychopath, when they become content with what they've done, will have their outlook changed once they accept their actions."

"When Bundy was being interviewed just before his execution, he said he didn't reach his peak until his final murder spree. That's when he was a prime predator, in his words."

"And?" Ripley asked.

"And that's when—" She stopped herself. "Oh my god, the Chi Omega murders."

"The what?"

It fit, almost perfectly. For all his infamy and notoriety, Bundy's murders were largely ordinary as far as M.O. and methodology went. It was the sheer scale of his crimes and victim count that made him the figure of absolute evil he was today.

She'd done it, she'd cracked the code. She'd seen into this unsub's mind and extracted his thoughts and plans. There was excitement running through her, euphoria even.

"In 1978, Bundy invaded a sorority house in Florida. He attacked four women in the span of fifteen minutes, killing two of them. These murders were completely different from anything else he did. It was theorized that he was suffering a psychotic episode and just lashed out. This was a taste of the *real* Bundy. No superficial charm, no manipulation. It was pure, uncontrolled chaos."

Ripley slammed her hand on the desk. "God damn, of course. I remember that. Four attacks and two murders in one sitting. If our unsub copied this, it would be a huge escalation from his past murders and it's something unique to Bundy. Rookie, I think you might be right, and if that's what your gut is telling you, then that's how we're going to play it."

Ripley opened the office door and summoned Harris in. "Sheriff, we know where this guy is going to strike next," Ripley continued. "Are there any dormitories nearby?"

"Dorms? There are no dorms around here. The nearest college is a hundred miles away," said Harris.

Ripley was typing away on her laptop. "It will be somewhere where young girls spend a lot of time, and ideally live there. It doesn't necessarily have to be related to an educational system. Our killer just wants to emulate the Bundy crime scene, so anywhere with young girls which is away from the public eye will be his target."

"An orphanage? Girls there up to sixteen years old."

"No, these women will be between eighteen and twenty-one."

"What's stopping him breaking into a house party, or just a place he knows four girls live?" Harris asked.

Ripley jumped in, looking up from her laptop. "I just checked the land registry system. There are no houses with that make-up of residents in this town at all. There are two homes with two female roommates of similar age, but that's all. Have your officers contact them and put them on alert, but we're confident he's going to target four women at once."

"Why? If Ted only killed two, why are we looking for four?" Harris asked.

"Bundy had every intention of killing every woman in that sorority house that night in 1978," Ella said. "If he hadn't been interrupted, he could have killed upwards of nine women in a single setting. Our unsub will try and do exactly the same. As well as paying tribute to him, he will happily one-up Bundy if he can too."

"Gotcha," said Harris.

"A year after the incident, one of the girls who witnessed the Bundy attack committed suicide. Bundy even nonchalantly took credit for that too."

"Hold your horses," said Harris, snapping his fingers. "Now that you mention suicide. What about a halfway house?"

"That could absolutely work. Is there one around here?" Ripley asked.

"Sure is. There's a nonprofit organization that helps troubled ladies. Domestic abuse, mental problems, drug addiction, and the like. You know the type I mean?"

"Do the girls live in-house?" asked Ella. "Do they sleep there? He's going to attack them while they're sleeping, otherwise there's no way he could kill four women in one situation."

"Absolutely they do. Well, not all of them, but a lot of them. It's nothing fancy, just a few beds, some food, and a shower. The owners are golden. They take in a lot of the young girls we help if there's nowhere for them to go."

Ripley and Ella locked eyes. Ella could tell Ripley was thinking the same thing as her.

"That's it. That must be it. Is it the only halfway house in town?"

"Only one I know of. Nothing else like it."

"Let's get going," Ripley shouted, grabbing her jacket. "We need to get there before the residents get to bed." They headed out into the main area of the precinct. Harris moved over to his desk to grab his keys. Beside them, his cell phone was ringing.

"Hold on, it's one of my guys," he shouted. "Hello?"

Ella and Ripley moved toward the door, but Harris held up his hand in a *wait* motion.

"Got it. Thank you," he said, hanging up swiftly. "Agents, one of my guys just got a hit on Dr. Richards's license plate. But the officer is halfway across town and can't get there real quick."

"Where was Richards spotted?" Ripley asked.

"Saint Mary's Hospital."

Ella's eyes widened in alarm. "That's where Alex is." She turned to Ripley. "He might be going to finish him off before he commits his Bundy murder."

"Serial killers don't like loose ends. I think that's exactly what he's going to do. Sheriff, can you get cars to the hospital right away?"

Harris ran over to his desk and checked his system. "No ma'am. Nearest squad to Saint Mary's is us."

"What about the halfway house? Who can you get there?"

"Zero right now. Half an hour? Two squad cars."

"Fuck. Call hospital security and give them a description of Dr. Richards. Have them track him down, and have them keep Alex's room secure. I'll get to the hospital."

"What if he's gone by the time we get there?" Ella asked.

"I'll go alone," Ripley said. "You go to the halfway house. If he's not at the hospital, I'll come straight to your location, okay? You'll have officers there in thirty minutes, too."

Ella didn't like that idea at all. "You want me to go alone? Are you kidding me?"

"No. One way or the other, one of us is catching this guy tonight."

CHAPTER TWENTY THREE

It was a night for death, but Mia was determined to throw a wrench in the works.

She sped toward Saint Mary's Hospital as the sun descended and streetlamps took over. The whole journey, her thoughts were on Ella and the halfway house. Was there any possibility they were wrong about this whole thing? If so, had she just sent a rookie into the waiting arms of a serial killer. There was no time to lose, even if it meant Ella having to go alone. Harris had remained at the station since they still had Clyde in the holding cells. Until another officer got there, he couldn't leave him alone.

No. Her gut feeling was that this was their guy, and her instincts had led her to success more times than she could remember. Besides, they'd made the decision and there was no turning back now.

Mia maneuvered the early evening traffic and sped up the small incline onto the hospital parking lot. She drove to the front area right outside the doors and jumped out of her vehicle.

The reception room was a warm orange, with around five people sitting quietly staring at the cell phones glued to their hands. A child sat cross-legged on the floor zooming a toy car around in circles. Mia approached the main reception desk and banged on the glass. There was no time for politeness.

"I'm with the police. I've already called in an alert. I'm here to meet your head of security."

Her words naturally drew the attention of the waiting patients, but Mia ignored their stares. The receptionist pulled out a walkie-talkie and crackled it on. "She's here," she said. "Send her through," a voice responded instantly. The receptionist stood up and gestured for Mia to follow her. She did, leading her to a side room that said STAFF ONLY. There was an African-American gentleman inside staring at a number of monitors.

"Ms. Ripley," he said, offering his hand. "I've spent the past ten minutes scouring every room for someone matching the description the police gave me. I've found nothing so far, at least not on the live cameras."

"Thank you. Has anyone tried to approach the unit Alex Bauer is being held in? Anyone at all, even if they don't fit the description?"

"Not a soul. I've got a security guard standing at the entrance and he tells me it's quieter than a hybrid up there."

"Is there anywhere in the hospital the cameras don't have eyes on?"

"Just the long-term units up on the top floor. The folks up there practically live there and there's some legal issues around recording them all day. Feel free to go and check it out if you wish. Staircase is just out there to your left. I can keep an eye down here."

"All right, thank you," Mia said, rushing back outside into the hospital reception. She followed the guard's directions and found a spiraling staircase which she climbed to the top floor. It was a long shot, but was there perhaps a possibility Dr. Richards might be hiding somewhere in the hospital? Might be aware that the hunt was on for him?

The top floor was eerily deserted. Mia's footsteps traveled across the marble floor down a long, narrow hallway and ricocheted off the barred windows at the far end. A signpost told her that the corridor led to the Children's Critical Care Unit. She peered inside, seeing a small room with only six beds, only one of which was occupied. The young girl in the bed was sleeping.

Mia backtracked and continued down the hallway, arriving at the Intensive Care Unit, the only other long-term care ward on the floor.

She pushed the buzzer and a receptionist's voice came through the speaker.

"Hello, are you here to visit a patient?"

"No, I'm with the police. We're looking for a Mr. Richards. Security should have put an alert out for him."

A moment of confused silence followed. "We haven't received any security alert, ma'am, but Mr. Richards is in here."

"What? He's in there?"

"Yes. I'll let you in."

A loud buzzing sound followed and the double-doors clicked open. Mia jumped through. She turned to her left to see a young blonde receptionist eyeing her from behind her desk.

"Bed thirteen, honey. Mr. Richards is over there." She pointed with her pen.

"What? Bed?" Mia began to speculate, but she could come to no logical conclusion in her head.

"Can I ask what this is about?" the receptionist asked.

"No." Mia said, turning and heading in the opposite direction.

The rooms began at twenty-eight and descended in number, although they were less like rooms and more like cubicles separated by white partitions. In each cubicle was a bed and a TV suspended in front of it. There were few signs of life inside the unit, except for a nurse helping an elderly gowned woman to a nearby toilet.

Mia followed the cubicles down until she found number thirteen. She came to a halt in front of it and locked eyes with the man sitting in the bed. They held each other's gaze for an awkward amount of time.

"Hello?" he asked, his gruff voice startling her. He was wearing a white gown, with an intravenous cannula sprouting from his hand. Another tube ran from his mouth into a machine behind him. His face was entirely without hair. No beard, no eyebrows. Mia placed him at around sixty-five years old.

It was just a patient named Mr. Richards, not the man she was looking for. "Sorry, mistaken identity, sir. I hope I didn't disturb you."

But a different voice came out of the shadows, startling her further.

"Agent Ripley?" it asked.

Mia felt the adrenaline and instinctively reached for her gun and handcuffs. Standing before her was Dr. Richards, dressed in a plain white T-shirt, jeans, and holding a vending machine coffee. "It is Ripley, isn't it?" He held up his spare hand with his palm out. "Whoa, you're scaring me. Everything okay?"

Something told her that things weren't exactly as they seemed.

"Dr. Richards, what are you doing here?" she asked, loosening her grip on the cuffs. "We've been looking for you all day."

"Looking for me?" he asked. He slid himself into a chair next to the old man in the bed. "Why have you been looking for me? I left work early to see my dad. We had a new body in this morning but I didn't have time to perform an autopsy. I'm back in the morgue tomorrow if you want to come see me in the morning?"

My dad. Mr. Richards, Mia thought. "This is your dad?"

"Don't sound so surprised," the elderly man jumped in. "I'm a wreck now but I looked just like him thirty years ago, I swear it," he laughed.

"Correction. Thirty-one years ago," Dr. Richards said, pointing to a banner hanging off the right-hand partition. In her haste, Mia had completely overlooked it.

On a silver ribbon with gold letters were the words HAPPY 64th BIRTHDAY TOM.

"You left early to celebrate a birthday," Mia said.

"Yeah. Dad's been in intensive care for a few months. Most nights I just come sit up here and hang out." Dr. Richards nodded toward the television. "What's with all these reality shows? What happened to good old-fashioned TV?"

"Like *Baywatch*," added Richards's father. "I tell you, if cancer doesn't kill me then those girls will."

"Dad, stop saying that."

Mia watched on in confusion as she thought the whole thing through. She could not come to any conclusion other than the simplest one: their presumption that Dr. Richards was their killer had been incorrect.

While it was by no means definitive proof, Dr. Richards didn't look like a killer at all. He was welcoming, approachable, passive. His skin was pristine; no visible wounds whatsoever, and she knew Alex Bauer had jammed a key into the killer's face. This certainly wasn't a man who was involved in an altercation the previous day. She couldn't identify a violent bone in his body, despite his profession. He fit the physical description but nothing more.

"Sorry, Agent Ripley, but you haven't told me what you're doing here," Richards continued. "Is everything okay?"

Mia took a moment to consider whether she could tell Richards the truth. She glanced at his father in his bed. No, it wasn't the time or the occasion.

"Yes, everything's fine. I was actually downstairs visiting someone, but then I saw your car in the parking lot outside."

"You... recognized my car?"

"Toyota Camry, right? I saw it the other day at the morgue. Only Camry I've seen around here. I guess being an FBI agent makes you remember stuff like that."

"Sure, I bet it does."

Mia hoped the lie was convincing enough. "I thought you were perhaps here for professional reasons, and I'd never have interrupted you if I'd have known you were just seeing your dad." She turned to Richards's father. "Happy birthday, sir. I'm sorry we had to meet under these circumstances."

Mia waved her goodbyes as she ran out of the Intensive Care Unit into the hallway. She pulled out her phone and dialed Ella's cell as she continued down the spiral staircase and back outside. "Pick up, damn it."

No answer.

Two calls followed with the same result.

She dialed Harris instead. He picked up on the second ring.

"Sheriff, we need to get to the halfway house right now. Is there someone there to take over watch duties?"

"A night shift officer just got here. I'm on my way."

Mia jumped in her car, backed out of the parking lot, and sped off into the night. If Dr. Richards wasn't the killer, then the actual killer was almost certainly at the halfway house. Mia realized that she might have sent Ella to her death.

CHAPTER TWENTY FOUR

The alleyway smelled of gasoline and cigarettes, but its location was ideal for what he had planned. The big finale. The magnum opus.

He made the two-mile journey on foot, as he had done with all of the others. The ones who left their vehicles at home always evaded detection for much longer than those who didn't. He was one of the smart ones, one of the elite. America hadn't seen a spree like this in decades, and tomorrow morning, after the dust had settled and the high was dissolving, he'd up the ante once more.

Oh, he had big plans for a follow-up, but no murder would be involved this time. No, they involved the press and the media. The murders might stop or they might carry on, he wasn't sure yet. But what he was sure of was that within the next few days, the world would know of the bayou copycat murders.

He idly wondered what they'd call him. The Replicator, the Imitator, the Mimic Killer? He had originally thought about assigning his own designation, like Jack the Ripper, the Zodiac, and BTK, but he decided against it. It came across as trying-too-hard, he thought. Let it play out naturally.

He had all the proof he needed in his home. Photographs of every dead body. Trinkets he'd prized off their corpses, mementos he'd stolen from their homes. Locks of their hair, pieces of their fingernails, even a swab of human flesh. He'd have his doubters for sure, but no one could deny that it was him and him alone who pulled off this masterful scheme.

He put one hand in his pocket as he casually leaned against the wall. He fingered the small piece of metal he found. He clasped it between his fingers and pulled it out, then clenched it tightly in his palm. It was the metal key ring he'd stolen off the stupid kid who'd manage to escape his wrath, the lucky little shit who had no idea that he'd signed on for a life of living hell when he fled that house.

He had kept the key ring for the same reasons as he had the others, but every time he looked at it, it didn't bring up the same feelings as the others. It didn't excite him. It only reminded him of his failure.

After the incident, he'd spent around twelve hours wallowing in anger, punching panes of glass until his knuckles bled. How could he have been so careless as to let the kid escape? He should have planned better, executed better, made sure the exits were bolted shut, not taken as many risks as he did.

The frustration of his botch had lasted until the morning after the murder attempt, when he'd all but bled every ounce of rage from his body. He had thought of what Jeffrey Dahmer once said: *killing was a means to an end*. The act of killing was secondary; it was everything that preceded it which he enjoyed. The torment, both physically and mentally, the power struggle, the act of playing God.

This was all still very possible. One of his victims was alive, and while the kid might know what he looked like, he didn't know his name or his location. That meant he could torment him for the rest of his days from afar, perhaps one day return to finish what he'd started. Hell, if he was intense enough, maybe even push the stupid kid into taking his own life. How sweet it would be to kill without even being present. How many others could say they did that?

He returned the key ring back to his pocket and felt it press against his leg. He brought it with him to remind him of his failure, and this time, to do better. This whole experience had been an intense learning curve, one which he'd flourished in by his own admission. Even the best ones made mistakes. Almost every high-profile serial killer had that *one that got away*. Dahmer had one, BTK had one. Hell, Bundy had countless. It was expected. One could even argue that it was necessary in order to perfect the craft of killing.

Tonight was his chance for redemption, and to meditate and act on what he'd learned. There would be no errors, no flaws in his plan. He wasn't going to fail again, especially not during the most important tribute of all. Tonight, he'd do what few serial killers ever had or ever would—take multiple lives in one night. There was every chance he'd even outdo his idol. Three was the goal and any more would be a bonus. What better way to celebrate Ted's birthday than bringing his most twisted crime to life once more? If he added a new shine to it, then even better. History would repeat itself, but it would be rebooted for the modern era.

He positioned himself in the shadows where the alleyway ended and main street began. He told himself he would be in there at 1 a.m. and out before half past. Bundy did it all in twenty minutes and he would too. It was now 12:56 a.m.

Leaning against the wall beside him was a large, sturdy piece of oak firewood he'd specially procured. Exactly the same weapon Bundy had used to cave in the skulls of four unaware young girls. Nothing else would do.

Twelve fifty-eight now. He'd been watching the building for nearly an hour and hadn't seen any of the rear windows light up. They were all sleeping, no doubt.

It was time to move in. Time to put the master plan into motion. He picked up his weapon and moved stealthily toward the Maya Rehabilitation Center for Recovering Women. He'd seen at least six women enter the building over the past hour, and what excited him more than anything was that no one, not even himself, knew how many would be leaving.

***

The center was a detached building flanked by a metal fence which backed onto the alleyway he was hiding in. He'd spent some time at this center himself years ago, back when it was a place for AA meetings. All this time later, they still hadn't fixed the two broken bars in the fence.

He squeezed himself through, making sure not to clang his weapon against the metal bars. The entryway led him into a patch of overgrown grass, still soaked from the evening's downpour. In the trees above, nocturnal creatures sang their midnight songs to him. He heard an owl hoot in the distance, and was sure he saw a cluster of bats flutter around in a distant oak tree.

And then silence, broken only by his footsteps as he reached the patio area. There were some old appliances littered around, a broken washing machine, an uprooted toilet, and a round table with an ashtray in the middle. There were four chairs dotted around, and one still had a coat hanging off the back of it.

Next came the door handle. He clicked it, expecting it to fall open as it used to do back in the day. But he felt resistance.

He tugged on it harder. Nothing.

Shit, he thought. There must be another way in somehow, he reassured himself and approached a large window looking into the center's lounge area. He squinted, unable to identify much. He considered breaking the glass, but didn't want to draw any attention himself. He could try the front door, but that was always locked.

It's going to have to be brute force, he thought, pressing his hands against the window to scope their durability.

But as he did, he saw a flicker of light from inside. A beam, like a flashlight.

Fuck. He ducked down out of sight, panicking. Was it one of the women who lived here? Had they seen his face?

His legs began to tremble as he felt that pang of frustration rise through him once again. The same one he felt when the stupid kid got had gotten away. The thought of failing again made him clench his fists to the point he couldn't feel his fingertips.

What would Bundy have done? he thought to himself. *He would have outsmarted them. He would have used the situation to his advantage. He would have thought on his feet.*

His eyes locked on the jacket hanging from the chair. An idea came to him.

He reached out, grabbed the jacket, and approached the back door. He made sure his log was out of sight. He knocked on the door.

In his peripheral vision he saw the beam of light return. This time, it was right next to the window. Whoever was inside had seen him, but he didn't turn to meet their gaze.

Shuffling on the other side of the door. Beyond the frosted glass, he saw a figure appear. Stocky and wide-shouldered, dressed in blue from head to toe.

Security guard, he thought.

A voice boomed out. "Who is it?"

Time to turn on the charm. "My name's Theodore. My sister lives here. She left her jacket at my place this evening. I'm just returning it."

A brief silence. "At this ungodly hour? How did you get into the back area?"

He put himself in character. He thought of Bundy again. "Her meds are in the pocket too. She needs them. I knocked on the front door but no one answered."

Another pause. "I didn't hear a knock."

"I only tapped lightly. I didn't want to wake anyone up."

"Okay," the guard said. "Well, just leave the coat on the step and I'll get it in a second."

"Thank you," he said, purposely placing the coat back on the chair. "It's on the chair when you're ready."

"Who does it belong to?" the guard asked.

Names rushed through his head. Could he give a vague description? No, the guard would know he was lying. He needed a name. He took a stab in the dark.

"Abigail."

He watched the guard's distorted shape move to and fro behind the frosted glass. "Okay," he said, finally. "Thanks. Now please leave the premises."

He nodded, unsure if the guard could even see him, then he stepped away from the door. He went around the side of the building, out of sight of the guard. He checked the wall for windows or security cameras and saw none.

He waited. Biding time was a virtue of the functional psychopath, he told himself. Impulsiveness was a fool's game.

He squatted down against the wall, listening for any signs of life. He caressed the wooden log in his hands, feeling its rigidity and sturdiness. He gently tapped it against his own knuckles to test its battering power.

The idea to give the weapon a name crossed his mind. *Sam,* he thought, the same name as the dog which possessed David Berkowitz. That would do.

Suddenly, he heard the door handle click. He grasped his weapon tighter and took in a deep breath. The cool night air seeped into his lungs and sharpened his focus. He heard the door hinges creak, then the guard's footsteps hit the concrete.

He thought of Alex. How he was somewhere out there now, still alive and breathing. He harnessed the rage, channeled it into a lust for savagery, then rushed out from his hiding place toward the security guard.

He saw terror in the guard's eyes. The same terror they'd all shown. He swung his log directly at the man's face, his surprise appearance making the guard freeze in shock. The attack connected, momentarily blinding the guard and sending him off his feet to the floor. He had no time to scream or run or fight back.

165

He perched himself over the guard, lifted the wooden log high in the air, and brought it crashing down again.

Silence took over.

His hands were shaking. The adrenaline was pumping. He was God again. He dragged the man's body into the shadows and stuffed him in a small gap between the building and the fence. An act of mercy, he thought. This poor sucker wasn't part of the plan, but he had to die for the cause.

"That makes one," he said. "Now, how many more do we have in here?"

And he walked into the center.

CHAPTER TWENTY FIVE

Everything was dark inside, one rung below pitch-black. He could make out faint shapes around him and was able to steer forward using them as a guide. His eyes gradually adjusted to the darkness, and then the layout of the building, hibernating somewhere in his long-term memory bank, came cruising back to him, He recognized the room's general arrangement, although furniture had been replaced and new areas had been added. But he was able to maneuver himself to the main area, the communal room, without issue.

There was a carpeted floor now, with a small TV and a few two-seater sofas dotted around. A lemony scent clawed at his nose as he recalled the building layout again in his head. There was a small upstairs area from what he remembered, so he decided to check up there first. There was every chance the living quarters were located there.

He ascended the stairs as unobtrusively as he could, making sure to step on the part of each step closest to the wall. It was always the quietest there—something he'd learned from a prison interview with Ramirez.

He found himself on a small landing walkway littered with boxes. He saw wholesale amounts of canned food, water bottles, rice. Survival essentials. He navigated past them, coming to two doors.

Thud.

His alert heightened. There was someone else here. He looked down and saw he'd kicked one of the smaller boxes by accident. Did he make that sound?

No. There's someone else in the building. Someone's awake.

He gently opened the first door, finding a room with a single toilet. He moved to the room opposite. It opened into a much bigger area. More storage and a few pieces of old gym equipment. He strolled around, enjoying the nature of his presence here. He was a trespasser, a predator on the hunt. He'd read that many serial killers committed their murders in a kind of detached haze, and were sometimes unable to recall the finer details of them.

But he wasn't going to let that happen. He wanted to savor every moment of his crimes. He wanted to live in the moment. Who knew if he'd ever do this again after tonight?

Another thud.

He spun around, his attention drawn to the far wall. There was a mirrored cupboard. He approached it and scrutinized the reflection staring back at him. He had specks of blood on his forehead from when he'd killed the guard. He wiped it with his sleeve.

The cupboard gently shook on its tracks at the top and bottom of the door. But there was no breeze in the room, no airflow from any open windows.

Someone was in there.

He readied his weapon and gripped the door handle. He pulled, but the door didn't slide as he expected. His touch rattled it again. This must have been what caused the thudding, he thought.

He continued yanking. Still nothing. Up above, he saw that the door had come off its rollers. He pulled harder, moving the door less than an inch.

It was stuck.

Thud.

Another, but it wasn't from this room. It came from downstairs.

He took one last look at his reflection, impressed with his image. With the log in his hand, he looked fierce, dangerous. He could see that picture on the front of a book cover one day, he thought.

He returned downstairs, finding a laundry room, a kitchen, and a small toilet area. He moved back into the communal area and then into a narrow hallway with a wooden floor. Four wooden doors stood before him, each declaring a hollow inspirational quote painted in stylized lettering.

When things feel like an uphill struggle, think of the view from the top.

A smirk spread across his face. *What a load of shit,* he thought to himself. *These women are at the bottom of the barrel and they're going to die there.*

His pulse elevated to levels he hadn't felt since he first strangled the girl in the car. He thought about that first kill for a moment, reveling in the excitement, the stimulation. Some serial killers had said that the first was always the best, and that they'd spend the rest of their careers trying to re-create that first high. He fully believed this to be true, especially after having experienced it firsthand. However, he also believed that if one could exceed the enjoyment of the first, then that experience would take center stage in his fantasies.

He pushed the door open with a small creak, revealing four beds parked in each corner of the room.

All of the bedspreads were perfectly made. No one was inside them. All empty.

The frustration rose up inside him, but he calmed himself and exited back into the hallway. No, there would be no failure tonight. He moved to the next door in line.

Don't be ashamed of your story. It will inspire others, it said.

"It certainly will," he whispered, and carefully pulled on the handle. It opened silently, uncovering a room laid out exactly like the first. His eyes dotted from bed to bed, feeling the sickening pang of frustration once more.

No. Only three were empty.

In the bed furthest away from him, he saw an arm hanging over the edge of the bed. He made out the familiar outline of a person lying on their side. Long hair hung down to their shoulders. It was clearly a woman. She was slim, young, maybe early twenties—just how he liked them.

He checked his watch. 1:08. Eagerness built up inside him. His hands began to shake with excitement, vibrating the oak log clenched in his fist. He breathed deeply to calm himself. He thought of his hero, and how he'd killed the Chi Omega girls in almost total silence as not to disturb the rest of the house. He was going to do the same.

***

Ella ran to the front door of the Maya Rehabilitation Center for Recovering Women and tried the doorknob. Locked.

She took a step back and scrutinized the building's layout, desperately thinking of a way to get inside. Beside the front door was a pointed metal fence. She barely even registered it for a second before she'd clasped her hands around the sharp rim and pulled herself up over it.

169

It dug into her hands, almost excruciatingly, but scaling fences like this was something every agent had to do in their careers—or so they told her. Once she'd elevated herself, she put her foot between two of the ridges and then jumped over into the back outdoor area.

She shook off the pain and hurried to the rear entrance. The door was lodged open with a coat jacket.

The thoughts began to whir in her mind. Was this door always lodged open like this? Or was this a sign of intrusion?

Then something hit her. Her senses picking up on a scent. The same odor she'd found at the past three crime scenes. There was blood in the air. She could feel the coppery traces in her nose and on her tongue.

There was no doubt about it.

The killer was here.

She drew her pistol and stepped into the building. Harris had already called and told the center to be on high alert, but given it was the early hours of the morning, how much of that information had been taken on board was unknown. Ella remained as silent as she could, keeping close to the walls and checking the corners as she navigated them.

She entered into a larger space, the temperature dropping a degree or two. It was a carpeted lounge, Ella realized. She stopped and listened to her surroundings. She held her breath. She familiarized herself with the building's pitches. Water running through rusted pipes. Rain hammering against the old flat roof. Heavy winds beating the single-glazed windows.

A floorboard creaked somewhere.

She kept herself in the moment. Sharpened her wits. She tried not to over-think, as she had done before. The families of the dead needed her focus to be laser-sharp.

The same creak again.

It wasn't beneath her feet. It was up above her, she realized.

Then footsteps, all along the ceiling. Not rhythmic, but slow and methodical.

She steadied her thoughts, but instead of keeping her position, she moved to the adjacent hallway where she saw a little more light seeping through. In the narrow hallway, there was a row of windows which let the light from the outside streetlamps. It wasn't much, but it was preferable to pitch blackness.

She waited, her gun perched waist-high, ready to assume her shooting stance at a moment's notice. She looked around, seeing a row of doors with motivational slogans slapped across them.

Ella wondered if anyone was inside there. If something violent was about to go down, they needed to know. Worse yet, Ella needed to know if anyone in there had already been attacked.

She tried the first door she came to, finding four beds. Suddenly, she heard the creaking of stairs. Whoever was out there was descending the staircase slowly, as if purposely trying to keep their presence unnoticed.

Ella heard him, *felt him.*

She went back into the room and hid amongst the shadows. Whoever it was edged closer to her. She heard him enter the bedroom next door, then leave as quickly as he arrived.

And then he was outside the room she was in. Barely a few feet away. She smelled the warmth of his body heat, heard his lungs expand and collapse.

The anxiety crept up on her, clouding her vision and causing the surrounding darkness to expand and consume her. She tried to calm herself, but she struggled to control her reactions. Here she was, alone with a man who had committed multiple homicides without remorse. What if something went wrong? What if he was smarter than her? What if he was one step ahead of her already and she didn't know it?

She felt one of the beds beside her. Her thoughts turned to her father, murdered while he slept. Was this history repeating itself? Was this the haunting of life's fragile symmetry fating her to die in the same way her father had?

The man entered the room, his silhouette a black cloud tainted with the blood of innocents. For all her determination and for all her resolve, Ella froze, rendered motionless out of some combination of terror and anxiety. She couldn't see or hear or contemplate. This wasn't some crime she was reading about in a textbook, this was real life and potentially the end of it. This was how she'd be remembered; a rookie agent murdered in the field by one of history's most abhorrent serial killers. She'd die tonight, and her name would be in books about this man for years to come. That would be her legacy, and then one day, someone would say her name for the last time and she'd be gone for eternity.

It felt like she was in a dream state, ready to wake up to reality any second.

But she didn't.

And the man approached her, wielding something high above his head.

Her last thoughts were of her father.

***

He walked cautiously over to her, stopping briefly near each bed so that if she awoke, she'd assume it was just another girl in the house retiring to sleep. He moved within a few feet of her, close enough to smell her unique scent. Every woman had one. Whoever this poor girl was had an odor of vanilla to her, perhaps through scented hand cream or shampoo. He wouldn't have time to learn anything about her, so he made up a quick profile in his head to help add a layer of personalization to her death. He'd found that it made the kills much more enjoyable.

She was a secretary, he thought. Low pay, low responsibility, low happiness. Brought to this center through domestic abuse at the hands of her ex whom she spent years trying to shed, but always went back through some misplaced sense of affection. He beat her, but protected her at the same time, maybe.

He'd find out the truth about her identity when he read about her in the news, but for now, she was a victim and nothing more. A part of history, helping him cement a legacy to rival that of his heroes.

With a surge of adrenaline he lifted the oak log high above his head and positioned his shot right in her temples. All it would take was one solid thud and she'd be gone. Soundless, painless.

Chaos was a heartbeat away. He slammed the log down, aiming for her head.

But the figure moved.

Panic set in. His legs began to quiver. Blind rage filled him from head to toe. "What the fuck!" he screamed.

The lights switched on overhead, and there she was standing by the wall, pointing a gun at him.

"Game over, you son of a bitch," she shouted.

CHAPTER TWENTY SIX

Ella held the shot in place. He was cornered against the wall. The only way past was through her, and even with all her fear haunting every inch of her body, there was no way she was going to miss.

"Freeze. Don't you dare move, got it? Drop your weapon to the ground—now!"

The man in front of her did as she asked, dropping the piece of wood onto an empty bed. He kept his gaze on her, and his demeanor remained upright, dominant. It worried her.

"Good. Now, listen to me. I'm an FBI agent with Special Firearms Honors. That means I can shoot you in the asshole from a mile away, and I've got my crosshairs right in the middle of your skull. If you move an inch, I'm going to blow your head clean off. Do you understand me?"

There was no response.

"I said: Do you understand me?"

"Yes, sweetheart," the man said.

"Call me *sweetheart* again and I'm going to circumcise you with a bullet. Okay? You're a very wanted man, and I'd have no hesitation in taking you back to the precinct in a body bag. Dead or alive, we don't give a shit."

There was unbridled rage in her voice, loathing in her words, and she knew that the best way to subdue this man was through intimidation. If she showed an ounce of weakness, he'd pounce, and there was no way that was going to happen.

"Get on your knees and put your hands on your head," she shouted.

He did as she asked.

Where the hell is Ripley? Ella thought. *I don't want to risk cuffing him on my own, and I want to keep him alive. Keep him talking.*

This was her dream scenario, her blissful nightmare, and yet all she felt for the man before her was hatred and repulsion. He was an organic serial killer, a true psychopath in his natural habitat, the

173

rarest of predators in the annals of crime, and yet the fascination was minimal. She had no desire to talk to him or get into his head. That would come later, if ever. Right now, she wanted him cuffed and behind bars. He *wanted* her to be fascinated by him, and the last thing she wanted to do was give him the satisfaction.

But who was this man? When she'd seen his vague outline as he entered the room, she was sure it was him. Same height, same profile, although his distinguishing features were concealed with a black hoodie. Even so, she was positive it was the man she'd profiled it to be.

The man nodded with a smirk.

"Who are you?" she asked.

"Who do you think I am?"

"Pull that hood down. Let me see you properly."

Slowly, almost teasing her, he revealed his face in full.

It wasn't Dr. Richards; it wasn't anyone she'd seen before.

It stunned her into silence. Once again, she'd been wrong. Her profile had led her here, but she'd gone the wrong route toward the perpetrator's identity. She felt like an amateur, assuming that the first name she'd come across was the unsub. Looking back, it was a stupid move. She cursed herself inside.

Whoever this man was had a deep gash around his right eye, the result of his fight with Alex, Ella thought. He was the most average of men; skinny, with low cheekbones and a thick mane of black hair. He had faint stubble around his chin and upper lip, and although his face was a little haggard, there were signs of youth and vitality in there. His mouth was pulled tightly into a grimace and his skin was flushed red.

Ella had spent her life studying people just like the man now standing with his back against the wall in front of her, but there was something unexplainable about the moment she found herself in. To look at this guy under any other circumstances, she'd assume he was maybe a construction worker, a postman, an outdoorsy type who loved to get his hands dirty and go home to his small family in their three-bedroom townhouse. Then, if she got talking to him, she'd wonder about his life story. Was he a sports fan? Did he have financial problems? What was his upbringing like, perhaps he was in the military, maybe he was a gifted math genius as a child?

174

Everything was ordinary. Nothing about the man before her was monstrous. She could hardly believe that he was responsible for any misconduct, let alone the hellacious slayings of multiple people.

Kemper, Ramirez, Gein, Dahmer, Gacy, Bundy. They were monsters to her because she was already well aware of their history before she looked into their life stories. She studied them through the lens of presumed evil, which, although she didn't like to admit it, tainted and distorted her perception of everything about them.

And yet, the man in front of her lived in the same world as she did. He walked the same roads and was a slave to the same impulses. She and he were bonded in humanity, and yet he was somehow different, through some biological fault or twisted perception of the world. She knew now that all of her research and knowledge could never allow her, or anyone, to truly penetrate the mind of a serial killer. They could try their best to emulate their thoughts and patterns, but that was all it would ever be—emulation.

Serial killers were not ordinary people, but ordinary people were serial killers.

"I'm your son," he said, finally.

"What?"

"I'm your brother. I'm everywhere."

"Oh. Shut the fuck up. I'm not interested in quoting Ted Bundy. But the fact you're spewing out his bullshit when there's a gun pointed in your face tells me everything I need to know about you."

"And what do you know about me?" he asked. "Do you think you can get inside my head just because you did some training, maybe read some books?"

Ella slowly edged toward the doorway to block it off in case he tried to flee. "I found you in here, didn't I? I've never met you before and I predicted this based on the brutal shit you've already done. I think that qualifies as getting in your head, yes?"

The man laughed. "Go on then. Tell me how you did it. How did you guess I'd be here?"

"I'll give you the short version. Edmund Kemper, Richard Ramirez, Ed Gein, Jeffrey Dahmer, John Wayne Gacy, and now Ted Bundy. Same victim type, same location, same methodology. No other places around here with a bunch of girls living."

He lowered his hands and leaned against the wall behind him. "You noticed that, huh?"

"Of course."

175

"I'm curious," he said. "At what point did you make the connection?"

Ella adjusted her stance to let him know she was still honed in on him. "Not until your third kill. But you obviously had it all planned out, right?"

"No, actually." The man shrugged. "The idea just came to me after I strangled that hitchhiker bitch. I realized I'd copied Kemper, so I just thought *fuck it,* I may as well go for the big six. It wasn't until halfway through I realized it was coming up to Bundy's birthday."

"You decided to kill six people on a whim?"

"Hah, you could say that. Life gets a little boring around here. Sometimes you need to inject a little serial murder to liven things up," he laughed. "Still, I'm impressed that you managed to guess I'd be here tonight. Which one was your favorite?" he asked.

"Favorite?"

"Your favorite murder."

"Normal people don't have favorite murders. Not all of us are inept losers who live vicariously through the monsters of the world. Some of us learn from them, and then catch the people who copy them."

"And yet you knew I'd mimicked Gein, Dahmer, the others."

"It's called research."

"No, it's called morbid fascination. I can see you now, with that gun pointed at me, part of you wants to pull that trigger and shoot me between the eyes. But another part of you wants to sit down with me and talk for hours, am I right?"

"No."

Leaning against the wall, he slid down toward the floor to a squatting position. Ella kept the crosshairs pointed at his forehead. "Lies. You know we've probably both read the same books, watched the same documentaries. We've consumed the same information, and yet here we are on two opposite sides of the table. Weird, right?"

"Keep your hands where I can see them. Don't you dare move them from on top of your head, you piece of shit."

The man did as Ella asked. "Whoa, what's with the foul language? Do I make you nervous?"

"Not in the slightest."

"People only curse when they're scared. Are you scared, Agent?"

Ella was almost numb with fear, but she made every effort not to show it. She kept herself steady, made sure that no part of her was quivering. She kept her eyes locked on him and didn't deviate for a second. She only prayed that her faking was a good enough substitute for the real thing.

"Shut up and stay on the ground. I'm the one with the gun, right?"

"Are you sure you're an FBI agent? Your right knee keeps jittering. Your pupils are dilated. You keep furrowing your brow. You know what that tells me? It tells me you're scared. You're new to this job, aren't you?"

"You say anything else and you're going straight to hell."

But he ignored her. "What is it you're scared of? Never detained someone before? Waiting for backup and worried they've forgotten about you? That must be a terrifying thought, isn't it? You're all alone in here with a pure psychopath, and the only way out is to become a murderer yourself. You're worried doing that would make you no better to me, not to mention all of the knowledge you could extract from me when I'm behind bars."

Ella gently pulled the trigger a little tighter. The more he spoke, the more she was worried that the only way out would be over his dead body. She didn't want that. It would feel like a slap in the face to his victims' families. Death was easy. Life imprisonment wasn't.

Intimidate him. Let him know you'll pull the trigger if you have to.

A silence lingered in the dorm room. She saw something in his face change. "Question, is there anyone else in this house?" he asked.

"Not a soul," she lied. Truthfully, she didn't know herself. "Sorry, but you're not getting your precious Bundy murders tonight."

He smiled. "I could still get one."

"Really? Because I've got six bullets with your name on it."

"Bullshit. You want me alive."

It frustrated Ella that he knew what she wanted. How did he know? Psychopath's intuition, Ella thought.

"I couldn't give two shits if you live forever or die today," she lied.

177

"So, what are you waiting for?" he asked. "I'm right here."

"The police will be here any second," she said, praying that her words might somehow make it true. Truthfully, she had no idea if Ripley, Harris, or anyone else was indeed on their way. What if they were still searching for Dr. Richards at the hospital? What if they'd taken him in for questioning?

No, there was no way they'd abandon her like that. Ripley promised she'd get here once she'd scouted the hospital.

Her thoughts took over, and for a brief flash, her laser focus on the suspect's head slipped. Her Weaver Stance dipped for just a second, and the suspect noticed.

A moment of weakness was all it took.

The man reached out, grabbed the oak log off the bed, and swung it toward Ella's hands. It collided against her knuckles with a sickening thud, sending her handgun flying out of the room.

CHAPTER TWENTY SEVEN

He lashed out toward her and struck her around the side of the head, sending Ella out of the bedroom and onto the rough hallway floor.

Her vision blurred as an excruciating, throbbing sensation relieved her of any capable thought. For a second, she was immobile. Time stood still for longer than seemed possible.

And then he was above her. Between his legs, she saw her Glock 17 lying on the distant ground, out of reach. Suddenly, the oak log came toward her again, threatening to obliterate her skull into a thousand pieces.

Ella threw up her forearm, blocking the blow and then sliding out from underneath the man above her. She jumped back to her feet in one swift motion, ignoring the overbearing ache in her skull and the shrill ringing sound in her ears. She found herself at the end of a hallway shrouded in darkness. There was a brief filter of light coming from the bedroom she'd hidden in, but not enough to brighten the entire corridor.

She felt closed in, with the only escape being out into the blackness into the waiting arms of a serial murderer. Suddenly, she heard heavy breathing. A figure emerged from the shadows and launched into her again, but Ella skirted around him and ran back into the bedroom. She dropped down and searched for her handgun.

It wasn't there. Of course not. It was in the hallway.

Footsteps again. "Looking for this?" He appeared at the doorway, now brandishing a weapon in each hand. He pointed the gun at her and laughed. "Looks like I'm gonna get my kill after all. An FBI agent and a hot young bitch all in one? Things have turned out better than expected."

It was the first and only time in her life she'd stared down the barrel of a gun. She thought back to the shooting range, all the newbies she saw who had clearly never handled a firearm in their lives. They all struck the same pose. This guy's was no different. Ella could tell he'd never touched a gun before.

She took the chance.

"You're not going to kill anything with the safety catch on, are you? You moron."

There was no safety catch on, but he didn't know that. Doubt crept into his face. She saw it instantly, and the moment his attention dropped, Ella flung herself toward him and grabbed him by the wrist. She maneuvered beside him as he frantically pulled the trigger, firing two shots into the floor. She brought up her knee and slammed it into his spine as she pulled his entire body backward. He remained on his feet, but Ella was able to push the gun from his hands.

His elbow came from nowhere, striking her temple and sending her back out into the hallway. Ella realized that he was physically competent, unlike her profile suggested. He was fast, rugged, and fought like a street thug. She could tell he wasn't formally trained, but he had strength.

Realizing this, she felt panic set in. She composed herself and focused, but a moment of weakness overcame her. He turned around and charged at her, pushing her against the wall with a heavy crack. His fist lunged at her, but Ella managed to duck. He hit the window, cracking a pain of glass and bringing back reddened knuckles coated in crystalline shards.

Ella stumbled into the communal room where blackness reigned. She tried to get her bearings, but suddenly felt a hand around her neck. No air could get into her lungs. Her body fell weak and her legs began to tremble as the man smothered her, lowering her to the ground as he suffocated the life from her. He put his body weight on hers, keeping her pinned down. She couldn't move.

She'd always heard that when death was coming, you knew it. Worst of all, you accepted it as an inevitability. She could do nothing but think back to the techniques to use when being choked from her old martial arts classes, recalling only one. But if they would give her some extra seconds of life, she was going to take it. There would be no death tonight, not hers, not his.

She pressed her tongue against the top of her mouth to bow out the underside of her chin. It created a minor space between his thumbs and windpipe, and she felt a slight relief. It awarded her a few seconds of clarity, which was enough to let her subconscious recall a second technique. The most powerful technique in the book—providing it was used on an amateur. Given his lack of handgun ability, Ella could only assume that his fighting skills weren't up to par either.

Through the agony and torment, Ella smiled. She looked her attacker in the eye and did her best to grin.

If you kick and scream, that just tells them it's working.

The hesitation inched in. His grip loosened as he readjusted his position, believing that he was doing something wrong. In the fleeting moments, Ella was able to take in a heavy breath. Less than one second was all it took.

With renewed vigor, she pushed his one arm flush against his body and leaned to the right. He launched his fist toward her face, but she'd created too much distance for him to hit. Ella used the momentum to roll aside, pushing him off her and down onto his back in one swift movement. With her free arm, she thrust her elbow into his nose, feeling bone and cartilage shatter with a nauseating crack. A fountain of blood gushed forth, coating the man's face with a crimson mask. She followed up with more punches, pounding until her knuckles bled. One crack to his left eye renewed the injury left in place by Alex, nearly dislodging his eyeball from its socket. The man cried out in pain, pathetically trying to kick Ella off and protect himself, but she felt nothing. No pain or remorse. She reached behind, caught his leg, and twisted his ankle to an angle which no human bone could endure. She kept the pressure on his knee so that his leg wouldn't rotate with the twist, and like wet tissue paper, his ankle bone snapped, incapacitating him in a heap on the ground.

Ella collapsed off him, scrambled to her feet, and ran back to where she'd dropped her gun. She scraped the floor, finding various debris, eventually landing on her pistol. She picked it up. When she returned, he was trying to crawl away. Ella stood there, blocking the exit.

"No way out."

They locked eyes once more, him on the ground and her standing tall. Any fascination she once felt was now overridden with fury. Her body felt like it could break at any second, much less her mind. To come face to face with a serial killer had been something of a morbid fantasy since she was a little girl, and to catch one was something that could surely never happen in her lifetime. Now, both of those fantasies felt infantile. There was nothing special about the man before her, and every fiber of her being told her that the world would be better off if he was six feet in the ground. It took all her willpower, all her moral fiber, to not lodge a bullet between his eyes.

He rolled onto his back, streaming with blood and seemingly about to breathe his last breath. "You know what Bundy said? When they caught him?" he shouted between breaths.

Ella trained the gun at his forehead one more time. "Yes. I do."

"Tell me."

"He said *I wish you'd have killed me.*"

"Kill me right now. I want you to." He scowled at her. "Come on, try it. Killing feels incredible. Don't you want to know how it feels?"

"No," she said, although the truth wasn't quite as clear, even to her.

"If I'm locked away, they're going to write letters to me. You know that, don't you? I'm going to be an icon. Like Bundy was to me, I'm going to be to them. We serial killers are your sons and your husbands. We're everywhere, and there'll be more of your children dead tomorrow. Why not kill me now, so I don't inspire anyone else?"

Ella pointed the gun between his eyes. She squeezed the trigger gently until she was at the biting point.

"You want me to do it?"

He laughed maniacally, hammering his fist on the floor beside him. "Fuck yes I do. I'm not going to prison."

Ella moved closer, gun trained on him. She brought it down and pressed the barrel to his forehead.

"No!" screamed a voice from behind. A horde of footsteps sounded alongside it, thundering in from the patio area. "Ella, don't you dare shoot him. Yield the gun. It's over."

Ripley appeared with Harris close behind. Ella dropped back onto the floor, keeping her gaze on the man she'd been inches away from killing.

Ripley and Harris both rushed down to the suspect and restrained him. Harris locked him in handcuffs. Ripley ran over to Ella and gently lowered her gun. She said nothing, but no words were needed. Ripley wrapped her arms around Ella and held her as tears filled her eyes. Beyond the distant broken window, blue and red lights illuminated the early morning streets. Two more officers arrived, entering through the front door this time. They helped

Harris escort the suspect to his feet. He struggled to stand up on his surely broken ankle.

"Are you hurt?" Ripley asked.

Ella wiped her eyes. "From head to toe."

"Come on. We have to get you to the hospital."

Ripley walked Ella out of the center and into the cool night air. The fresh trickle of rainfall felt good against her face, soothing her wounds and bringing her back into the real world. There would be no death tonight, at least not in this town.

Three squad cars sat on the pavement outside the recovery center. Harris and two officers crowded around the suspect as they gently loaded him into the backset. Ella realized that after everything she'd been through with him, she didn't even know his name. She wasn't even sure if she wanted to know.

"Hold on a second?" she asked Ripley. "I just have to do something."

Ripley nodded and waited by her vehicle. Ella walked over to Harris and the other officers. The back door of their car was still open.

"They always look so different in chains don't they?" Harris said. "Want to say anything to this creep before we lock him away for good?"

But he interrupted her before she could speak. "Oh, I think we'll be seeing each other again."

"No, we won't," she said, slamming the car door shut in his face. "I've got better things to do." She turned and walked back to Ripley.

"What was that about?" Ripley asked, unlocking the car.

"You told me not to romanticize these people or this job."

"I did, and I stand by it."

"That was me not romanticizing it," Ella said. She'd always thought that the day she came face to face with a serial killer would be the most insightful and captivating experience of her life. But it had happened, and it was nothing like she imagined. She'd always imagined serial killers to be a different breed, like they harbored a secret about life which no one else knew. She thought they'd have insights which went beyond the most hardened philosopher.

But the man she'd fought with was not special or memorable or fascinating. He was human, like her and Ripley and everyone else she'd met the past few days.

"Good," Ripley said. "Now you're really learning."

"I'm not going to let these people consume my entire life anymore," Ella said. "Now let's get out of here."

CHAPTER TWENTY EIGHT

It was ten o'clock in the morning on a new day and the world looked different, she thought. She'd had spent the night recovering in Saint Mary's Hospital after being treated for her injuries, and her diagnosis was that she'd be back to full health after a few days' rest.

She had a room with a view, and outside she saw the first sun since she'd arrived in this strange little part of the world. The events of the previous night, and in fact the past five days as a whole, didn't seem real to her yet. No doubt they would in time, but even with the soreness around her throat and the scars on her cheek, it felt as though she'd dreamt everything, from the plane ride here to the horrors of the night before.

A nurse popped her head into Ella's cubicle. "Ms. Dark, you have a visitor."

Ripley walked in, dressed in a casual jeans, a loose-fitting top, and brown jacket. Ella had never seen her so informal. "Still alive, Rookie?" She took a seat on the edge of her bed. "What's the verdict? Will you live to fight another day?"

"I've got a damaged windpipe, a few bloody knuckles, and a couple of scars on my face. He concussed me too. I've got to take some antibiotics for my throat injury and after that, I'll be good as new. Well, almost."

"You did an incredible job. A lot of people would have shot him right there and then, out of fear and convenience. But you kept him alive for us. An alive suspect is always better than a dead one. That's something I probably should have told you, but there's no better teacher than experience."

A part of Ella wished she'd shot the man dead as soon as he entered the dorm room. She knew that when the dust settled, she'd recreate the scene in her mind over and over again, playing out every possible result. "I know. That's why I did it."

"You're gonna be playing the what-if game a lot over the next few months, and maybe even the next few years. What if he'd escaped, what if he'd have gotten to the dorms before you. Things like that. There's no cure for it, you just have to meditate on it and get past it. But someone of your strength should be able to do exactly that. You took down a killer single-handedly. Not many people on earth can say that."

"If you hadn't shown up, I might have killed him."

"I've shot more people than you've had hot dinners but you don't see me bragging."

Ella laughed. The moment hung in the air. "Who was he, anyway?" she asked reluctantly.

"His name was Austin Creed, worked on an alligator farm around here. Neither the sheriff nor any of the officers on the force had heard of him before. He was a total nobody. No criminal history, no DNA in the database, absolutely nothing. To look at his life, you'd think he was a model citizen."

"Have you spoken to him?"

"Yes, while you were relaxing in bed, some of us were working," Ripley joked. "He confessed to everything. Sang like a canary, even. Once they know their game is up, they can't wait to confess. This guy blurted it all out without asking. He knew all of the intricate details of the crime scenes, even told us how he found all of his victims. Harris and a few officers went to his house this morning and found jewelry and ID cards belonging to the victims. We talked to some of his neighbors and co-workers too. No one had a bad word to say about him."

"What was the house like?" Ella asked, curious.

"If I saw that house under other circumstances, I'd assume this guy was your run-of-the-mill everyman. It was as normal as normal can be. Well kept, clean. He even had a chirpy little dog running around. Pup was well looked after too, by the looks of it."

"Was the dog's name Crunch?"

Ripley shot her a look of surprise, then held her hands palm up. "Yes. How did you know?"

"Bundy's dog was named Crunch."

"Well, that just confirms things even more," she laughed. "He's our man, no doubt about it."

"Thank God," Ella said.

"God had nothing to do with it. This was all you."

Ella stretched her legs, feeling a little numbness in them. "But my profile was completely wrong."

"No, it wasn't. A psychological profile is a diagnostic tool to guide and predict, and that's exactly what yours did. It's not rigid science, despite what some textbooks might tell you."

"I think I found that out the hard way."

"Creed was a loner, a manual worker, lived in the area and had a rough childhood. In fact, the only thing that wasn't accurate was the history of sexual deviances, and just because there are no records of any sex offenses having taken place, it doesn't mean they didn't happen. You were close, and sometimes that's the best result you can hope for." Ripley stood up. "Anyway, are you ready to get out of here? There's a flight back to D.C. in four hours. I bet you're dying to get home."

"Just waiting for the doctor to discharge me, then I'll be good to go."

"All right. I'll be waiting downstairs."

***

Before Ella made her way downstairs to the hospital foyer, she made a detour to the fourth floor. She didn't know if she'd find him there still, and she didn't know if she'd get in trouble for doing so, but she tried regardless.

Most beds were empty, perhaps a side effect of being located in such a backwoods town, where population was low and sickness was considered a weakness. She followed the path from memory until she arrived at the same bed she had only two days ago. She found him fully dressed and ready to leave, much like herself.

"Alex?" she said. He looked up in surprise. The kid looked much better than he had the last time she saw him. His neck was almost free of marks and there was a healthy glow to his face. All of his bandages were nowhere to be seen.

"Oh hey, Agent," he said. "Wow, you look nearly as bad as me," he laughed, nodding toward the cuts and bruises on her cheek.

"I've been in the wars, just like you. The same war, in fact."

Alex's eyes enlarged. He blinked a few times. "What? Seriously?"

"Seriously."

"Did you…?"

"Catch him?" Yes. I got him. Well, *we* got him."

Alex curled his hands into a fist and punched the air. "Yes! Holy shit, that's awesome. Did you kick his ass?"

"Something like that. You loosened him up for me." She smiled.

"What's going to happen to him?" Alex asked, his tone a mixture of excitement and worry.

"At the very least, he's never getting out of prison. At most, lethal injection."

"The death penalty?" Alex asked.

"I'm not supposed to tell you this, but I know how it feels to be haunted by something your entire life. The man who attacked you was a serial offender. Before he got to you, he'd killed four people. You were meant to be his fifth, and I was nearly his sixth."

Alex's lips parted, his jaw nearly falling loose from his skull. "A serial killer? I escaped a serial killer?"

"You did. Not many people can say that."

It was clear Alex wasn't sure how to respond. "Shit me. I guess I should play the lottery tonight since luck is on my side," he said.

"There was no luck involved. You fought him off. Be proud of yourself."

"Who was he? Someone who lives round here?"

"A local. That's all I can really say, but I'm sure you'll hear everything on the news pretty soon. I hope you didn't need your car back any time soon because the police are going to need it as evidence for a while."

Alex chuckled. "That car was a piece of shit so I'm glad to be rid of it. I don't care about that, but I just wish I could get my key ring back. Do you think I could? Once the police don't need it anymore?"

Ella saw something change in Alex, like he was suppressing something. "Maybe. Was it important to you?" she asked.

Alex shrugged. "It was a present from my mom when I got my first car. She died a couple of months later."

"I'm sorry to hear that. Unfortunately, the police didn't find any key ring when they searched the suspect's house."

A dispirited Alex shrugged again. "Figures. Ah, well. Shit happens."

"I understand how hard it is. When I was a kid, someone took something from me too, and all I've ever wanted was to get it back. I've spent over twenty years dreaming that one day it'd come back, and that feeling when you wake up and it's not there hurts like nothing else."

"Sucks, right?"

"It does, that's why I couldn't hand this over to the police," Ella said. She pulled a rectangular piece of metal from her pocket and dropped it on Alex's bed. The engraving said: ALEX, NO MATTER HOW FAR APART WE ARE, YOU'LL ALWAYS BE IN MY HEART.

Alex saw it and immediately covered his mouth with his sleeve. He let out a sound, half-laugh, half-cry. He moved his sleeve up to his eyes as sobs took over.

"What the...? Where did you get it?"

Ella shrugged. "That's what a real magic trick looks like," she laughed.

Truthfully, Ella wasn't sure. The previous night, as she was being escorted to the hospital, she reached in her pocket and found the key ring there. It was possible she scraped it off the ground as she hunted for weapons during their battle. Perhaps she took it from him as she pummeled him half to death.

"Thank you so much. I don't think this is an accident," Alex said, holding back pressurized tears. "This ring saved me. I know my mom was looking down on me when that freak tried to kill me. It was her who intervened."

Ella smiled. "Do me a favor? Don't tell anyone I gave you this."

Alex heartily shook his head. "It's our secret. Thank you."

For the first time in the past week, Ella felt nothing but positivity. She saw the fruits of her hard labor. She saw a little of her in Alex, but Alex was now free of the shackles that would have kept him held back for the rest of his life had this killer escaped. She knew she'd made a difference to the lives of the victims' families, but being able to see real tears of joy, real gratitude in front of her, was a prize like no other. For the first time, she felt like this whole thing had been worth it. Justice had been done.

It might not heal the mental wounds, Ella thought, but it was a token that he'd fought through a hardship and lived to tell about it. No doubt Alex would hear of the recent murders on the news, and perhaps be bombarded with retellings of them for the rest of his life. Hopefully, this small trinket would let him remember his trauma as a victory.

***

She watched Alex leave the ward with his father while she held back, grabbing herself a quick machine coffee to charge her before the long journey back home. As she waited for the machine to finishing whirring, a shadow engulfed her. Someone appeared behind her, too close to be a stranger.

In the reflection of the vending machine, she saw that same blurry profile she had the previous day.

"So, you thought I was a serial murderer, huh?" a voice said.

She spun around and came face to face with Dr. Richards, the man who she'd wrongly assumed to be the killer. Ripley had filled her in on her incident with him the night before. A look of defeat and embarrassment spread across Ella's face.

"And I was wrong. I'm so sorry," she said, praying that he wasn't livid about her predictions. His eyes were inflamed red. She suddenly felt incredibly guilty about ever assuming his guilt. "How'd you find out?"

"My first clue was the twenty notifications I got when my phone got a signal."

Ella smiled in defeat. "Just that?"

"No. My second clue was when an FBI agent came storming into my dad's room looking for me."

"Oh," Ella chuckled. "Well, I guess that gives it away."

"Just a little bit."

"Honestly, I'm so sorry. Your receptionist told me you were celebrating a birthday and that led me down a wrong path. It's totally my fault. Don't blame the police or anyone else for this."

"It's fine. We get it wrong sometimes. God knows I've made a few mistakes in the autopsy room, and you know what? Mistakes are always forgivable if you have the courage to admit them. You have, so thank you."

Ella didn't expect such a response from someone she'd assumed was a murderer. "I appreciate you being so understanding. A lot of people wouldn't be, in your situation." She smiled.

"It's cool. You don't learn anything from being perfect. Anyway, I won't keep you. I'll let you get on."

Ella thought on it. She desperately wanted to stay and talk, wanted to apologize for making potentially life-altering assumptions about someone she barely knew. "Tell your dad I said happy birthday," she said.

"Thank you, but I can't. He passed last night."

"He died? Oh my god, I'm so sorry." Her guilt doubled, hitting her hard in the stomach. "Are you okay?"

"Yeah, I mean, I lost him a while ago, if I'm honest. It's been a long time coming. I'm just glad I got to spend some time with him before he went."

"That's as much as you can ask for. Memories are the diary we carry forever. As long as he's in your heart, he's with you. It's the same place I keep my dad, too."

"Then I'm sorry to hear that, but it sounds like we have a lot in common. It's a shame you're gonna have to leave soon."

"Right now, in fact. My plane to D.C. leaves in a few hours."

"Shame. Wish I could come with you. I've never been to D.C. What's it like?"

"It's overcrowded and it smells like sulfur, but I think you'd love it," she joked. "You should come out. I can see if there are any coroner positions available if you want?"

"That would be great. And if there aren't?"

"Then I'll see if there are any serial killer positions available instead."

They both laughed. "Do that. I've still got your number from last time," he said.

"Actually text me this time, okay? I'll be waiting."

They said their goodbyes and went their separate ways. Ella had no idea if she would indeed see him again, but a possibility was better than nothing at all.

EPILOGUE

Ella opened her eyes and found herself thirty thousand feet in the air. She was sitting cross-legged in a white leather seat, and beside her was a flight attendant pouring drinks for people across the aisle. Opposite her, Ripley was staring narrow-eyed at a laptop, hammering away at the keyboard.

Ripley caught her eye. "Sorry, did my typing wake you up? I hate doing these reports so I type them like I'm mauling an ants' nest."

"No, not at all. I guess I'm still exhausted."

"It's no surprise. When we get back, take a few days off, then see how you feel."

The prospect of returning back to life in the Intelligence Unit felt a little strange now. Not like it was beneath her, but that she felt she'd contributed more to the betterment of the world in the past few days than she had for the past twenty-eight years. But even so, with wounds like these, was this the life she wanted for herself in the future? Did she want to end up like Ripley, jetting across the country and consuming the details of the most disturbing crimes in America on a weekly basis?

Until today, she would have said no. But the feeling she got when she told Alex that she'd caught the monster who would have no doubt haunted him forever was something she'd never forget.

Ripley shut her laptop with an unnecessary slam. "Would you do this again, Dark?"

Ella peered out the window and watched the tiny buildings below dissolve into nothingness. Clouds appeared beside her.

"I don't know. Why? Would you want me to?"

"That's not my choice. You do remember what I said? About not romanticizing this stuff?"

"Absolutely."

"I mean what I said. Your talents can be used elsewhere, so don't think you have to do this again. Edis will want you back out here when he reads my report. I've got no doubts about that, but it's your choice and it stays that way. Don't let him talk you into anything."

"I won't. Thank you for the advice, but honestly, it's a tough decision. Part of me says yes, part of me says hell no."

"If you have any questions about it then come to me any time, okay?"

Ella thought about it for a second. "Well, there is one question," Ella said.

"Hit me."

"A few days ago, you said you'd only ever chased one copycat killer in your whole career."

Ripley sat back in her seat, clearly anticipating what was to come. "I did."

"Who was it? Because I don't know of any copycat serial killings whatsoever in the US. At least none which have been substantial enough to warrant FBI investigation."

Ripley chugged a small whiskey miniature and looked up at the seatbelt sign pinging above her. She removed hers.

"Back in 1995, I caught a guy named Lucien Myers. You know about that?"

Ella did. Lucien Myers had slayed five women in the rural areas of Iowa. He was little known outside of true crime enthusiasts, but his crimes remained some of the most sadistic in modern history. "Of course. You got an award for catching him."

"Correct. Everyone knows Myers, but what a lot of people don't know is that in 1998, someone was inspired by Myers's crimes. Inspired enough to mimic them."

"Oh, no, I didn't know that."

"Probably because it never reached the serial stage. But a guy, or more like an obsessed fan, reached out to Myers in prison. Myers gave him my name, and after killing a woman in Iowa, he came for me."

Ella tried to imagine what life would be like, living day-to-day in the knowledge that you were being hunted by a vengeful monster. Accidentally finding herself in the crosshairs of one had shaken her soul to its core, but being actively pursued by one was a horror like no other. Worse yet was the notion that you *didn't know* you were being hunted by someone whose mission it was to torture and kill you. A great deal of sympathy, combined with a newfound respect for Ripley, came over her.

"And he got you?" Ella asked.

"He got me. I was abducted in a van and taken to an abandoned shack. I woke up tied to a chair with a table of surgical weapons in front of me. He told me to pick the weapon which would kill me. He said if I didn't choose, he'd use them all. Exactly the same as Myers did to his victims."

Ella quickly realized exactly why Ripley didn't want to talk about this before. Ella had consumed the details of hideous crimes which went beyond human comprehension more times than she could count, but there was something about Ripley's retelling of the details that struck her differently. Now, there was no detachment between Ella and the grisly details. She couldn't keep a vicarious distance. Not only did she have to consume the details directly, she had to also deal with the emotional fallout of the victim. She realized that things were different for her now. Would it be like this with every case she covered from now on?

"Jesus. That's... I didn't know, I'm sorry for bringing it up."

Ripley checked her phone, then laid it beside her and looked out the window. There was a long silence, neither of the agents wanting to break it. Ella worried that she'd upset Ripley by bringing all this up.

"I've never told anyone what really happened," Ripley continued, much to Ella's relief.

Another silence followed. Ella badly wanted her to continue, thinking maybe that hearing Ripley's trauma would help numb her own.

But Ella couldn't bring herself to say anything more.

"Honestly, I should have retired right there and then, but I kept on trying to catch the bad guys. I hoped that if I slayed enough monsters, I'd eventually conquer my trauma, rise above it."

"But it doesn't work that way," Ella finished.

"Not at all. That's why whenever I hear the term copycat, it brings it all back. For seventeen years, I've suffered through flashbacks, nightmares, sickness, hallucinations. It made me feel detached from the people I loved the most. It pulled me apart from my ex-husband and my kids. Like I said, it's not that I didn't believe your theory from the start, it's that I didn't want to."

Ella took it all in, now seeing Ripley in a different light than before. She didn't choose to be how she was, she was made that way through hardship and distress. Ella felt a great affection for her, but one steeped in compassion. She felt like there was an opportunity to offload some of her own grief, but felt hesitant to do so. Ella didn't want Ripley to think she was trying to outdo her. She didn't want Ripley to think that her own trauma was comparable to hers.

But revealing her past might make Ripley see her differently. The same way Ella now saw Ripley in a new light, with new sympathies and respect. There might never be a better time to do so.

"A few days ago, you asked me why I became an agent. I didn't really tell you the truth."

Ripley turned her attention away from the window and looked at Ella. A look of concern spread across her face.

"No?"

Ella took a deep breath and thought of the best place to begin. Should she tell her what she definitely knew, or what she *thought* she knew? Should she include the grim details, or just the overview?

"When I was five years old, my dad was murdered. Why, or by whom, I have no idea."

Ella realized that as far as the facts went, that was all she had. All of the visions, nightmares, and theories she had were surplus. But even so, it was a relief to finally say the words out loud. For all she'd thought about these events over the past twenty-three years, divulging the details actually felt a little strange.

Ripley's look of concern turned to compassion. Ella saw a sense of realization in her, like she'd known there was something traumatic in Ella's past all along.

"That's terrible, Dark. Don't feel like you have to divulge the details if you're not comfortable with it."

"There's not much else to tell, and even though I have to relive the scene most nights in my dreams, I still don't know how it truly happened. Some days, I'm sure that I walked into my dad's room in the middle of the night and saw the killer standing over his body. Other days, I'm sure I found his body in the morning. It's all a total mess."

"That's called an acute stress reaction. You witnessed a life-changing event and your primal response mechanism is addressing it any way it can. I get the same. Sometimes I dream my trauma from start to finish, but certain things are a little different. It's reached the point where I'm not sure what really happened and what didn't."

A comfortable silence was suspended between them, despite their mutual confessions. Ripley broke it first.

"It's funny, really. We're both here for the same reasons."

"I guess we're not so different after all," Ella said.

A flight attendant placed two coffees on the table between them. "Latte with cream," Ripley said. "I ordered it for you while you were asleep."

Ella smiled her thanks. She sat back and gave thought to the idea of doing all of this again, in another state, with another psychopath in her sights. She knew she couldn't make such a decision with haste, but if she did do it all again, with Ripley by her side, then God help some of the criminals they'd meet.

Ella turned to the window and caught her reflection. It still surprised her to see her face decked in cuts and bruises. It was a face she barely recognized at all.

But something told her that she'd be seeing that face again in the future.

NOW AVAILABLE!

GIRL, TAKEN
(An Ella Dark FBI Suspense Thriller—Book 2)

"A MASTERPIECE OF THRILLER AND MYSTERY. Blake Pierce did a magnificent job developing characters with a psychological side so well described that we feel inside their minds, follow their fears and cheer for their success. Full of twists, this book will keep you awake until the turn of the last page."
--Books and Movie Reviews, Roberto Mattos (re Once Gone)

GIRL, TAKEN (An Ella Dark FBI Suspense Thriller) is book #2 in a long-anticipated new series by #1 bestseller and USA Today bestselling author Blake Pierce, whose bestseller Once Gone (a free download) has received over 1,000 five star reviews.

FBI Agent Ella Dark, 29, is given her big chance to achieve her life's dream: to join the Behavorial Crimes Unit. Ella has a hidden obsession: she has studied serial killers from the time she could read, devastated by the murder of her own sister. With her photographic memory, she has obtained an encyclopedic knowledge of every serial killer, every victim and every case. Singled out for her brilliant mind, Ella is invited to join the big leagues.

Victims are being found murdered in the Pacific Northwest, their bodies strung up high in the branches of Redwood trees. It is presumed to be the work of a serial killer dubbed "The Artist Killer." Ella feels so close to catching him, feels certain she has read of similar murders—but this time, her knowledge fails her.

Can she catch a killer without her talent?

Or will it return to her too late?

A page-turning and harrowing crime thriller featuring a brilliant and tortured FBI agent, the ELLA DARK series is a riveting mystery, packed with suspense, twists and turns, revelations, and driven by a breakneck pace that will keep you flipping pages late into the night.

Book #3 in the series—GIRL, HUNTED—is now also available.

Blake Pierce

Blake Pierce is the USA Today bestselling author of the RILEY PAIGE mystery series, which includes seventeen books. Blake Pierce is also the author of the MACKENZIE WHITE mystery series, comprising fourteen books; of the AVERY BLACK mystery series, comprising six books; of the KERI LOCKE mystery series, comprising five books; of the MAKING OF RILEY PAIGE mystery series, comprising six books; of the KATE WISE mystery series, comprising seven books; of the CHLOE FINE psychological suspense mystery, comprising six books; of the JESSE HUNT psychological suspense thriller series, comprising fourteen books (and counting); of the AU PAIR psychological suspense thriller series, comprising three books; of the ZOE PRIME mystery series, comprising four books (and counting); of the ADELE SHARP mystery series, comprising six books (and counting); of the EUROPEAN VOYAGE cozy mystery series, comprising six books (and counting); of the new LAURA FROST FBI suspense thriller, comprising three books (and counting); of the new ELLA DARK FBI suspense thriller, comprising three books (and counting); and of the new A YEAR IN EUROPE cozy mystery series, comprising three books (and counting).

An avid reader and lifelong fan of the mystery and thriller genres, Blake loves to hear from you, so please feel free to visit www.blakepierceauthor.com to learn more and stay in touch.

BOOKS BY BLAKE PIERCE

A YEAR IN EUROPE
A MURDER IN PARIS (Book #1)
DEATH IN FLORENCE (Book #2)
VENGEANCE IN VIENNA (Book #3)

ELLA DARK FBI SUSPENSE THRILLER
GIRL, GONE (Book #1)
GIRL, TAKEN (Book #2)
GIRL, HUNTED (Book #3)

LAURA FROST FBI SUSPENSE THRILLER
ALREADY GONE (Book #1)
ALREADY SEEN (Book #2)
ALREADY TRAPPED (Book #3)

EUROPEAN VOYAGE COZY MYSTERY SERIES
MURDER (AND BAKLAVA) (Book #1)
DEATH (AND APPLE STRUDEL) (Book #2)
CRIME (AND LAGER) (Book #3)
MISFORTUNE (AND GOUDA) (Book #4)
CALAMITY (AND A DANISH) (Book #5)
MAYHEM (AND HERRING) (Book #6)

ADELE SHARP MYSTERY SERIES
LEFT TO DIE (Book #1)
LEFT TO RUN (Book #2)
LEFT TO HIDE (Book #3)
LEFT TO KILL (Book #4)
LEFT TO MURDER (Book #5)
LEFT TO ENVY (Book #6)
LEFT TO LAPSE (Book #7)

THE AU PAIR SERIES
ALMOST GONE (Book#1)
ALMOST LOST (Book #2)
ALMOST DEAD (Book #3)

IF SHE FEARED (Book #6)
IF SHE HEARD (Book #7)

THE MAKING OF RILEY PAIGE SERIES
WATCHING (Book #1)
WAITING (Book #2)
LURING (Book #3)
TAKING (Book #4)
STALKING (Book #5)
KILLING (Book #6)

RILEY PAIGE MYSTERY SERIES
ONCE GONE (Book #1)
ONCE TAKEN (Book #2)
ONCE CRAVED (Book #3)
ONCE LURED (Book #4)
ONCE HUNTED (Book #5)
ONCE PINED (Book #6)
ONCE FORSAKEN (Book #7)
ONCE COLD (Book #8)
ONCE STALKED (Book #9)
ONCE LOST (Book #10)
ONCE BURIED (Book #11)
ONCE BOUND (Book #12)
ONCE TRAPPED (Book #13)
ONCE DORMANT (Book #14)
ONCE SHUNNED (Book #15)
ONCE MISSED (Book #16)
ONCE CHOSEN (Book #17)

MACKENZIE WHITE MYSTERY SERIES
BEFORE HE KILLS (Book #1)
BEFORE HE SEES (Book #2)
BEFORE HE COVETS (Book #3)
BEFORE HE TAKES (Book #4)
BEFORE HE NEEDS (Book #5)
BEFORE HE FEELS (Book #6)
BEFORE HE SINS (Book #7)
BEFORE HE HUNTS (Book #8)
BEFORE HE PREYS (Book #9)

BEFORE HE LONGS (Book #10)
BEFORE HE LAPSES (Book #11)
BEFORE HE ENVIES (Book #12)
BEFORE HE STALKS (Book #13)
BEFORE HE HARMS (Book #14)

AVERY BLACK MYSTERY SERIES
CAUSE TO KILL (Book #1)
CAUSE TO RUN (Book #2)
CAUSE TO HIDE (Book #3)
CAUSE TO FEAR (Book #4)
CAUSE TO SAVE (Book #5)
CAUSE TO DREAD (Book #6)

KERI LOCKE MYSTERY SERIES
A TRACE OF DEATH (Book #1)
A TRACE OF MUDER (Book #2)
A TRACE OF VICE (Book #3)
A TRACE OF CRIME (Book #4)
A TRACE OF HOPE (Book #5)

Made in the USA
Las Vegas, NV
27 July 2022